Change of Heart

A Gwen Arthur Novel

Olivia R. Burton

First Edition, 2019

ISBN: 978-0-99763333-9-9

Peacock Deceiving a Suitcase
www.PeacockDeceivingASuitcase.com

OTHER TITLES

Gwen Arthur Series
Mixed Feelings
Business With Pleasure
Cold Feet
Hollow Back Girl
Change of Heart

~

Bone to Pick
Flesh and Blood
The Writer's Overnighter
Gut Feeling
Suckered In
Split Second

The Preternatural PNW
Rattle
Metal
Knell

~

Throb
Murmur

COLLABORATIONS
Passage Through Moonlight
The Godfather's Naughty Daughter
Song of the Argyle Goddess
Belladonna Clasped
Cash Grab

Olivia R. Burton

CONTENTS

One

It was a Saturday and someone was banging on my door before ten in the morning. What the hell was the meaning of this and who was I going to have to kill to get back to sleep?

Ages passed, eons, entire dynasties and eras came and went as the banging continued to ruin my morning and finally, when the banging didn't stop and neither of my pillows could muffle the sound, I gave in. Ungainly and angry, I untangled myself from my sheets, stumbled out of bed and across the room right into my door frame. Still half-asleep, I yowled as my shoulder protested.

The banging stopped, making me hope for a moment that my door had called a truce, apologizing who whomever it had pissed off. Perhaps they'd leave me and my home in peace and I could get back to my pleasant dream world where I enjoyed rainbow booze and a plate piled high with fancy sweets. As I came around the corner into the living room, I found Mel's face pressed against the glass of my front window. Mood plummeting, I paused at the end of the hall, staring at him with anger boiling inside my pudgy belly.

Spotting me, Mel jolted, pounding spastically on the window, and then dove back to my door. I heard him try the knob as if my mere proximity would have unlocked it.

"Goddammit, Mel," I spat, storming over to yank open the door and give him a piece of my mind. My rage hiccupped, confused by the Mel standing outside my door. Distress radiated off of him, greasy and thin, like hot oil without the ability to scald. It lapped against my skin and I stepped back, not only because it was gross, but also because something was very wrong. The distress was human and, despite the fact that he was usually a werewolf, so was Mel.

"What's wrong with you?" I demanded, something tiny in my mind panicking, flinging itself against the inside of my skull like a terrified bird. Without giving an answer, he pushed in past me, arms coming up to cross over his impressive pecs.

"I'm freezing, for one," Mel chattered, pacing with long steps to the opposite side of my living room before turning back to face me. He was huddled around himself in a way I'd never seen before, wearing a pea coat I recognized. It was a stylish thing I'd seen keep him warm in an autumn graveyard in the rain. Yet now, it looked as useless against the cold as a napkin. "Shut the door."

Shutting the door against my better judgment, I stayed where I was, wondering what had just forced its way into my home and if I was going to regret allowing it in. Well, I already regretted it, but that wasn't to say being attacked or gnawed on wouldn't make me regret it more.

"Well?" Mel demanded, throwing his arms up in the air as if I was the problem here.

"What?"

"I need help! You need to fix it!"

"I need to fix what?!" I argued back, though I was pretty sure I knew what he was talking about.

"I'm human!" Mel wailed, before pacing to the left toward my guest room. Lost, absolutely clueless about what he expected me to do about this, I watched him as he crossed my living room twice more. Mel is taller than me by a fair amount; if we stand close enough, I have to crane to look up into his attractive face. He's got blue eyes, dark hair, a superhero jaw, and thick, expressive brows. Our friendship had bloomed despite my empathy, which kept me from being comfortable around his werewolf emotions unless they were magically dampened. Despite the fact that feeling him usually makes my skin want to crawl off into corner and drown itself, I like looking at him. He's built like a statue of a Greek god and part of why he's so insufferable is that he knows it.

"I don't know what happened!" Mel whispered desperately, making me realize I hadn't responded. "I just—I woke up and I can't smell anything and I can't see anything and my hearing is shot and I can't shift!"

Squeezing my eyes shut for a moment, I shook myself out of my half-asleep thought process and looked back up at Mel. He was glancing over at me every so often as if I was going to announce the solution to a problem that I wasn't even sure I wanted to fix. No matter how hard I poked him with my empathy I could not detect even a hint of werewolf in him. Standing there with him pacing in my living room was no different than standing next to any human.

Was I dreaming, I wondered, taking a quick second to inspect myself from my dark, chin-length hair down to my plump hips crammed into too-tight, stained pajama pants. Had the fun dream about fancy pastries turned into a nightmare where something that looked like Mel weaseled its way into my home wanting to eat my face instead of nail me like the real Mel would have?

The human world at large isn't aware of preternatural creatures and, since I'm human—albeit somewhat enhanced—I'm not entirely aware of everything out there, either. I wasn't dreaming, I decided as Mel continued to fidget, and I knew I wasn't going to be of any help to him alone.

"I'm going to make a call," I said. Lifting a hand, I jabbed a finger toward him. "You: Sit. Stay."

Mel threw me a snarl, stopped pacing. "I'm not a dog."

"Not now, you're not."

"Not *ever*," he growled. It made me smile, breaking through my worry. If this was something impersonating Mel, it was doing a damned good job.

"This may be the earliest booty call I've ever gotten from you," Owen Reid purred into the phone in lieu of hello. "Unless you've switched time zones since the last time we spoke."

"Nope, still in Seattle. And, sadly, this isn't a booty call."

"Who are you and what have you done with Gwen Arthur?"

I laughed, but catching a look at Mel's annoyed expression sobered me up. "Uh, yeah, so. Mel's here and he's got a problem. Apparently he's human."

"Apparently?" Owen asked, his voice plain. I wasn't near enough to feel his emotions, of course, but something about the absolute lack of emotion made me think he didn't like what I had to say. "He's there, in your home I'd assume? And you're alone with him?"

"Yeah."

"Do me a favor. In your right nightstand I've tucked something at the back. Grab it for me."

"For you?" I asked, teasing him to cover the fact that his casual tone had me on edge. Leaving Mel hunched on the couch pouting, I did as Owen said, heading back to my room. He wasn't my boyfriend, exactly, but we were involved. Occasionally, when I'd been a very good girl or the universe was feeling very sorry for me, he'd show up and we'd get down and dirty. The last time we'd seen each other, things had gone to shit and we'd nearly been murdered by mermaids, but the sex had been good.

Apparently, some time when I hadn't been looking, he'd pirated my nightstand drawer and, because I hate to clean and have no reason to snoop through my own shit, I hadn't noticed. Tucked into the back of the drawer was a dagger, a medieval-looking thing with symbols down the blade and a handle that looked too intricate for something jammed into a nightstand in a sugar-addict's bedroom.

"Whoa," I said, shocked at the weight of it, how beautiful it was, and preemptively worried for what I was going to be expected to do with it.

"You see the fourth symbol, the one that looks like a circle with a …" Owen stopped and I got the feeling he wasn't sure what to call the thing slicing diagonally through the circle.

"A stalk of wheat?" I suggested. Owen let out a small snort.

"Yeah, that works. Go into the living room, slice open Mel's thumb and check the symbols."

"You want me to *what?*"

"If any symbol except that one lights up, get the fuck out of there."

"I'm not going to cut Mel open!"

"I'm not asking you to gut him like a fish," Owen said calmly. "Just his thumb. Any part of him will work, actually. I just figured a digit would be easy enough. Besides, if he protests, doesn't that say something as well?"

"It says he's someone who doesn't want to end up bleeding all over my hardwood. Which, by the way, I don't want either."

"Gwen," Owen said, and this time I could hear the emotion in his tone. It rang of frustration clear as day. "You called asking my advice. I'm a few states away so I can't do much in this moment except offer to interpret the results of this test. If you don't want to test his blood I can't help him."

"You can't … Facetime him or something and tell me anything?"

"He looks like Mel and, I'm assuming, feels human, right? So what am I supposed to do from here?"

"I … uh." I didn't have an answer. Owen knew his preternatural stuff and if poking Mel with a sharp, metal stick was the only thing he could suggest, I probably didn't have a choice if I wanted answers from him. "Okay. Hold on."

I whirled around, headed into the living room, and jolted as Mel burst to his feet and demanded, "Did you figure it out?"

"Here, gimme your hand."

"My hand?" Mel asked. Without question, trusting me like a child trusts a teacher, Mel stuck out his palm, offering me his flesh. I'd never cut anyone open before and I wasn't really sure how to do so with Mel. I'd sliced myself open in the kitchen dozens of times, but I hadn't ever really paid attention to how hard or what angle. Swallowing, I set my phone down on the coffee table, took Mel's hand in mine and grimaced up at him. I had tried for a smile but I'm confident I'd failed.

"Remember, you asked for this," I warned, before slicing the knife across his thumb and, by complete accident, the meaty part of his palm. Mel stood still for a beat, looking down at my handiwork, confused by the blood that welled. We both seemed confused by it, actually, like we'd just walked into the room and found two entirely other people acting out this weird, slightly witchy ritual.

Then he gasped, screeched, and wailed, "What the hell?"

"Sorry!" I yowled, jumping back, dropping the knife, then pointing spastically to the bathroom. "Don't bleed on the floor!"

Clutching his bloody hand, Mel stared at me, jaw dropped, for a few seconds, before darting off to the bathroom. I heard the water turn on, heard him yelp in pain, and I wailed quietly, feeling sick with guilt. Distantly I could hear a voice repeating my name rhythmically for a bit before I remembered I'd left Owen on the coffee table.

"I did it!" I announced into the phone. "Now what?"

"Look at the knife. Is anything lit?"

"Um." I crouched down to look at it, flipping it with one finger as if holding it might bleed me too. "Nothing's lit up."

Owen was quiet, completely absent of sound as if he'd hung up or ceased to be. I could hear something faint in the background, like a hotel room heater, so I knew he hadn't actually hung up on me, but it was just as jarring as if I'd been abandoned.

"What?"

"This isn't good," Owen said simply, steel edging his voice. "Especially since I can't help right now. The job I'm doing, it's not something I can walk away from. I'm going to make some calls and see if I can find anyone who can help you right now, but if I can't find anyone, Mel may just have to wait until I'm done."

"What's wrong with him?"

"Gwen, I need you to promise me something."

"I'm not cutting anyone else open."

"Don't tell Chloe."

"What?" I asked, a laugh fracturing my voice, confusion burbling to the surface of my psyche, even as Mel's pain, exasperation, and anger still jabbed at me from across the room. "Don't tell Chloe what?"

"About Mel. If I can't find someone else to help you, then you have to wait until I can deal with it."

"Why?"

Owen sighed, a rare sound of disquiet coming from him. "That's … more than we have time for now. But I can say that, if this is what I think this is, Chloe trying to solve this herself could put her in a lot of danger. This isn't something she's equipped to deal with, not anymore. Well," Owen spat and there was disgust there. "Maybe not ever."

"But you're equipped?"

"Probably not."

"What about Mel?" I asked, turning away, lowering my voice. "Is he going to be okay?"

"Waiting won't make it any worse, I can tell you that."

"Won't make what any worse?" I asked, still quiet. The water turned off in the bathroom and I could feel Mel moving closer, coming back into the living room.

"Losing his soul," Owen said simply.

Olivia R. Burton

Two

Owen promised to make some calls and get back to me and I let him go, trusting him to do his best to help Mel get his wolf back. Owen was a mercenary by trade, a badass with a gun and sexy abs who could fight off mermaids and stop succubi. If anyone could fix Mel's problem, it was definitely Owen.

Despite all that, I couldn't just sit around, not with Mel in the state he was in, and not on an empty stomach. Mel admitted, after some prodding, that he couldn't remember the last time he'd eaten either, and as I plied him with bandaids and anti-bacterial cream, I came to a decision.

"We'll go see Madeline."

"You think she can fix me?"

"Do I think she can give you your soul back?" I asked, scooping the pile of wrappers into my hand and carrying them to the trash. "No. But she's pretty smart and we helped her deal with Norma, so maybe she'd be willing to offer some sort of advice."

"I'm not missing my soul," Mel said, inspecting his bandaged hand with a scowl. "Your boyfriend doesn't know what he's talking about."

"He usually knows exactly what he's talking about, but he's not my boyfriend," I protested. Mel lifted his gaze to me and I couldn't read his face, or the exact pitch of his emotions. We watched each other quietly for a few moments before I stepped as wide around him as my narrow kitchen would allow, and jerked my head. "I'm gonna get dressed."

"What if she can't help?" Mel asked quietly, as I hit the doorway.

"Then at least you will have bought me breakfast and some hot cocoa."

Mel snorted, amused despite the situation, and I grinned as I rushed to my room.

"Have a seat, I'll order."

"Get me hot coffee. Like, really hot. I'm freezing."

"That's because you're wearing the thinnest jacket ever made."

"I don't need—I don't *usually* need anything else, okay?"

"Just go snag a table."

The Internets is my favorite place to overeat pastries, despite the fact that it's often crowded to the ceiling with people. I don't do well around lots of emotions, mainly because I don't just perceive them, but I often take them on. When someone's standing next to me feeling mad, I get mad. I take in their stabbing rage and—well, I get angry at the pain of having to stand next to them, firstly, but it doesn't stop there. I start thinking of things that make me mad or, barring any thoughts about red-light runners, litterbugs, or restaurants that fail to notify me before I order that they're out of the advertised desserts, I invent things to be angry about.

As a result, going into a crowd is like walking into a circus filled with screaming children, clumsy knife-jugglers, a stampede of elephants, and carnival games where the aim is to shoot my eye out instead of that of some wooden clown. Only, all of those things are emotions and I'm stuck in a tent with them.

The Internets is different, though, probably because it's owned and nearly constantly occupied by a succubus. Madeline isn't much to look at but none of that matters to anyone who comes near her and, really, why should it? She's a nice lady who gives discounts on snacks and coffees, stays open late, and puts up with my inability to properly calculate a tip.

Plus, part of her being a preternatural creature that feeds on sex is that she exudes a pleasant aura or pheromone or something that makes everyone within her orbit just a little bit content and horny. It works out well for me and my stupid empathy and not just because the joint takes up the whole bottom floor of my office building.

I'd finished placing my order and was handing over my credit card when Madeline stepped out from the kitchen, her gaze directly on me.

"Gwen," she said, more seriously than I'd heard in awhile. "What's happened?"

"What do you mean?" I asked, pausing with a chocolate muffin part way to my lips. It would take my card a second to process; I could probably get half the carbs down in that time.

"Mel," she said, before moving away from me to let herself out from behind the counter. I glanced back at Mel, set the muffin down, and grabbed a pen to sign. Apparently stuffing my face would have to wait.

She got to the table before I did, and I paused next to her, unsure if I needed to leave the two of them alone. "Got your coffee."

"What happened," Madeline repeated, to Mel this time.

Mel reached out for the mug with one hand, gesturing wildly with the other. "I don't know! I just woke up this morning *human*!"

"You're not human," Madeline said, before noticing me standing there. She gestured for me to have a seat, and then looked back to Mel. "But you are missing part of your soul."

"Told you," I said, finally taking a bite of my muffin. Mel turned to me, his jaw obstinately set, before he looked back up at Madeline and relented. "You can tell that?"

"I can guess that's what's the matter," she corrected. Leaning down as if she wanted to get a closer look at him, she lowered her voice. "We've joined in the past, I know the way you should taste. It's different, wrong. It's … you, but human. Sweeter, sure, but wrong."

"Sweeter?" I asked, mouth full of chocolate. Madeline nodded but didn't look over.

"It's almost as if someone else has fed on you, nearly drained you, but there's no claim, no mark. This wasn't another one of my kind."

"Thank god," Mel said, a shiver of panic running through him. As if to settle himself, he grabbed his mug, took a deep gulp, choked, exploded with shocked pain that hit my chest like spikes, and coughed out steaming coffee. It spattered the table, my muffin, and Madeline's hands. I swore at him unintelligibly around my breakfast but Madeline only stood, pulled the rag from her apron, and mopped the coffee off herself and the table.

"Careful," she said so mildly I laughed. "Coffee's hot."

"Scalding!" Mel yelped, hanging his mouth open and panting like a dog. I almost spat my muffin at him laughing at the irony, but kept the observation to myself. "Why would you serve this to anyone!?"

"It's the same temperature we always make it. You're just not a werewolf at the moment."

Mel sucked in a breath as if to argue, but only sank back against the booth, depressed instead. I frowned, feeling a little bad for him, and took a moment to let him pout, inspecting my muffin for coffee damage. Deeming it still edible, I crammed the rest into my mouth and waited to see what would happen next.

Madeline gave Mel some time, before she patted his hand. "You don't know how this happened?"

"No idea. I just woke up weak and pathetic."

"And you can't think of anyone who could have done this to you?"

"I didn't even know someone *could* do this to me! Even when N—" Mel faltered and I felt the same nostalgic sort of pain from earlier slither through him. "Even when I was fed on before, it didn't feel like this. I wasn't human."

"No," Madeline agreed, keeping mum on mentioning the other succubus who'd threatened not only Mel's life but also her own in a roundabout way.

"Looks like you'll have to find out, won't you?"

"Is that how I fix it?" Mel asked, looking up at her expectantly.

"I can't say. I would assume, however, that knowing what a problem is helps one solve it. Once you know why you're effectively human, you might be able to reverse it."

"It's too bad you can't just get your brother or Sarah to bite you and turn you back," I suggested. Mel frowned at me but it was more sad than disappointed.

"We don't precreate that way."

"I know," I assured him, before grinning. "I met the pups."

Mel smiled at that, his sour mood no match for the thought of all his nieces and nephews.

"We'll figure it out," I assured him, suddenly filled with pity. My usual annoyance with Mel's very existence couldn't hold up against the very human sadness and worry swirling through him. Sure, being an empath often makes me an asshole, causing me to reflect the negativity back on the people exuding it, but it makes me nice sometimes too. I'm never unsure if someone's suffering and having to feel said suffering sure as hell makes me want to get rid of it, sometimes to my own detriment.

Rarely, but it's been known to happen.

"What's our first step?" I asked Mel as we got back into his car. He turned it on immediately, blasting me with the heater that I'd forgotten he'd left maxed. I winced at the vent. February in Seattle is chilly, usually the last blast of frigid ice and snow before it goes back to a constant, dreary drizzle, but this was overkill. "I suggest we buy you a new coat."

"I don't need a new coat," Mel said, even though he was huddled into himself, teeth still chattering.

"Yes you do. Where's the nearest REI?"

"Gwen, I don't plan on staying like this. I'm not going to buy a winter coat I'll never need again."

"Yes you are or I'm not helping you. If we're going to be—actually." I cut off, realizing a serious flaw in his original plan of showing up pathetic and human on my doorstep. "Why did you want me to help you?"

"What do you mean?"

"You woke up as a human—at an ungodly hour, by the way—and decided I was the one who should help you?"

"It wasn't ungodly, it was five. What time do you wake up?"

"Oh a Saturday? Ten? Noon? Seven if Chloe is feeling particularly sadistic and wants me to work out."

"Do you stay up until four, or something?"

"We're not having this conversation," I snapped. "This is about you and the fact that you thought coming to a therapist would be the right way to solve your very strange and confusing problem. Why not go to Chloe?"

Mel's gaze dropped and his shivering ceased. He was quiet for awhile, as if truly perplexed by my query. "I … I don't know. I just panicked and thought of you."

"Because you wanted to talk through your feelings about your father?"

"My father's great. Look, I don't know." Mel turned his attention to his massive vehicle, put it into gear, and pulled out into traffic. "I just … You're human; I figured … I didn't think about it, really."

"Why not Chloe? She's got her shit together way better than I have and she's way more qualified. She used to be … What was it, the Hammer?"

"Gavel," Mel corrected automatically.

"Yeah, she used to work for some Fairy, she's got that sack full of magical whatsits and doodads, and she *likes* getting up early. Why did you show up at my place?"

"Well, maybe I thought you'd be nicer to someone suffering a great injustice, someone weakened, someone in trouble."

"Who the fuck do you think you're talking to?"

Mel glanced over, saw that I was joking, and laughed. "Fair point. Look, I don't know. We worked together at Tough Love, you saved me from Norma—"

"That was Owen."

"Well, you *know* Owen. Maybe that's it, I was just using you to get to him."

I made a thoughtful sound, realized he was getting on the freeway toward downtown and that we were probably going to REI like I'd suggested.

"Good. Then, since I'm your savior, do as I say and buy a coat."

"Savior?" Mel snorted. "Even human I could take you in a fight."

"You burned your mouth on a moderately hot cup of coffee."

"… Shut up."

"I will if you buy a damned coat. It won't do anyone any good if you freeze to death before you spontaneously turn back into a werewolf."

"You think that could happen?"

"Dear god I hope so."

Mel laughed and went quiet as we drove. After a bit, I caught him glancing at me as he took the exit I'd expected him to take. "You're sure you don't like me better human?"

"I still don't even know if I like you at all."

Mel went silent then, glowering at the road ahead as I chuckled to myself. I let him stew for awhile, taking the time to try to formulate a plan for exactly how I was going to help him if I couldn't call the only local person who would have the tools, resources, and good ideas to fix everything.

"So walk me through your day," I said as Mel and I stepped out of REI into the brisk Seattle air. "Did you run afoul of any covens or fall into a vat of Instant Human?"

"It was a normal day," Mel said, leading me back toward the car. "No witches or weirdly specific vats of goo."

"But walk me through it. Humor me."

"You humor yourself enough."

"I *am* hilarious," I agreed, before whacking his arm with the back of my hand. He winced but I knew I hadn't done it hard enough to do any damage. "Go. What's a typical day for Mel Somerset? You—what?—wake up, stare into the mirror for six hours making kissy sounds and admiring your abs, open the phone book to list out the next ten women you need to sleep with to get all the way through it—you're up to the Qs, which you're very proud of."

Mel climbed into the car silently, eyeballing me, but letting me ramble as I did the same.

"You take a photo of the list, tuck the original into your wish box—which is covered in brightly colored pictures of unicorns!—and then it's time for breakfast. Seven raw eggs, a bowl of dry protein powder, an entire package of goat sausages, and a jug of fortified orange juice. Am I right?" He didn't answer. "Naturally you shower after that, letting your four-thousand-dollar, automated closet pick out your outfit, and then it's back to the kitchen where you hydrate with sixty-four ounces of water and slurp down some sort of supplement that you were promised would make your dick bigger."

"Hey," Mel snapped, finally taking issue with my assessment of his character. The dry protein powder, analog phone book, and six-hour preening didn't bother him but this was too far. "You know for a fact I need no help in that arena."

"Oh, it's the size of an arena now, is it? You should see a doctor about that."

"I saw two yesterday, in fact, and they each gave me a thorough physical."

"Okay, don't get gross. So you had two dates yesterday?"

"I wouldn't call them dates, but I had three, in fact. Two … encounters—"

"You banged some aliens? With giant grey heads and sticky fingers?"

"Do you want to hear about my day or not?"

"Not if you had sex with sticky-fingered Martians."

"Gwen."

I lost it, doubling over laughing at the defeat in his tone and the gravelly annoyance filling the cab. When my laughter trickled into giggles, I did my best to clear my throat and gestured for him to continue. He watched me for a bit longer, the parking time limits be damned, before he sighed and spoke.

"I woke up, I went for a run, as I always do. I showered, had breakfast, looked over my caseload for the day, headed into the office. I did some research, broke for lunch, met with my first lover, then went out to surveil. Around five I met with my second lover, then headed home to prepare for my date."

Mel went quiet then, ending on a note of finality, as if that was all that needed to be said. I knew I didn't want details of said date, but that couldn't have been the entire day. If he'd woken up at home before tearing over to my place, then he'd either had the date stay over, or gone somewhere and come back after.

"And then?"

"You said you didn't want me to get gross—not that sex is gross, especially not sex with me."

"I bet sex with you gets gross sometimes," I argued, certain I could predict how open-minded he was to the whims and fetishes of possible partners. "But I don't even mean that part. Did you go to pick her up? Did she come to you? If you did pick her up, where did you go? Did you eat at any new places? Was there a mustachioed man in a dark trench coat slinking after you at any point? Did you go furry and get magical paint thrown on you by a vegan, what?"

"We …" Mel faltered and I felt a little flutter of panic. "We went on a date. I came home and slept. That's it."

"Is it?"

"It … I came home and went to sleep."

Something there, I thought, frowning at him. "Did you shower first? At her place? Where *was* her place? Or did you just get it on in the backseat of this thing?"

"I came home …" The fluttering panic flapped like a bird and I winced, my arm twitching as if I'd meant to lift my hand and protect my face from beating wings. "And went to sleep."

"So you came home and went to sleep," I said, knowing that wasn't the whole story, even though he was insisting it was. "So let's go to your home, check it out."

"Why?"

"Because if that's where you ended up after your date with this woman, maybe there's a clue. What would you do if this was a case you were investigating for someone else?"

Mel watched me, his beautiful face a mask of uncertainty. Nerves still flapped in his gut, joined by helpless confusion. I wasn't sure where any of it was coming from, if it was just a side effect of being human or if something more sinister was afoot. Before I could ask, he swallowed hard, took a deep breath, and then started the car. We drove in silence.

Olivia R. Burton

Three

Mel lives in the forest, deep down dirt roads between towering trees, amongst nature befitting a dude who can shift from a beefcake into a nearly jet black wolf. He still hadn't explained what his plan would have been if he'd been hired to investigate some other poor schmuck being robbed of his identity, but I hadn't pressed. He was shaken up and even without his werewolf emotions, that was hard to sit next to.

When we got into his place, I took a look around, considered the dark woods, rich fabrics, and stylish lines of his small home, and then gestured vaguely.

"Well, where should we start?"

"I have no idea," Mel admitted, looking around with disappointment plain on his face. I sighed, wishing I could rid him of the beating thumps of defeat hitting me in the chest. It took me a moment before I realized that, oh hey, I could.

"Gimme your hand," I said, closing in and reaching for him.

"Gwen, human or not, I'm really not ready for marriage." I rolled my eyes, grabbed his hand without waiting for him to give it, and took a deep breath. Before I could try anything he said, "don't cut me open again."

"Does it look like I've tucked a samurai sword up my sleeve?"

"Maybe you'll use that sharp tongue of yours."

I grinned up at him and we shared a small laugh that eased the tension just a bit. The emotional connection, as you'd expect, is stronger with touch and, before I flexed my empathy to draw unpleasantness out, it beat against me like a child smacking me with a pool noodle. Then, when sucked in, it was briefly worse, then briefly better, and then unpleasant again. I moaned, dropping his arm, feeling the pounding inside me now, fighting like it wanted out, and I had to do a quick run around the kitchen island to calm myself.

I'd only learned a few months ago the my empathy was more than just a sponge that could sop up small amounts of emotion. When visiting my family and dealing with a slightly murderous tree, I'd realized it's more of a vacuum. I'd always known it sucked, but never how literally.

As I let out a wail and shuddered out the last of Mel's disappointment, I came to a stop near the fridge, flexing my hands. "You good?"

"I guess," Mel said, confused. He watched me quizzically for a bit, before looking around as if everything should be different. "What just happened?"

"Don't worry about it. You got any chocolate?"

"Sure," he said, moving to his pantry cabinet. "What kind?"

"Milk. With marshmallows. Or caramel. Ooh, or *both*."

Mel tossed me a pack of caramel cups that I greedily tore into, munching away the last of the discomfort that I was always left with after stealing emotions. Mel wouldn't stay in his improved state forever, but hopefully it would last at least long enough for me convince him to start helping and stop whining.

"Okay. Now. Where do we start?"

"I don't know," Mel said again, though unbothered this time. I swore, throwing my arms up into the air.

"Never mind. Tell me about your dates."

"I thought you didn't want to hear."

"I don't want to hear descriptions of breast size or sex sounds, but gimme a general rundown. You're sure all the women you bothered yesterday were on the level?"

"I'm certain all the women I *treated* were on the level, yes."

"Even the newbie?" I said, ignoring his incorrect assessment of his sexual abilities. "The other two are clearly nuts, but if you've boned them before and come out of it still furry, I guess they're probably fine."

"Veronica was normal. I've slept with plenty of women before, Gwen. You among them, in fact, and none of them have ever caused anything like this. Not for me, not for any other werewolf I've ever met. It's not the women. Or the sex," he said, as if anticipating some nasty comment.

Tossing the wrapper in the trash, I figured I'd at least get to snooping and hope he'd follow suit. "Still, tell me about her."

"You jealous?" Mel asked as I opened the first cabinet.

"Only of the women who *haven't* had to sleep with you."

"Because you know they still get to experience the joy fresh for the first time?" I rolled my eyes and moved on in my search. Mel laughed, pushing on. "I don't know. She was pretty, young, maybe mid-twenties. She doesn't live locally, but she's in town on business. I met her at work, actually. We were both on the elevator and started chatting. She gave me her number, then headed off to her meeting."

"What's she do?"

"Consulting."

"Descriptive."

"I wasn't looking to get input on my branding," he spat, "so we didn't talk much about work."

"What did you talk about?"

"Does it matter?"

I thought about it as I considered the living room and then dropped down to peer under the couch. Mel kept an immaculate household, somehow, and I wondered if he had a maid and if maybe I should get one. There were probably at least a dozen candy wrappers and old Skittles tucked under *my* couch.

"I guess not. So, tell me about the date."

"We went out, we had sex, I came home."

"Descriptive," I deadpanned again, getting to my feet and deciding I would move on to—as much as it pained me—his bedroom. Mel followed, still not commenting as I moved about, pulling open drawers in his walk-in closet, rifling through his hanging clothes, looking under his bed, and moving around to check the second nightstand. He did laugh when I let out another uncomfortable wail at seeing a cutlery tray filled with neatly organized sex toys, but he didn't offer to show me how to use them, so I just shut the drawer and kept snooping.

"It's really awkward," I said as I stepped into his massive bathroom. "Pawing through your stuff while you just silently watch me like a perverted ghost."

"Why am I the pervert? You're the one eyeballing my vibrators."

"You're the one who has them!" I argued. Mel lifted a brow, smirk firmly planted on his full lips, making it clear he knew I was the vibrator calling the kettle black. I quickly changed the subject. "Uh. Tell me more about Veronica and your date. I assume you went out but didn't immediately have sex right outside her hotel room door."

"No," Mel said, but didn't offer anymore.

"Good god, Mel. You've never been shy about your sex life before, why start now?"

"There's just nothing to tell!"

"There's nothing to tell?" I argued, pushing to my feet and kicking his vanity shut. "You know, I'm doing all the work here. You're not giving me anything—don't look at me like that, I'm not interested in your vibrators—and you're not helping me look. Why am I doing all the work when you're the one who's so worried about being human? I'm fine with being human."

"I already told you, there's nothing to tell about my date."

A flutter of panic wobbled in his gut, piquing my interest. I closed in on him, watching him as I pressed. "Why did you come to my house this morning?"

"Because I'm human!"

"And you thought maybe it was my fault?"

"No, I want you to fix it."

"You want *me* to fix it? Mel I've had a remote control that's been out of batteries for, like, three months because I'm too lazy to buy more. What the fuck are you talking about?"

"I just woke up, realized I was human, and came to your house. I don't know."

"Why don't you know?" I asked, crossing my arms as if they could stop the fluttering panic from reaching into my own chest. "You woke up, realized you were human, and thought ... what? Gwen will fix this? Gwen—the human whose arm I nearly chewed off after she got herself stuck in spider poop—is who can fix this confusing and unfathomable problem?"

"Look. Look. *Look*," Mel said, anger jumping to the front of his psyche, rushing to his defense as if it could actually help anything. "If you don't want to help me, I'll—I'll—I'll ..." Instead of finishing his sentence, he just threw up his arms and stormed off to cross out into the bedroom. "You're being a real bitch about this."

"Why didn't you go to Chloe?"

Mel stopped storming, facing the wall, as confusion bubbled up in a fizzy mess, overflowing across the floor to burble around my feet. I watched him, genuinely intrigued by his reaction. Mel was never this unsure, never this bothered. The only time I'd seen him this out of sorts had been when he'd been rejected by Mrs. Quottrich, my most miserable client. The old bat had acted as if his polite advances had been physical assault and it had sent him into a tailspin. He'd been under the influence of a succubus then, but apparently this time was different. There was no Norma in his brain, and his soul hadn't just been chewed up by a magical creature who feeds on sex.

Now, I had no idea what was going on, but it was really messing with his head.

"Why didn't you go to Chloe?" I repeated, as Mel turned to glare at me.

"Are you going to help me, or not?" he asked, sidestepping the question. Instead of pressing, instead of making the impotent anger and panic in his guts worse, I held up my hands in surrender.

"I'll help."

He sighed, but remained a storm of disharmony. After a few moments, giving him enough time to calm down a bit, I headed into his room to meet him, and jerked my head toward the hall.

"Come on.,"

"Where are we going?"

"I have an idea," I said, deciding I didn't want to give anything away in case it spooked him. One thing that seemed consistent about Mel's state was that, despite insisting he wanted to get his wolf back, Mel seemed singularly dedicated to steering clear of anything that could actually help do so.

I wasn't sure how to get him to cooperate except to treat him like a dog who needs to take medicine but hates the taste. Metaphorically, I was gonna have to mash the solution to all this into a hunk of cheese and chuck it at him from a distance.

I let Mel drive his stupidly massive Suburban, but gave him directions as he went. He didn't catch on to where we were headed and I hoped he never would. Once we were on the freeway, once his guard was down and he was feeling better, I felt a wedge of curious puckishness bump out of him.

"Tell me about your boyfriend."

"I don't have a boyfriend," I said, not bothering to look up from my phone.

"So the man you see semi-regularly isn't your boyfriend?"

"Nope."

"*Owen's* not your boyfriend?"

"No. Why, does that bother you?"

"I guess it just surprises me a little that you're a casual sex girl."

"I'm not a casual sex girl, Somerset. I'm a casual sex *woman*."

Mel rolled his eyes and I pressed on before he could get out the word eking through his vocal chords.

"How do you know I see him semi-regularly?" I asked, hoping we could leap-frog the subject of my sex life and somehow move on to something else.

"You show up at the office smelling of him here and there. It's not a hard link to make."

"You sniff me at work?"

Mel laughed. "I sniff everyone at work. Not really on purpose, it's just part of being a werewolf."

"What's Chloe smell like?"

"Usually whatever shampoo she's using. And whatever person she's been with. Lately it's that … uh, Izzy, I think."

I groaned, shaking my head as the subject of Chloe's weird, otherworldly boyfriend came up. I like Izzy, I guess. He's … nice enough. But there's nothing human about him, he'd brought with him a cat that I was now forced to work with, and he steals most of the sweets I get my hands on, both in and out of my house, whether I let him in or not. Mel laughed.

"You don't like Izzy?"

"I don't … know how to deal with Izzy. He's weird and unpredictable and eats my sweets."

"So he and Chloe aren't exclusive, then?"

It took me a moment to realize Mel was making a lewd joke but when I did, I whined, sick at the suggestion. "Gross!"

Mel laughed, cheered by my reaction—and off the subject of Owen and my sex life, thank god. "What, isn't Izzy cute enough?"

"Izzy isn't human."

"Neither am I and you jumped into my lap."

"I didn't—" I couldn't *really* argue that point. Yes, I'd spent ages avoiding Mel and being annoyed by his interest in me but, when it had come down to the actual deed, I'd been the one who'd started it. "You're different."

"How?"

"Izzy isn't ... He's like ... He's like a particularly stupid dog. You may be the one who can wag his tail, but I can't even begin to imagine sleeping with Izzy. He's in no way a sexual being."

"Gwen, has no one ever explain to you where puppies come from?"

I snorted. "I know dogs have sex, but I would never have sex *with* a dog. It's—Izzy and I aren't ... Just drop it, okay? Let's talk about something else."

"Like your boyfriend?"

"I swear to god, I will roll down a window and jump out."

Mel cackled, delighted by my frustration, but he didn't press.

We arrived at Merrin's building, found parking as easily as ever, and headed up the dirty staircase to her floor. The building was old and poorly maintained and I'd stopped bothering with the elevator awhile back. It usually didn't work but when it did there was a horrible metallic sound that made me want to pee myself.

Merrin Smith is a witch, a tiny, flighty redhead who drifts in and out of reality but somehow still manages to survive in the world by reading tarot cards, palms, tea leaves, and whatever else hippies and bored, jobless rich people are into. Chloe and I used to check on her, throwing her money here and there or bringing her food, but a little over a year ago she'd gained some sort of Fairy keeper. Since then, we hadn't had much contact with her, but I was hoping Evadne would at least remember me and let Merrin help me.

She didn't like Mel much, but maybe now that he was human she'd chill out.

"We should have taken the elevator," Mel said, panting a bit. I wasn't much better off, though I really should have been the only one complaining. I've got an extra forty pounds on me and my idea of pushing myself to my own limits is to grab the remote from the other end of the couch using only my socked feet. Mel, however, is beefy and built and, like he said, he goes for a run every morning. Three stories shouldn't have turned him asthmatic.

"We're almost there, Somerset. Perk up."

"She'd better be able to help me. I don't think I can live like this. It's torture."

I snorted, amused at his assessment of being human, and patted him on the back as we hit the landing. Mel took a moment to catch his breath, seeming genuinely bothered by the state of his fitness, but I pushed on, headed down the hall. It was a cacophony of emotions, people crammed four or five to an apartment in most cases, with the occasional lone grump tucked deeper into the building. This, as well as arguing, loud music, the smell of weed, and barking, distressed dogs were all typical of Merrin's place.

We got to her door as it opened and a small, puffy toddler ran smack into my knee, bouncing back onto her diapered bottom without so much as a blip in her emotions. She struggled like an upturned turtle to get up, while her mother approached, watching us as she bent down to stand the kid up.

"Can I help you?"

Confused, I glanced past her into what I thought had been Merrin's apartment, and then back to her. She was suspicious, confused, and a little annoyed, though the slice of that had been present before we'd walked up. Her husband glanced over from his space on the couch but didn't offer us greetings or ask who we were.

I smiled kindly, trying to ease her suspicion. "Hi! We came to visit a friend, but I think we might have mixed up the apartments. It's been awhile since we saw her."

"Oh, well, we just moved in a few weeks ago."

"Ah, that explains it," I said, glancing down as the kid did her best to peer up at me from within layers of warm clothes. "Sorry to have bothered you."

"No problem," the woman said, leaning down to heft the kid up into her arms. "I hope you find her."

"Thanks!" Leaving her to carry the kid off in the direction we'd come, I steered Mel down the hall, just aiming to give her space so she wouldn't feel threatened. When we were far enough away, I stepped around to face him. "Well, there goes that idea."

"When did Merrin move?"

"A few weeks ago, apparently."

"Where did she go? Can you call her?"

"Mel," I growled, the emotions of the building sparking in my brain, short-circuiting my patience. "I know what you do. And no, I don't have her number. She had a home number here, but Chloe has it. I don't think I can ask for it without letting on that something's the matter."

"And why can't you tell Chloe again?"

"Why didn't *you* tell Chloe?" I argued, annoyed at his annoyance. As if this was all my fault and I'd begged him to let me solve his stupid problem. "You came to me!"

"I already explained—Look, let's just try to find some other way to fix things."

"Like what?" I challenged, feeling twin spikes of rage jab out of the apartment behind me, as voices rose and the clear sounds of an argument followed. I didn't know the language, but anger isn't hard to translate.

"I don't know."

"We could call Sarah, Julien? What about your other siblings? You've got like a hundred, right?"

"Just three. I don't want to bother them."

"You don't want to *bother* them? Mel, you're human!"

"I know!"

Another spike of anger hit me, thumping into my spine with a sharp pain that I recognized as jealousy and hurt as it sliced through the back of my heart. Before I could consider throwing up my mental shields or controlling myself, frustration with Mel and his whiny lack of interest in solving his own problem took over and I lashed out. Without meaning to, without even really knowing what I was doing, I punched Mel as hard as I could in the shoulder.

My fist cracked, Mel grunted, and we both swore. "Shit!"

"Fuck!"

Cradling my hand, guilt sloshing around in my guts, I turned away, swearing quietly to myself, trying to overcome the anger that still crackled through me, the shame roiling in an oily mess in my belly, mixing with Mel's shocked hurt and insult.

"What the hell?" he croaked, cradling his arm.

"Shit, shit. Sorry. Shit. I don't—sorry."

"Why'd you hit me?"

"I don't know, I just—we should get out of here. It's—Come on. I'll buy you a cookie."

"A cookie?" Mel demanded, insulted. I laughed bitterly at the annoyance in him and shook my head, lifting my hands to rub the frustration out of my suddenly tight face.

"I don't know. I want a cookie when things go wrong. I don't know. We just have to get out of here."

"Can we try the elevator at least?"

"If you want to risk it, sure. It's around the corner."

"I know where it is."

The elevator didn't work, just as I'd thought, but we found a stairwell closer than the one we'd taken up. We made it back to the car without coming to blows again, and when we got in, Mel immediately started stripping.

"What are you doing?" I demanded, panicked for reasons I couldn't articulate.

"I think you really hurt me," Mel mumbled once the jacket was off. He tucked his arm out of its sleeve and out under the shirt so he could inspect his arm without getting completely shirtless. "No bruise yet, but it really hurts."

"Sorry," I said again, still feeling bad. "The people behind me were having a screaming match, the couple below them were decidedly *not* having a screaming anything, and you pissed me off."

"I pissed *you* off?"

"Mel!" Snapping, worrying suddenly that I might hit him again, I smacked my fists into my own thighs, growling out a rumbling string of curses, and then took a deep breath, forcing myself to calm down. I had no idea what to do or how to help Mel. He wouldn't—or couldn't?—tell me what had gone on the night before; he insisted nothing strange or unusual had happened, and the only people who would know where to start were unavailable to me. Mel put his shirt and jacket and more effective jacket back on, and then started the car. We sat in heated silence for a few moments as I tried to formulate a plan.

We needed to trace his steps, to figure out what he'd gotten himself into that had turned him human. I'd watched a million hours of television in my lifetime. Some of that crime solving, procedural shit had to have leaked into my brain. Even if it was all bullshit, at least it was somewhere to start.

"Gimme your phone," I said reaching out. Mel didn't answer or do as I asked. When I looked over at him, he was frowning at me, suspicious. Frustration bloomed in a mushroom cloud through my chest once more and I threw myself at him, digging into his pockets as he tried to fight me off without hurting me. I got the upper hand, though, when he tried to shove me back with the hand I'd sliced open and the pain made him jerk back. I found his phone, dropped back into my bucket seat, and found it locked. Like a genius, I aimed it at his face to unlock it as it suggested, and then began to search through it.

Four

His message apps were curiously void of any mention of the girl he'd supposedly met the night before, despite being filled with evidence of many, many other romantic encounters. He had work notes, personal notes, saved images that I didn't look too closely at, but no real evidence of who he'd met.

"Did you erase the stuff about the date?"

"No," Mel said, his own curiosity piqued. "Why?"

"Because I can't find anything about it. How did you know where to meet her?"

"Where to meet her?" Mel asked. I sighed, giving up. Clearly he couldn't remember, even though he didn't seem aware he didn't remember. Every time I'd tried to get a direct answer about his date, he'd found some way of evading. Maybe whatever had happened to him had affected his memory as well.

"Though that wouldn't do anything to your phone, would it?"

"What?"

"Shut up." Trying something else, I started opening apps I'd use if I was going on a date. Yeah, Mel didn't date like I would and I didn't date like most other women would, but surely there had to be some similarities. I checked his search history, found the last week empty, checked his dating apps, and finally went to his maps app. "Bingo!"

"What did you find?"

"Where you went last night."

"Where I went last night?"

"Just drive, Mel." Sighing, I set the phone on its magnetic cradle on the dash, and pointed to the directions there. "Just follow the directions. This is the last place you searched for yesterday, so it has to be something."

"You're sure?"

"It's literally the only thing I can think to try right now, okay? Just humor me. Or, stay human forever. I don't care."

Petulant annoyance jabbed out of Mel and into my side, but he started the car and we were on our way.

We got to the hotel, pulled into the underground parking, and I thanked my stars that I hadn't been the one driving. Downtown Seattle sucks to drive in normally, but the closer you get to the Space Needle, especially on a weekend the worse it gets.

"I don't think I actually was here last night," Mel commented as we found a spot.

"I don't trust you," I said, unbuckling. "You don't seem to know what the hell's going on, really."

"I know exactly what's going on," Mel grumbled, though he didn't elaborate. We headed to the little elevator vestibule, hitting the button even as I felt the thing descend, filled with people. I frowned, trying to figure out why the cluster of patterns felt familiar, and found myself still frowning into the car as the doors opened and a group I knew all too well saw me, paused, and then shrieked.

Well, one of them shrieked. The rest let out a manly rumble of pleased recognition. Rita Stemple, small, dark-haired, and eclectic as hell, flung herself out of the elevator, crushing me to her as if trying to suffocate me. Everything in me melted a little, feeling strangely comforted by the fact that she still smelled the same as she had in college. The rest of the group filed out, filling the tiny room with happy surprise and, to my horror, one awful slither of smugness that only barely masked a wriggling, slimy thread of insecurity. Studiously ignoring the slither, I did my best to focus on Rita's glee at running into me after so many years.

"G-Spot!" she yipped, pulling away to grin hugely into my face. I laughed, caught up in her glee, though I would have been happy on my own. Of the whole damn band, she'd always been my favorite. "Guys, it's G-Spot!"

She stepped aside as Jason pushed forward, brushed his blond hair back from his long face, and pulled me into an awkward hug.

"How you doing, man?" he asked. I melted a little; Jason is gorgeous and always has been. Age had been good to the angles of his face and it seemed he'd started dressing himself. Ten years ago he'd let Lance do a lot of his clothes shopping, just out of laziness.

"I'm good," I said as Dennis and Harvey came forward and Jason stepped back. "You guys look great." I took the hugs happily, patting backs, rubbing shoulders, agreeing that it was wild we'd all run into each other, in this of all places, until the final member approached. My insides turned to lead. Lance smirked, looking down on me with his mud brown eyes, and I couldn't decide if I wanted to hit him or carve open the earth and let it swallow me up. He looked the same as he had in college, though definitely aged a bit more than the others.

I couldn't imagine what I'd seen in him back then and it wasn't because he'd changed for better or worse, either. He was still bone skinny, tall as a stop sign, dressed like a pretentious asshole, and slightly unwashed. Eighteen-year-old Gwen had been such a stupid idiot.

"G-Spot indeed," he purred. No, I reconsidered, I definitely wanted to hit him more than the other thing.

"Who's your buddy?" Rita asked, probably sensing the fact that Lance was moments from getting a knee to the groin.

"Oh, sorry," I said, taking the excuse to get the fuck away from my ex. "This is Mel."

"I'm a huge fan," Mel said, giddy but playing it cool. "It's really great to meet you. Are you in town for a gig?"

"Yeah! We all came in early to catch up with friends and fam, though," Rita said, pulling him into a hug as if they too were old friends. "So nice to meet you, man. I knew we'd run into Gwen. Didn't I tell you? I told them."

Dennis nodded. "She said it, like, ten times. We're all headed to lunch, if you want to join us."

"Yeah, wildcat," Lance purred, desperate for my attention in a way that would have made me laugh if it had been anyone else. "Come with us."

"*Don't* call me that," I hissed before I could control myself.

"But you're feral in the sack," he murmured, his voice deliberately gravelly.

"I'll go feral on your face," I growled.

"Oh-kay!" Rita interjected, diving between us, as if honestly worried I might claw Lance up or bite him and give him rabies. "If you can't join us now, you should at least promise me we'll meet up before we leave, okay?"

"Oh, of course."

"I lost my old phone, but lemme give you my new one." Without asking permission, in classic Rita form, she grasped along my coat, looking for my phone. I let her, meeting Dennis' eyes over her shoulder as we both laughed at her overzealous lack of tact. He'd filled out since college, grown enough that it threw me. His brown hair looked sun-streaked and he had a pretty good tan, which wasn't on brand with what a computer-obsessed homebody he'd been when we'd known each other a decade ago.

"You still talk to Stan?" he asked as Rita fished my phone out of my pocket and made a happy sound when she found it wasn't pass-coded.

"Sometimes, yeah. He was around last year, actually."

"Cool, can I pass long my number through you?"

"Yeah, of course."

"Thanks, Gwen."

"Come on, guys," Rita said, handing my phone over to Dennis. "I'm cavernous right now. My stomach's gonna turn into a black hole at any second. Mel, it was so nice to meet you. Lemme know if you want tickets to the gig, both of you."

"We might be out," Harvey cautioned, but Rita just waved him off. We too shared a shrug of, "oh Rita," and I considered if Harvey was actually taller or if the weight he'd managed to lose just made it appear so. Dennis tried to hand my phone back, but Rita grabbed it from him, manhandling me to put it back where she'd found it, before hugging me tightly against her.

"It's so, so good to see you!"

"You too," I said, squeezing her back. "I'm sorry we can't join you, we've got some stuff to handle here."

"Anything we can help with?" she offered, her black hole stomach forgotten in an instant.

"Nah, Mel here just got shitfaced last night, left some stuff and we're on the hunt for it."

"You want my key?"

I laughed. "Your key?"

"Yeah, I always get four in case these idiots lose theirs. You need one to get around. Here, take it."

"That's okay, I'm sure we can—"

She was already shoving a key into my hand and hugging me again. "Okay, we're off. Text me and we'll make plans for dinner!"

"Okay," I agreed, knowing it was futile. Rita stepped back, hooked her arm into Lance's, and dragged him toward the exit. I felt a great love for her in that moment, especially as he threw a wink back my way and mimed, "Call me."

"I don't even have your number, you moron!" I yelled as Rita dragged him out into the garage beyond. Dennis barked out a laugh and his glee nearly covered Lance's spike of frustration.

"You slept with Lance Krieg and you didn't want to sleep with me?" Mel asked as the elevator doors closed.

"I didn't want to sleep with you because I slept with him. I knew you'd be just as bad in the sack."

"Ah right, I forgot you're delusional."

"I—" Cutting off before I could argue, I considered that maybe he had a point. I'd dated Lance and slept with Mel. Clearly my judgment and sense of reality was badly skewed. "Let's just see if we can find anything helpful."

"You don't want to talk about dating a famous rock star?"

"He wasn't famous when I knew him. None of them were. They were friends, they played sometimes, but they hadn't really decided to make it a thing yet."

"So you were young?"

"Young and stupid."

"Some things never change."

I glared up at him as the elevator doors opened. He winked and stepped out into the lobby, looking around. A family hustled over and I held the door open so they could get all sixty-eight pieces of luggage, three kids, and a stroller onto the car, and then stepped up near Mel.

"Well. You were here yesterday."

"I'm still not certain of that," Mel said, looking down at me. I felt curiosity burble from across the room and turned to see what was interesting. An employee was watching Mel in a way that made me think she might know something. Mel noticed too, following my gaze, but attraction curled within him. That was a pretty normal reaction for a werewolf, especially Mel, but it made me realize that I hadn't really felt it so far that morning. Usually you couldn't keep Mel's libido in check but this morning he seemed no hornier than an old woman playing dominos.

"Mr. Somerset?" the woman asked as we approached.

"Mel," he said, holding out his hand. "And you are?"

"I have something for you," she said, turning to head toward the desk. Her dismissal was clear, an obvious indication that she hadn't been eyeballing him because of his pretty face or big muscles.

"She has something for you," I teased. "But it's clearly not the thing you want."

"Perhaps I already got it."

"And sex with you is so unmemorable even *you* forgot you had it?"

Mel glared at me but, lacking a comeback, chose instead to follow the desk agent. We waited for only a few moments before she came back around and handed us an envelope.

"Your companion left that for you this morning, said you'd be back to pick up the rest of your things before noon."

"My companion?"

"Veronica?" I asked, figuring Mel's brain would continue to glitch if expected to produce actual information about the woman he'd slept with. In any other man it probably wouldn't have shocked me that he'd forgotten the name of just one of the hundreds of partners he'd had, but Mel was different. He could be a dick, sure, but he did seem to genuinely make connections with the women he enjoyed. I'd seen him run into his ex-partners in the past and none of them had ever taken a baseball bat to his windshield or punched him in a fit of rage.

Well, I guess I couldn't say that about myself.

"Yeah, I think so."

"Thanks," I said, grabbing Mel's arm and steering him away, eager to see what treat the woman he'd slept with had left him. It was probably just a Dear John letter, but I had a feeling it was going to be more than that. "Open it, open it!"

"Calm down," Mel chastised, but did as I said. Inside was a key packet and a key. Nothing else. "I guess we're going to 534."

"I guess we are."

Like Rita said, we needed a key to get upstairs, but now we had two so we made it just fine. We headed down the hall in silence, passing by rooms full of tourists and business people, housekeepers, and maintenance techs. I wasn't really sure who the employees milling about were, actually, but I made a strategic guess to keep my brain from jumping to unhappy conclusions.

I couldn't figure out why, but I had a real bad feeling about what we were about to do. I couldn't put an actual name on the feeling of dread starting in my gut, but I didn't like it anyway. We hit the room, Mel slipped the key into the lock, and we both watched it turn green. Without hesitation, Mel pushed open the door, slowly as he called out, "hello?" No one answered and no lights were on, so he pushed the door open the rest of the way.

I couldn't see what had happened exactly, but when Mel grunted and gasped, I jolted, yelping. A moment later, Mel stumbled back, glanced at me with shock and confusion, and then toppled as his eyes rolled back in his head. The door tried to shut, bumping against his feet as my eyes finally took in the sight of the arrow sticking out of his left arm.

Five

Mel was bleeding and I was doing nothing. I didn't know what to do, really. I'd never actually seen anyone get shot before, not with an arrow, anyway.

"Mel?" I asked quietly. I didn't really expect him to answer, though I guess I didn't really expect anything at all.

"He's out," a familiar voice said as a wobbly, sweet jiggle of irritation rounded the corner down the hall. "Let's get him inside."

I looked over, still unmoving, as Chloe's boyfriend Izzy strolled casually over, dumped the last of a bag of loose candies into his mouth, and then stuffed the wrapper into his pocket. Where the *hell* had he come from?

"North Dakota," Izzy said, though I hadn't spoken aloud.

"What?"

"Grab the other leg. We've got, like, a minute before Cynthia's gonna call the cops."

Hopping over Mel's leg to bump the door open, Izzy grabbed Mel's foot and then gestured wildly to his other.

"Who's Cynthia?" I asked hollowly as I did as he requested.

"Head of Marketing for the Durham-Driscoll group. Heave!" On his order, Izzy yanked, pulling Mel's leg. I did the same and, within a moment, the door was shut and we were alone in the room. Dropping Mel's limb unceremoniously, Izzy waved his arm toward his face. "Kiss him."

"Excuse me?" I asked, dropping his other leg. Izzy had already turned away, moving to a spent crossbow balanced on top of a stack of paper reams on top of a narrow table that had been pulled away from the wall. As if it wasn't a deadly weapon, Izzy knocked it onto the floor as he passed.

"It's princess toxin. You gotta wake him up."

"I'm not gonna kiss him."

31

"Then you're gonna have to carry him out. Or drag him out. Either way," Izzy said disappearing into bathroom. "You're gonna get noticed!"

"I don't want to kiss him!"

"We both know that's not true," Izzy said with a toothy grin, exiting the bathroom. Izzy's a fair, sharp-featured creature who looks human but the resemblance ends there. He's easily distracted, way more powerful than I could exactly comprehend, and equally as useful as he is frustrating. "Don't you remember the magnets? Princess Mel. I told you this would happen. Now get down and pucker up. I'll get this thing."

Just as casually as he'd knocked the crossbow to the ground, Izzy yanked the arrow out of Mel's arm, stopping the blood flow that tried to start with a wad of paper towels. "Ah, man. I forgot the bandaids. Ah well, we can use a pillow case. Winter War style!" Grabbing my hand and pressing it over the wad of paper towels, Izzy popped to his feet, spun around to face the bed, and yelled something intense in another language.

"Was that … Swedish?"

"Finnish. Keep pressing. And kiss him, for the love of Cheese-Its."

I looked down at Mel, slack and beautiful, unconscious and bleeding, and considered my options. Izzy hadn't told me why he was here, but asking him probably wouldn't change that. He's easily distracted and usually withholding. He knows his magic, though, and the Princess Mel bit did sound vaguely familiar. I could only assume he knew what he was talking about and pressing my lips to Mel's was the only way to wake him up.

"Goddammit," I grumbled.

"He usually does," Izzy said, before ripping a pillowcase in half.

"What?"

"Just—actually, hold off." Dropping to his knees, wads of torn cotton in hand, Izzy started manhandling Mel roughly. He hummed happily as he half undressed Mel, getting his arm free of his new jacket and the useless older one. I sat back on my heels as Izzy performed battlefield triage, wrapping Mel's arm in quickly-bloodied cloth, tying it off, and then added more and more layers until no more blood flowed.

"Is he gonna be okay?" I asked as he finished.

"Oh yeah, we just need a healer."

"Where do we get one of those?"

"Uh." Izzy paused, tipping his head back as he stared at the ceiling with a slack jaw, apparently considering the options. "No, never mind. Constance is in Texas this week. We gotta just wait."

"For what?"

"To see what happens."

"So he's just gotta live with being shot?"

"That's what you humans do, isn't it?"

I frowned, unable to argue. Healers existed and man were they handy. But in general, they weren't out in the world, advertising their skills and using them to save random idiots in random hotels.

"Whoa," I said suddenly, stiffening, realizing exactly what had happened. "Whoa!"

"Just caught on, did you?"

"To what?"

"You tell me."

"Oh my god, Izzy." Izzy snort-laughed at my frustration, but kept stuffing Mel back into his clothing, getting him to fighting shape. I sighed, realizing he was going to be exactly as cooperative as usual, and pressed on. "Whoever left the key for Mel wanted him to get shot right?"

"Sort of. You would've done, or Chloe if she'd caught on."

"Is that why you're here? In case it had been Chloe?"

"Chloe wouldn't have walked into that stupid trap. She's smarter than that."

"So why are you here?"

"You needed help."

"Technically Mel needed help."

"You couldn't have gotten him in here without me."

"I'll give you that."

"Now kiss him."

Rolling my eyes, I looked down at Mel, realizing that it was probably time to stop being squeamish and just do it. If Izzy said this was the only way to wake Mel up—

"Do we have to wake him up?"

"Eventually, yeah, I think he'd appreciate it."

"Well, I mean, he hasn't been real useful so far. What if we just leave him here and we go figure this whole thing out while he's safe and sound?"

"Not in the cards. Well." Izzy dipped his gaze as if just noticing a bug scurrying across the floor by his knees. There was nothing there. "Oh, hey, didn't see that one there. But, no, you should do this on your own."

"Why can't you help?"

Izzy just snorted, and I got the feeling he thought I was making a particularly absurd joke. I rolled my eyes, realizing I wasn't going to get what I needed out of him. This was't unusual, of course. Izzy could show up at random, help here and there, but mostly he seemed a step out of reality. According to Chloe, he lived sort of out of time, riding the edges of every possible timeline. He'd made comments during our time together that led me to believe that maybe sometimes he *couldn't* help, if only because he just had no idea what was really going on.

"Okay. So, what? I wake Mel up and you just poof out?"

"I gotta see a goblin about a unicorn."

"I … Really?"

Izzy nodded spastically, as if the meeting excited him and I just sighed. I probably didn't want the details and I was certain he wouldn't give them anyway.

"Do you have any advice, at least?"

The smile disappeared from Izzy's face, his gaze darted up past my shoulder, and he went stiff. His expression twitched, his pretty features warping ever so slightly toward pain and anger. Swallowing, worried that whomever had set up the trap for us was sneaking up behind me, I turned slowly but found only the couch.

"Don't tell Chloe," Izzy said after a bit, pulling my attention. "If Owen can't get hold of Florence, just wait for him to get out here."

"Who's Florence?"

"Just promise." Uncharacteristically serious, Izzy held my gaze, pleading with me. His entire psyche, the whole gelatinous wobble of it was vibrating, every one of his emotions in turmoil, crawling over each other in a way I hadn't ever felt from him before. It made me nervous, made me consider that things were really bad, and that I was in *way* over my head.

"I promise."

Izzy grinned, his emotions settled into a pleased jiggle once again, and he reached out to boop my lips. "Pucker up."

Giving in, I took a deep breath and bent over Mel, bracing myself on his shoulder. It was a mild kiss, just my puckered lips on his slack mouth. I jerked when I felt consciousness rush in, yelped when Mel's body went rigid and his arms came up in a panic. He bumped me but Izzy was quick, pressing his arms back down before Mel could do either of us any damage. Recognition covered his face before I felt shock and pain take over.

"Take a deep breath," Izzy said. "And don't scream; Cynthia's out in the hall."

Mel whimpered, tried to reach his left hand to his wounded arm. When he hit the wound, he swore, the shock inside him warping to panic.

"What happened?" he demanded, trying to sit up. Izzy just kept pushing him back down, telling him no. Finally, frustrated with us both, Izzy reached out to grab my hand, pressing it to Mel's face.

"Calm him down, would'ja? If he gets up too fast he might faint. Unless you want a reason to kiss him again."

"No, no," I said, petulantly as Mel went, "What?"

Without waiting for Izzy to explain, and without trying myself, I flattened my palm on Mel's cheek and shoved my empathy inside him. It was like diving off a rocky crag into a tempestuous sea. Panic, pain, confusion, shock, and fear crashed against me and I shut my eyes against them. It was hard to get hold, at first; I'd been feeling emotions for as long as I could remember, but it was only recently that I'd learned about this stupid trick.

"Mel," I mumbled. I felt his attention divert slightly from Izzy holding him down as if he weren't half Mel's size, and the distraction gave me what I needed. I grabbed onto the emotions, slurped them out of him and into me. Mel went still immediately, but my eyes shot open.

I let out an uneven, panicked whine and jumped to my feet, fighting the urges now colliding within me. Did I want to pull open the window and fling myself out or drop into a heap on the ground and cry? Neither, I told myself. Or both? I could see the emotions at war within me and I could recognize which were mine and which were Mel's. Gulping in air, I did my best to cage those that didn't belong.

"What happened?" Mel croaked behind me. I twisted to face him, the action fast enough to make me dizzy.

"I'm okay," I assured myself desperately. "I just—I'm okay." I was still on edge but it wasn't so bad; I wasn't going to follow my first instinct to run around the room waving my arms like I had been called out of the audience on The Price is Right.

"What happened," Mel asked again.

"You got shot,." Izzy said, before leaning back and freeing Mel to move if he so chose. "So hang tight for a bit. The princess potion packs a punch. Heh." Proud of his alliteration, Izzy chuckled to himself.

"I did?" Mel asked, before trying to shift to prop himself up on his elbows. The second he moved his injured arm, he hissed in pain, falling back to the ground. "Dammit."

"You'll be fine. I bandaged you up good. Just don't sleep on it or do any weight-lifting."

"Okay," Mel said agreeably, unable to be too bothered by the situation, thanks to what I'd done. Refocusing on my panicked pacing, he jerked his chin. "What happened to you?"

"You happened!" Breathing out, I tried to remember that the agitation I was feeling wasn't my own. The emotions caged in my brain were smashing tiny fists on the bars, trying to break free. I didn't know how my father handled this so well, but it was clear I was going to need more practice.

"She's fine," Izzy said, before sliding his hand behind Mel to help him up into a sitting position. "Easy boy. Slow, take it easy." I continued to pace, trying to work out the feelings in my guts as Mel worked his way from prostrate to sitting cross-legged like a small child waiting for story-time. Once he was up, he turned his focus to me, blank, curious, but mellow. I still felt like peeling my skin off.

"I feel like I should be more worried about being shot," he said after a bit, his psyche trying to produce confusion but unable to put much effort behind it.

"You should be!"

"Gwen sucked it all out of you," Izzy explained. Shaking my head, I lowered it into my hands, took a deep breath, and forced myself to just breathe. Time crawled on as I did my best to calm myself, thinking only of my breath, of my beating heart. I needed to slow both of them down. Finally, as I started to finally feel like things were nearly under control, I heard shuffling. Mel had made it to his feet without passing out and I had managed to settle myself without slugging him or finding a staircase and flinging myself down it.

"Did I hear that right?" Tone sly, Mel stepped forward, lust rising in him as I rolled my shoulders. "What did you suck?"

"Get your mind out of the gutter."

"I'm just curious about what you did to me while I was unconscious and vulnerable, Miss Casual Sex."

"That's *Admiral* Casual Sex to you."

"A promotion, nice," Mel commented, winking, and turning to Izzy. "Well, now what? I assume you're here to help."

"I was," Izzy said, before reaching up to scratch behind his own ear rapidly like a dog. "And I have. Good luck, pals."

Abruptly, before either of us could argue or ask that he stay, Izzy bounced toward the door, letting himself out. Mel darted after him, opened the door before it had even latched, but Izzy was gone. I could feel it and Mel could see it.

"What the hell?" Mel demanded.

"That's Izzy for you."

"Goddammit. Did he know anything helpful at least?"

"Not really. He just told me that the arrow was probably supposed to kill you, and warned me against telling Chloe."

"That again?"

"Yeah, I don't know. Supposedly, someone named Florence might be able to help, though."

"Great, give her a call. Tell her I'll pay her whatever she wants."

"I don't know her. Apparently she's a friend of Owen's, and he still hasn't called me back."

"So call him, tell him to hurry up."

I sighed, shaking my head. "It doesn't really work that way. I could try, but I guarantee he won't answer or have anything useful until he's ready."

"Then what now?"

I looked around the room, really noticing it for the first time since we'd come in. It was just a hotel room, nothing special. Veronica, whoever the fuck she was, had told the desk agent that Mel had left some items to pick up. The place looked empty to me, but maybe we just hadn't searched enough.

"You really don't remember the room?"

"Not in the least. I've never been here."

"You're an idiot." Figuring it couldn't hurt to snoop, I moved to the closet, thought better of opening it while standing right in front of it, and took a step back. Carefully, using my toe, I nudged it open, but found nothing inside. There wasn't much else to look at, but I looked where I could. Nothing turned up, not even a stray hair, until I got to the mini-fridge. Taking the same precaution as I had with the closet, I stepped aside, opened it as carefully as I could, and let out a sound of confusion.

"What?" Mel asked, coming over as I grabbed the envelope tucked inside on one of the plastic shelves. He hovered close as I opened it and we both read it silently.

My condolences, Gavel.

"Hunh," Mel said, still unable to generate worry or panic. I swallowed hard, feeling that same spike of dread from before we'd come upstairs. I didn't recognize the handwriting, and didn't know for sure who had written it, but I had a sick, sick idea of who it might be. "Think it was meant for Chloe?"

"I know it was," I whispered, before I crammed it back into the envelope, tucking that into a pocket, and grabbing Mel's uninjured hand. "Let's get out of here."

"Where are we headed?" Mel asked, as we climbed into his car.

"Anywhere else," I said, suddenly more nervous about the hotel than I really had any reason to be. The damage was done, the trap laid had already hit a target and been taken out. I probably didn't have to worry. I'd called Owen, just in case, but he hadn't answered and I hadn't bothered leaving a message. I could tell him my theory when we spoke again later, hopefully when he had some good news to impart.

"Specific," Mel said, but started the car and pulled out of the garage. He'd grabbed a temporary spot and didn't have to pay, so we were back out on the streets pretty quick. "Mind if we stop by work?"

"Sure, anywhere's fine."

"I brought some files home last night and I wanted to drop them off, get them back into the safe."

"You brought them with you?"

"I planned to do some work this weekend but obviously that's not going to happen now."

"No, I mean to my place."

"Oh." Mel shook his head, realizing with a stab of embarrassment that he'd misunderstood me. "I never took them out of the car last night. So, yeah, unintentionally."

"Are they real secret? You investigating a senator or something?"

"All my cases are secret. That's why I'm called a *private* investigator."

"Hunh," I grunted. "Learn something new every day."

We drove in silence for a bit, Mel letting me stew on the note we'd found at the hotel. I had a hunch but it was a horrible one. If the person who'd left the note was who I thought it was, we were in real trouble.

"Hey, what'd your date last night look like?"

"Veronica?" Mel asked, glancing briefly over at me before taking the exit. "Why?"

"Just curious."

"I don't know, she was pretty."

"Specific," I said, hoping he caught the sarcasm. Mel grinned but didn't elaborate. After a moment, when I realized he wasn't going to, I pressed. "Mel, tell me what she looked like."

"She was pretty, you know? Why does it matter?"

"Because I don't think you can remember."

"Of course I can remember," Mel insisted, but that same familiar flap of panic wavered. "It just doesn't matter, okay?"

"I think it absolutely matters. Was she tall? Short? Fat? Thin? Redhead, brunette, blonde? Green hair, spiny face? Was she even human?"

"She was human," Mel said, but left it at that.

"I think you can't remember and you've got some sort of spell on you that's keeping you from really wanting to get your wolf back."

"No, I definitely want my wolf back," Mel growled. I felt a little sorry for him then, if only because that panic was really wriggling and the growl in his voice was so human it was painful.

"So tell me what she looked like, tell me what you did. Let's walk through everything right now."

"Right now," Mel said, pulling into a loading zone. "I have to get my files up to my office." Practically fleeing, Mel shoved out of the car, rounding toward the back. I got out as he opened the rear door and grabbed a cooler that I hadn't noticed. I wanted to ask what the cooler was for, but not enough to let it derail me from the topic. I chased him as he hustled toward the door, cooler in hand.

"You can't run away from this conversation," I said, catching up to him as he mashed the elevator button.

"I'm not running away from anything."

"Liar," I spat, as the elevator hit the first floor carrying a single passenger.

"Gwen, please," Mel snapped just as my brain realized it recognized the emotions in the elevator and panic bloomed in my gut. "Just drop it and stop being an ass."

The elevator doors slid open, Chloe caught my eye, and glee burst inside her like a balloon. "Hey guys!"

Six

Mel and I stared at her in mute horror for so long the doors started to shut. Laughing, confused at our stupidity, Chloe caught the doors, hopped out into the small lobby, and looked between us. Her gaze landed on Mel after a bit and she spoke, breaking the awkward silence.

"New coat?" Then, as it dropped to the bloody hole in his arm, as alarm drenched her in a chilly flood she asked, very calmly, "Or old?"

"Old," I said, trying to hide my panic, suddenly paranoid that I'd left the hotel note sticking out of my pocket and that, somehow, it too would draw Chloe's eye and she'd grab it. She'd grab it, read it, come to the same conclusion I had, and get herself killed trying to make it all right. "Halloween jacket. The idiot forgot it was stained."

"What's going on?" Chloe asked, knowing instantly I was lying. She didn't have my ability to judge emotions but she knows people and she definitely knows me, so lying to her was a wasted effort.

"I'm bringing some files back to my office," Mel said, his tone infinitely more casual than mine. There was worry in him but it paled in comparison to mine by a couple hundred shades. "Gwen's tagging along."

Chloe inspected us briefly, keeping her expression blank, but she was calculating, curious, worried. She knew something was up and, short of just turning and running away, I wasn't sure how we were going to stop her from learning what. Casually, without explaining what she was doing, she closed in, grabbed Mel's zipper, and yanked it down. I didn't realize until she slipped her hand into the collar of his shirt what she was doing and it made me feel so stupid.

"No necklace," she said, before reaching her hand down to Mel's, taking the cooler out of his grasp. "Come on, kids. Let's go back upstairs and talk."

We were silent in the elevator and down the hall to my office and the only reason I didn't try to run was that I could feel how worried Chloe was about both of us. I couldn't bear to make it worse by bolting out the door and down the street like a coward. Mel acted cool as a cucumber, though there was some anxiety in him as well. Chloe let us in, cooed to the cat who was curled up asleep on our couch, and then set the cooler on her desk. Rupert is giant ginger with stripes of golden yellow running along the thick fur coat, scary eyes, and a vendetta against me that I don't understand and hope never comes to fruition.

"What's going on?" Chloe asked as I watched the cat suspiciously.

"Nothing," I claimed, trying to sound as cool as Mel felt.

"So you and Mel are just hanging out, huh?"

"Just two friends, hanging out," Mel said. I winced, knowing she'd never fall for such a load of crap. Chloe nodded, lowering her gaze as if she was thinking for a moment and then leaned in close and pinched Mel's bandaged arm. Shock blew out of him, smacking me in the face and making me stumble. The rage, insult, and hatred that comes with physical pain jabbed me in my eyeballs as he jerked away from her and swore.

"Why are you bleeding?" Chloe demanded, before looking to me, a simmering anger trying to drown the concern that was clawing its way up out of her heart. "What happened to him? Why is he bleeding? Why are you together? Why aren't you *much* angrier about being near him?"

"Mel's human!" I yelped, confessing it all like a guilty child who's been caught egging the neighbor's house. Chloe could make me confess to most anything with her withering stare and serious voice but most of the power she held over me was rooted in our friendship. She and I are close, almost more bonded than sisters, and she takes care of me. I would do the same for her—if I wasn't a hermit who can barely handle doing my own laundry— even though she makes me eat vegetables and exercise.

I could feel her emotions, ringing clear as bells through me, and she was honestly worried that Mel and I were in some sort of danger. I couldn't leave her hanging, couldn't leave her dreading something she couldn't identify. Owen and Izzy had warned me not to tell her, but Chloe was reasonable, smart, competent. I was sure if I explained everything, told her Mel and I were working on it, that it was in her best interest to back off, she would. I was sure she would listen.

She never listens when I assure her I'm fine eating a fourth slice of cake, but maybe this she would listen to.

"Mel went on a date that he can't remember with a woman he can't remember and then he woke up human and came to my house and woke me up at, like, five a.m. and I called Owen and Owen had me stab him and then he got all freaked out and you're not supposed to know so we went to see Madeline and she said he's missing part of his soul and we went to a hotel and Mel got shot with an arrow and I found a letter and I think it's from Kincade and Owen said we can't tell you I'm sorry."

A storm of something I couldn't identify was swirling in Chloe. There was too much emotion there for me to immediately recognize it all and my focus on it distracted me from the fact that the cat had dropped off the couch to haul her massive, furry, ginger bulk across the room to rub against my leg.

I screeched, shocked at the sensation, and jolted away, smacking into Mel. He grunted, briefly panicked, and shoved me back toward my nemesis, who deftly skirted my stumbling feet and leapt up onto the desk. As Rupert pawed at Chloe, begging for attention, her tiny cat brain filled with smugness at having surprised me, I righted myself.

"I hate that cat."

"Do you still have the note?"

"What?" I asked, glaring Rupert down, before I realized what she meant. "Y-yeah." Chloe waited patiently for me to dig it out of my bulging jacket pockets and then inspected it. The storm inside her started to spiral, coalescing into a tornado of steely rage and insult. "You're supposed to stay out of it, remember?"

"You're going to solve this all yourself?" she asked, setting the letter on the desk and rubbing her hand down Rupert's striated back. The cat purred intensely, the sound as terrifying and loud as a truck barreling down the street aimed straight at me. I went tense as a bridge cable. Cats are unpredictable, nasty creatures, capable of affection and joy one moment, murderous glee the next, and unprompted rage the absolute nanosecond after that. I don't get along with cats and have been swiped at one too many times to trust them.

Rupert aimed her yellow eyes my way and I swear her mustachioed little mouth twitched briefly into a grin at the sight of my terrified jolt.

"We've been working on it," Mel said after a bit, when it was clear my standoff with the cat was keeping me out of it. "Gwen's had some good ideas, surprisingly."

"Like what?"

"Well. She searched my place—though she didn't find anything. And she searched my phone and found the address to the hotel … where I got shot. So, maybe they've been shit ideas, actually."

"Better than any you've had," I snapped, before clarifying. "Actually, you haven't had any ideas! You'd just yelled, 'fix it!' at me a whole bunch and refused to give me anything to go on."

"That's because you keep asking for irrelevant information!"

"Nothing I've asked you to tell me is irrelevant!"

"Stop fighting," Chloe ordered, shutting us both up instantly. Knowing her audience, she grabbed a handful of wrapped, candies out of the bowl on her desk and handed them over. They were sugar-free, but I grabbed at them greedily, unwrapping two and sticking them in my mouth before she could reconsider and take them away. Chloe sighed, staring at Mel with pity plain on her face. "How human are you?"

"Gwen's barely complained about being around me at all," Mel said, stepping up to pet the cat, who rumbled again and leaned in to nuzzle him.

"So, very human." Chloe sighed, letting her head fall back. She was quiet for so long I finished my entire handful of candy and was considering sneaking off into my office to grab some of the stashed sweets I'd hidden around the room. As I dropped my wrappers into the trash, she spoke again, her voice quiet, tense. "Owen said you shouldn't tell me about any of this?"

"He seems to think it's too dangerous. I don't know why. You two foiled Kincade's dastardly deeds last time, I don't know why this is any different."

Chloe didn't answer, but a wedge of heavy, nostalgic rage seemed to work itself out of her and into my chest. Something was bothering her, something that had happened in the past and carried a lot of weight. I'd felt the same sort of feelings from my clients as they were digging through their pasts, searching for important moments that might have led them down whatever path they were so desperate to veer off. Lowering her gaze, meeting my eye, serious as I'd ever seen her, she asked, "So, what's the plan?"

"I ... asked Owen to help."

"That's your whole plan?"

"I mean," I hedged, feeling guilty for some reason. "I didn't really call him with a plan at first, he was just the first person I thought to call. After he had me stab Mel, he seemed to realize something and told me I couldn't tell you. I had promise him. Now he's gonna be mad at me."

"He's not here, now is he? And ... if Mel's soul is missing, that's not something that we can just ignore."

"Owen said it would be fine to wait until he got here."

"But the sooner we can fix it the better," Mel said. I frowned over at him, despite the fact that he'd hauled Rupert's entire body up into his arms and was petting her into a content stupor. She was definitely more pleasant to be around when she was being loved on but I'd seen her happiness turn to anger in an instant and I just didn't trust it.

"I agree," Chloe said, pushing away from the desk. "Tell me about your date last night, Mel."

"We went out, we had sex, I came home and went to bed."

"That's it?" Chloe asked.

"That's all he remembers."

"That's not true."

"What did you wear?" Chloe asked, taking a different line than I would have thought of.

"Why?"

"Was it that coat?"

"He just bought that one," I said with a snort. "He was going to freeze to death in the other one."

"I mean the other one." Chloe said, before jerking her chin at Mel. "Take it off."

"You want my coat?"

"Yeah. I think it might help."

"How could it help?" I asked, before reconsidering. She was the expert, had apparently worked directly for some Fairy, running errands or whatever, before she'd come to work for me. I considered that a step down job-wise, but she seemed happy and I loved having her, so I didn't argue. "Never mind. Give her the coat, Mel."

"Only if you think you might have worn it last night," Chloe said, watching him with tactical curiosity.

"He was wearing it yesterday," I offered.

"Then let's give it a try. Strip."

Mel was looking between us, uncharacteristically unhappy about being the subject of discussion between two women. Usually Mel wanted nothing more than to be between two women in any way possible. Whatever had nicked his soul and fried his memory, however, had affected him in other ways too.

"Guys, it's just a coat."

"Then take it off and hand it over. Or I'll cut you out of it," Chloe threatened. Mel rolled his eyes, set the cat down, and did as she said. Chloe moved into the records room and then came back with the coat tied in a plastic grocery bag. "New plan: Mel, you hang here with Rupert, Gwen and I are gonna go check something out."

"Why am I staying here?"

"Because the cat needs company."

"Chloe," Mel sighed. She smiled at him, closing in to lean up and kiss him on the cheek.

"Just do as I say and everything will be fine. You can go up to your office, if you want, organize your files, do some work, whatever. We'll be back as soon as we can."

"What if I want to go home?"

Chloe was quiet, considering his request for a moment, before she eyeballed him. "Did you give your date your address?"

"She said she didn't have a car."

"That much you remember."

"I remember everything," Mel insisted. "We met here, made plans—"

"You met *here*?" Chloe asked, going tense all over again. Swearing quietly, she dropped the bag on her desk, and rushed into my office. Mel and I exchanged confused glances for a moment, waiting to see what was up, before she came back out with a gun and its holster in hand.

"What the hell?" I demanded, suddenly worried. "Where the hell did that come from?"

"It's just a precaution. Change of plans. We're all gonna drive to my place, Mel you're gonna keep Poopy company, and Gwen and I are gonna see a man about a coat."

A burp of dishonesty bumped out of her as she said, "a man," but I didn't question it. Chloe was much too keyed up to be messed with.

"Give me more detail about the hotel," Chloe said as we were on the way in her car to her place. She'd had Mel move his car into a more permanent spot so he wouldn't get towed, and insisted on driving us herself. I wasn't sure where her gun had disappeared to but I'd seen her use it before and trusted that she wouldn't accidentally shoot either one of us so I tried not to think about it.

"I went through Mel's phone looking for clues and couldn't find anything except that, in his maps history, he'd searched for this place downtown. So, we went and, like, right when we got there, we were spotted by an employee who recognized Mel. She—"

"No, no," Mel corrected snidely. "Not *right* after we got there. Right after we got there we were spotted by someone else. Several someones, who all recognized you, remember?"

I felt my cheeks go hot as I turned to glare at him, hating him more than I'd ever hated him, even more than when we'd been just work neighbors and he'd been an obnoxious werewolf who'd shown up daily just to rib me and make me miserable.

"That's not really relevant," I pressed, hoping he'd understand that I really, *really* did not want to discuss this particular ex with anyone, let alone with Chloe.

"What's he talking about?" Chloe asked.

"I'm talking about Eye Masters."

"The ... band?" Chloe asked.

"Yeah, apparently Gwen knows them. One of them in particular. she knows *real* well."

"Mel, you're human, which means I could actually murder you right here, right now."

"Too many witnesses," Mel said, grinning giddily. Witnesses be damned, I thought, briefly picturing myself climbing into the back seat and somehow shoving him out of the car and into the freeway.

"You know Eye Masters?" Chloe asked, eyeballing me in the exact same way she had when she'd found out I'd slept with one of her favorite authors.

"I'd really rather not talk about it."

"She slept with Lance Krieg."

Amused surprise spurted out of Chloe, splattering my skin and making me cringe.

"Death," I warned Mel. "Slow and bloody."

"*I'm* sorry," Chloe said, grinning. "You did what?"

"I really don't want to talk about it," I insisted, hoping she'd take me at my word and drop it. I should have known better.

"No, we're gonna talk about you sleeping with a rock star."

"He wasn't a rock star when I slept with him. Not legitimately, not in bed. It was a bad time, and I regret it intensely."

"So you knew him pre-band?"

"I knew him in college."

"In college!" More surprise, more glee, as Chloe whipped her head around to meet my gaze for just as long as she could without crashing the car. "You didn't!"

"I didn't what?" I asked through clenched teeth, knowing she'd made the exact connection I hadn't wanted her to.

"You *didn't!*"

"Oh my god," I moaned. "Can we just please just focus on Mel and his soul?"

"You're not weaseling out of this, young lady. Tell me everything."

"I'm saying nothing. I plead the fifth."

"Tell me everything or I'll hold you in contempt!"

"You can't do that!"

"I'm the Gavel, I can do anything I want!" The glee whipping off her skin was palpable. Since it was better than the anger or irritation from earlier, I sighed, considered that I could embarrass myself if it meant Chloe's mood stayed high. But god did I not want to talk about it or admit any of my wrongdoings. Sure, I wouldn't end up sentenced to death, but this was still going to feel as gross as confessing to some nasty crime in court.

"You said you weren't doing that job anymore, so you can't even call yourself that."

"It's a lifelong title, like how someone is always Mr. President. Now spill."

"Oh god," I moaned. "But after this, we're never speaking of it again."

"Overruled," Chloe said simply. Despite myself, I snorted, laughing for a bit. She grinned over at me and patted my knee and I gave in.

"I knew Dennis and Jason from classes, and had sort of seen Lance … from afar, unfortunately. I, uh, ran into him at a bar, back when I thought that was a thing I liked to do. Stan, for obvious reasons, did not want to come with me. Lance was into me, I was an idiot and we …" I trailed off, clenching my jaw and snarling against the truth that was about to come out of my mouth. "We went back to his place. Which was actually his and Jason's place, but at least he had his own room. It was the worst sex I'd ever had—worse than Mel, even." I felt the explosion of insult, but Mel said nothing.

"And Stan found out?"

"No," I said, dragging the word out as long as my breath would let me. "Well. Maybe. Later, but I don't think the guys would have told him. I—I just—I left Stan because I was a coward. Because I was an asshole. Probably because I was nineteen and therefore an idiot. I left because …" Swallowing the emotions welling up, I pushed on. "Because I couldn't bear to look at his face and tell him what I'd done and feel him hear what I had done."

Chloe turned onto her street and I could feel her pity, feel the look she was giving me, but I refused to see it, to take it in. She shouldn't have pitied me, I didn't deserve that much. I deserved disdain and disgust. Not pity. I was the one who'd fucked up royal, Stan had been the one who'd suffered. Sure, we'd gotten past it and could consider each other friends now, but that didn't erase the fuck up. It may have been buried deep in our past, but it was still there.

"I dated Lance for six months because I was trying to make it into something it wasn't. I would not have survived—or he wouldn't have—if it hadn't been for the rest of the band. After I ended it, I kept in touch with Rita and Jason for a bit, but it didn't last. Lance started getting them gigs and every time I talked to either of them, the band would come up and it would get weird."

"So he got the friends and you took your dignity and left?"

"Half of that's true."

"Everything's worked out, you know," she insisted, as she pulled up in front of her building. "You can let go of the guilt."

"Just because everyone's happy ten years after the fact doesn't mean I didn't do anything wrong."

"Yeah, but just because you did something wrong doesn't mean you need to beat yourself up about it forever."

"It's not a full-time job or anything," I said, shrugging jerkily. "I just beat myself up as a side gig."

"It's a shit gig," Chloe said, patting my knee. "You should quit and craft macrame owls instead."

Seven

Mel pouted the whole way up to Chloe's apartment, probably still pissy that I'd once again insulted the sex we'd had. Chloe let us into the apartment, gestured to the bathroom and ordered Mel to head in.

"Why?"

"I want to check your arm," she explained.

"You're a doctor now?" Mel said, gingerly sliding his coat off his injured arm and draping it over one of her bar chairs.

"I'm a concerned third party," Chloe said, before pointing to the kitchen and catching my eye. "Snacks in the fridge, if you're interested."

"When am I not interested in snacks?"

Mel made his way to her massive bathroom as I checked the fridge. Finding only date balls and fruit, I moved on to her cabinets, pulling through them with the foolish hope of a child. Search failed, hopes dashed, I headed into her tiny bedroom after her, finding her in her even smaller walk-in closet, stripped down to her bra and a pair of leggings.

"I think Izzy ate all the snacks. All I see are date balls and fruit."

"Those are the snacks," Chloe said, rolling her eyes and moving to a trunk tucked under her longer dresses.

"Oh. I thought you meant fun food."

"Vegans don't have fun food," she joked. "We just eat salad and cry."

I snorted. "You're a damned liar," I accused, pointing at her, even though she was facing away, crouched and unlocking the trunk with a key that looked older than my dead great grandmother. "I've had vegan cheesecake."

"In the community, we just call it 'cheesecake.'" I could hear the lock squeak and croak as she turned the key, but it popped open and she slid it off, pushing the thing open. Mel stepped up next to me, stripped down to

47

his skin, his nipples hard from the cold. My gaze scraped appreciatively over him but guilt swept away any lust that tried to gather when I saw that his injured arm had bruised heavily all around the wound, which twinned the bruise I'd punched into his other arm. Tearing my eyes away, I turned back to watch Chloe fiddling with something at the bottom of the trunk.

It all looked like something that should be sitting in an ancient castle in the middle of Ireland somewhere, not tucked under floral cotton peasant dresses on the fourth floor of a converted factory, or whatever Chloe's weird building had been before. Reaching in, Chloe pulled out a stiff, brown bustier scarred by age and use, and rested it on her knees as she unwrapped the many straps around it. I jolted when I realized she meant to wear it and pointed accusingly.

"You're vegan!"

She tensed briefly, looking to Mel and biting her lip as if she wasn't sure she wanted to explain further. "I am. This predates my veganism. It's not exactly something I can replace, either."

"Why? What is it?"

"Um." I felt a deep discomfort growing in her and, after clearing her throat, Chloe stood up straight in her baby pink bra, met my eyes. "It's enchanted werewolf leather. It'll protect me against pretty much anything that hits it. It doesn't cover everything, but a surprising amount of creatures go straight for the guts. And, bonus: I can wear it under evening-wear."

"Did you just say werewolf leather?" Mel asked, ignoring the joke about ballgowns.

"Yeah," Chloe tried for a harmless smile. "But it was … no one you knew."

Mel scoffed, instantly insulted, though I couldn't understand why. He wore cow leather all the time, so it's not like he could claim to be against using skin as clothes. Before he could accuse her of anything or protest, Chloe's cat Poopy slipped into the doorway, rubbing herself along Mel's ankle and making him jolt. I'd felt her approach, but her presence was somehow less offensive than Rupert's, so I'd just ignored her.

Apparently it wasn't me she was after, as she very specifically focused on Mel as she lifted her gaze. As far as cats go, Poopy was one of the good ones. Maybe even the only good one. I couldn't figure out if Chloe had spoiled her or trained her well or just gotten lucky in adopting her, she'd never really reminded me of a cat, despite her lithe black form, intense eyes, and sharp, sharp claws.

Even now, sitting with her tail at attention, staring up at Mel intensely, she didn't feel like a normal cat would. She wasn't annoyed with him or judging him; she just seemed curious and, oddly, a little concerned.

"Mel, I had this made for me by one of the fae years ago. It's not exactly easy to come by and I promise I wouldn't keep it if I didn't think I may need it to keep me alive."

Poopy gave a quick, squeaky meow from the floor, bonked his ankle a few times in rapid succession. Mel glared down at her, undeterred from his insult.

"You just watch your mouth, cat. She might make you into a pair of gloves."

Poopy let out a disgruntled purr, pushed to her feet with a flick of her tail, and turned to head back into Chloe's room.

"You think you'll need it to keep you alive?" I asked as Chloe strapped it around herself. It looked snug but flexible, hugging her ribs and curving up over her small breasts into wide V high enough that any aforementioned formalwear which was too low-cut would have shown it off.

"Better safe than sorry," Chloe said, a needle of dishonesty stabbing out of her. We stood in silence as she got dressed, pulling a loose shirt over the corset, strapped on a hip pack from the trunk, and grabbed socks from her dresser. "Come on, get back in the bathroom. Let me see if you need stitches."

"Are you qualified to diagnose that sort of thing?" Mel asked, moving out of the way so she could pass.

"*Qualified* suggests training I don't have, but I'm experienced enough to recognize a bad wound. Come on, Aurora, let's see how bad you're pricked." Tossing her socks on her desk as she rounded the corner into the bathroom, she moved to the simple vanity in the corner, pulled out the chair, and patted the back. "Sit."

"What happens if I need stitches?" Mel asked. Chloe just grinned.

"What weren't you telling Sleeping Beauty?" I asked once we were down the road in her car. Mel had sat patiently through the stitches, perhaps because he was trying to be manly to prove a point and possibly because Chloe had drugged him when he hadn't been looking. Either way, when we'd been ready to go, Chloe had convinced him to stay there with the cat. Plus—again, perhaps because he'd been drugged—he'd admitted he was tired and wanted a nap anyway.

She glanced at me, gave me a small, considering smile. "I have no doubt Kincade knows where he lives. I don't know how she found him in the first place, what she's doing in town, or if it's all one big coincidence that she went after Mel in the pursuit of something else, but I'm not chancing it. I don't want him going home—you either, come to think of it."

"Why not me?"

"She tried to kill you just a few weeks ago, so this could all be one big fuck-you that has no further consequences, or it could be … something much worse."

"Like what?"

That nostalgic pain and anger roiled up in her, whipping at my skin, scalding my insides, making me wince. Chloe took a deep breath, noticed I was uncomfortable, and tried to shake herself out of it. The storm calmed a bit, I slapped my shields up on the windows of my psyche, and hoped it was enough. We were quiet for a bit longer before I broke the silence.

"You don't think Mel could take Kincade in a fight?"

"Not human he can't. He's an idiot on a good day; right now, he's just baby mortal, unaware of what he can handle and what he can't."

"He burned the shit out of himself on some coffee this morning."

Chloe barked out a laugh, and the amusement tamed the storm even more.

"See? He's going to continue to work on werewolf habit until he either gets himself killed or learns his lesson. Kincade has tussled with creatures on Mel's level—his normal level—many times. I've fought her myself and she's—I hate to admit it, but she's good. She's skilled, quick, ruthless. Plus, she plays dirty. If Mel tried to go up against her as he is, he'd end up on his ass."

"If you're so worried about baby human Mel, why am I here? I'm just baby human Gwen."

"You can sense when someone's sneaking up behind you. Or, if someone standing smack in front of you wants to punch you in the face. Either way, you can duck or run."

"True, but if Kincade plays that dirty—Oh shit!" I flailed in my seat as my brain grabbed hold of a memory and used it to strangle me. I wasn't sure why it had come to mind then, what had called it up, but the memory of when I'd very first met the bitch wrapped around my throat and squeezed. I choked out "Veronica!"

"What?"

"Mel said his date's name was *Veronica*! When Owen and I ran into her the first time in Montana, he called her that. She got *very* cranky."

"Really?" Chloe squinted her eyes, calculating.

"Is that a thing? Did I do good?" I asked. Chloe smiled, but she wasn't entirely listening to me. After a few more seconds she lifted her elbow, gesturing vaguely toward me without her hands leaving the wheel.

"Call Owen, ask what they were doing when she went by Veronica."

"Okay," I agreed, reaching into my bag. "You think it matters?"

"It might. She could have certain names for certain types of jobs, or it could just be that she doesn't like him to use an alias when he knows her … Well." Chloe trailed off, glancing over at me. I felt a hint of discomfort in her but she took a breath and continued. "In my old line of work, and in Kincade's, Owen's, etc, you don't go by your given name to anyone. Names have power in Fairy and, even when it comes to humans, you don't want anyone to be able to track you down. You gave Kincade your name and she kidnapped you at gunpoint, remember? However, you may find people you trust enough to have repeated contact with. Owen was one of those for me, which is why he knows me. Though, he didn't know me as Chloe until he met you. Kincade is … not exactly trustworthy, but she keeps her word on the rare occasion that she gives it."

I was holding my phone, waiting to dial until she finished. I caught a hesitation in her and I held off, letting her continue if she chose to. After a few seconds, she smiled over at me.

"I used to go by Amina."

"That's pretty."

"It means 'trusted.' My mistress gave it to me."

"Ooh la la," I purred, wiggling my eyebrows obnoxiously. Chloe shook her head, let out a low laugh.

"My boss; not the other kind of mistress."

"What did you call Owen?"

"Actually, that's what he went by with me. I've heard him use other names, heard people refer to him by those names, but those are for him to tell."

"Wow." Feeling al little stunned at the fact that Owen had trusted me enough right off the bat to give me a name he only, apparently, gave other people in his business, I went quiet. Chloe gave me time to process, before clearing her throat.

"Call him. See if you can get any info out of him."

"Um, what should I tell him about you?"

"About you singing like a canary and telling me everything?"

"Yes, exactly."

Chloe smiled, but it was to cover up a guilty conscience. She didn't answer for long enough that I asked a question instead.

"Why is everyone so worried that you can't handle whatever's going on?"

The guilt in her grew, flooding out to ooze around my ankles and up my legs like a flood of molasses. I reached out to touch her arm, intending to take some of the guilt off of her before I entirely realizing what I was doing, but she'd put a coat on and, before I could touch her wrist, she pulled out of my grasp.

"Mel's soul is missing, right? That's … bad news. Remember Nysgrogh?"

I shuddered, pulling my arm back as if my entire body wanted to swallow itself and invert into a black hole just to avoid the memories of having dealt with a demon who'd been kidnapping children and who'd tied me up and practically bled me right into a vampire's mouth.

"Yes," I whispered. Chloe's guilt dissipated somewhat into pity.

"She was trying to take souls, right? Well, dealing with her wasn't the first time I've … come across someone trying to steal souls. I really don't want to get into it, but the first time … it went poorly."

"How—never mind." I shook my head, feeling the panic building in her even as that single syllable came out of my mouth. "You don't have to tell me. Just … If you can't, or don't want to deal with it now, you don't have to."

"I can't leave you and Mel to deal with it yourself."

I waved my phone as if I had the golden ticket. "Owen already promised to help. And Izzy said something about someone named Florence."

"I don't know her."

"Well, either way, you don't have to get involved."

"I think I do," Chloe said quietly. "I think I need to prove to myself that I can."

"Are you sure?"

"No," she admitted. "But I'm going to."

"So that brings us back to the original question: what do I tell Owen?"

"Tell him ... Um."

"How about I just don't mention it yet?"

Chloe looked toward me, a small smile curving her bow lips. "You're a terrible liar, though."

"Hey!"

"He'll never buy it."

"Then I just won't mention it."

"So what's your excuse for calling him?"

"I mean." What was my excuse? Shit. "Well. I mean. I realized she had the same name right? And I haven't heard from him in a few hours. And Mel got shot! So. All that's my excuse. Plus, you know, I like flirting with him."

Chloe chuckled, nodding a few times before gesturing loosely to nothing. "All right, then, get it girl."

Eight

Owen was predictably out of contact once again, so I sent him a text, mentioning the Veronica connection, describing how Mel had been non-fatally shot, and asking if he'd had any luck finding us help. I didn't expect an immediate reply, but I kept the phone out and in my lap for a few minutes after sending, just in case.

"Where are we going?" I asked as we hit Pioneer Square, with its narrow streets, totem poles, and brick buildings. Chloe pulled up to the curb, finding a lucky spot in a construction packed alleyway, and turned off the car.

"We're here. Hang here for a second. I'm gonna pay for parking." Chloe pushed out of the car before I could complain but that didn't stop me. I let out a grumbling sigh just for the hell of it, and watched her jog up to one of the meters. It only took her a minute before she came back with the window sticker and yanked open my door.

"Come on. I only paid for thirty minutes." Slapping the sticker on the passenger window, she wiggled her fingers at me. I draped my bag across my shoulder and got out. I followed Chloe's quick steps across the sidewalk, peering into windows as we went. When I noticed the direction in which we were heading, I made an interested sound.

"What are we doing? Are you buying me a snack?" Chloe shushed me, grabbing my arm and steering me toward a skinny stairwell leading down below street level. It smelled atrocious. "Ugh. There's nothing good down here."

"Yes there is. Come on." Producing a key from her pocket that I was pretty sure she shouldn't have, I watched her unlock the grated door, glance upward to make sure no one was following, and then grab my arm to drag me inside.

"I don't think we should be down here," I whispered as she shut the door. She just grinned, waved me on. Glee was fizzing inside her, a happy, bouncy excitement. It reminded me of my own mood when Chloe presented me with cake for lunch after depriving me of sugar all morning.

"The next tour won't be by for a few. If we hurry, we should be fine. Plus, once we get to Chiv, it won't matter. Come on." Chloe hooked her arm around me and dragged me through the musty underground city that used to be Seattle's street level in the 1800s. It still smelled like I'm sure it had back then, though I hoped the current bouquet wasn't from overflowing sewage.

I'd been on the Underground tour in college, but it had been so long I could honestly say I didn't remember much of it. Dark, dank, creepy: these things were familiar, but past that I couldn't tell where we were headed or why. I remembered a little souvenir shop at the end; maybe Chloe was going to buy me gummy candy shaped like rusted pipes.

"Why are the lights on?" I mumbled, hustling close. Chloe glanced at me as I bumped her elbow.

"There are tours that come through here about every hour. We're just taking advantage of their hospitality. And you don't have to whisper. There's no one else down here right now."

We moved past uneven flooring, crumbling walls, and support beams that had clearly been added to keep the streets above from compacting on our heads and ended up in a room the size of a large living room. The floor sloped downward at roughly the middle, leading to a dilapidated bar and a wall of pictures taken when you'd still been able to see the sunlight from where we stood.

As I paused to inspect the columns as if I had any idea of structural integrity, Chloe marched straight to the bar. Clearing her throat, she knocked twice on the top of it and called out something that sounded like an expertly trainer Opera singer being forced to sing in Klingon. It was guttural and musical all at the same time. After she finished, she rolled her gaze around the room intently.

A man appeared in front of her.

Ah, well, he looked like a man. For the most part. Built like a streetlight, he towered over Chloe, his waifish body decked out in a long leather coat, knee-high boots, and more straps than you'd need to keep down a grizzly bear. He was stylish with a top hat, a shiny gold vest, and a gold chain running from the button of his vest to one of his pockets. His emotions were bouncy and alive, like electric gremlins that had eaten too many Pop Rocks.

I swallowed thickly, suddenly nervous about standing so far away from the only person who could protect me from this newcomer. As I moved, baby-stepping along the floor in an attempt to get to Chloe without him noticing, I felt his emotions jump. He twisted to face me, baring pearly whites that literally looked like strands of bulbous pearls had been mashed into his gums in place of teeth. When he stepped toward me and held out a skeletal hand, Chloe spoke.

"Chiv." Her voice was a warning and I felt his emotions lash out at me, a rope of lightning that wrapped around my neck and tugged. I let out a small sound, fighting against the demand, leaning back like a dog resisting the pull of a leash. Smile still in place, he turned back to Chloe, reached up with lengthy, bony fingers and pulled his top hat off. The hair underneath was made of bluish, smoky wisps. I let out another small, uncomfortable squeaking sound, but neither of my companions so much as looked my way.

"Gavel," Chiv said as he dipped low in a bow. Even bent double, he was nearly as tall as Chloe. When he stood upward, he set his top hat back in place, tucked one arachnid hand into his shimmery, gold vest, while his other gestured toward her, palm up. "What is thy Mistress' will?"

"I'm here on my own business. I'd like to make a trade."

"Ah!" The rope of emotion around my throat dissipated, replaced by another throb, this one thankfully less insistent.

"I need the memories attached to this object." Chloe got Mel's coat from her bag, held it out. Chiv's emotions sparked again as he reached toward her. Chloe pulled the coat out of his grasp, her eyes going narrow. "You'll tell me the memories and I'll let you keep the object, as well as the memories—*minus* any names."

"No names? That may not be payment enough."

"They're interesting memories, I promise. I'll give you the coat to test. If you like the memories, you get to pass them along to me, then keep what you enjoy. Deal?"

He smiled at her, close-lipped this time, before he turned fully to face me. I felt his psyche whip out toward me again and it roiled in my guts, making me want to vomit just out of sheer terror. I was pretty sure my eyes were the size of hubcaps and I knew was shaking. My teeth were chattering.

Chloe's brain rumbled with irritation, but she said nothing as he looked me over. I jolted when he held his hand out toward me again. Chloe just sighed, but didn't try to stop him, which I resented.

"Hello," he offered. I lowered my gaze to his hand, clenching my own into fists. I had no intention of touching this electric creep.

"Chiv, do we have a deal or am I leaving?" Chloe asked. Could she not see that I wanted to pee my pants and run?

Hand still held out, Chiv twisted his angular face to look her over; the emotion still crackling along the skin of my throat got a little more restrictive but it only lasted a moment. The intensity of it, the unfamiliar pain of it kept me ignorant of exactly what it was, but I didn't have to understand it to hate it. Finally, he turned to face her full on, held out both hands.

"An alternate proposition."

"I'm listening."

"Your empath has a bit of fae gold in her pocket, something glowing with power, with spell, with intention. I will read your cloth, if I can inspect the precious stone."

"Gold?" Chloe asked, turning to me, perplexed. Shame swamped me, embarrassment drenching my spine in ice. I did have gold in my pocket but I didn't want her to know about it. It was my own guilty pleasure, something I'd tucked into my clothing for months, a little trinket that had become a security blanket for reasons I couldn't entirely fathom, but needed anyway. Seeing something in my face that worried her, she stalked over, putting her hands on me like a cop frisking a suspect. The insistent electricity frying my throat didn't dissipate as Chloe closed in, and I slid my gaze to the creature watching us, hoping it didn't matter that Chloe had her back to him.

When Chloe found the coin, lifting it in her open palm as if it needed to be displayed to the room, she met my eyes. After a moment, she took a large step back, watching me intently as I jolted to follow her.

"Why do you have this?"

"Uh," I groaned, shifting my weight. I felt my leg start to twitch as discomfort rumbled through my body. Between her attention and Chiv's, I felt like a misbehaving toddler. "I don't know."

"This is from the Lofriska. Why do you still have it? Why are you carrying it around?"

"I just … like it."

Chloe's gaze dropped to the ground, her expression screwing up to match the anger and regret rumbling in her guts. Swallowing hard, she plastered calm across her features again, completely seamlessly, and then turned to Chiv, holding the coin out toward him.

"Change of plans. Forget the coat. I want to know the history of this coin related to my empath. *All* the history that's touched her. You may view the memories, but they pass to me and you keep none. You can, however, keep the coin."

"Hey," I argued breathily, terrified of losing my little gold charm. When I grabbed at her desperately, determined to get my coin back, Chloe hissed at me like a mother cat. Confused, shocked, I shrank back. The electricity burning my flesh flashed through the roof, blinding me, hurting me all over, and I cried out, dropping. Chloe ignored me, still focused on Chiv, still holding the precious trinket toward him.

"Deal?"

"We have a deal." His voice was a liquid growl, elegant even as it clearly conveyed his displeasure. Chloe smiled brilliantly and dropped the coin, knowing somehow that he'd catch it like a snake grasping a bird in midair. Chiv tossed the coin back and forth between his palms twice before rubbing it between his thumb and forefinger. Something ached inside me, tugging hard at my chest like a thread connected directly to my heart. I groaned, letting myself sag to the ground.

Turning on his heel, the creature with the wispy hair and the elegant suit that reminded me of a lion tamer's get-up began to pace the dingy room. He weaved through the support beams as he did, his head nearly brushing the ceiling here and there. When he hit the far end, he twirled again, his eyes fixed on me. He flashed his round, opalescent teeth and pointed the coin my way.

"You have taken fine care of this trinket."

Chloe jerked her chin at him. "Are you ready to get on with it?"

"Oh, yes," Chiv purred, his eyes still on me. In an instant, he was standing in front of Chloe, smiling down at her. She didn't jolt, wasn't surprised by the quick movement, even when he pressed the flat of his palm to her forehead, the coin the only thing making contact between them.

Chloe rippled maniacally through a series of emotions that somehow felt familiar, as if I'd experienced them all myself in exactly the same order. It was a roller coaster, moving so fast I almost couldn't track her from the initial terror to the pockets of comfort, ecstasy, glee, annoyance, and myriad other emotions that swamped out of her. My stomach flip-flopped at the tumult but I managed to keep from barfing. By the time she finished, though, I'd listed to my side on the dirty floor and I couldn't stop groaning.

Chloe gasped when Chiv stepped back, my coin folding into his bony fingers while he watched her with a horrifyingly wide and tight smile.

"Thrilling," he murmured. Chloe grunted, squeezing her eyes shut, fisting her hands as she recovered. She was quick, practiced, breathing deliberately until she was outwardly calm. Inside she was still a knot of animosity, but standing in front of the Fairy she was cool as a cucumber.

"Nice doing business with you, Chiv."

"I am pleased to see you in the field again, Gavel. I look forward to future encounters."

"I don't," Chloe said, spinning to close in on me. Without a word, she grabbed my elbow, hauled me to my feet as if she had the strength of ten men, and led me back the way we came. I stumbled, needed to lean on her for support, but we made it out. Chiv's emotion stayed latched around my neck nearly until we made it to the car and it wasn't until it drifted away, caressing my psyche almost gently, that I recognized it as a gluttonous sort of non-sexual desire.

"I don't know what just happened," I croaked once we were out of Pioneer Square. "But I didn't like it."

Chloe didn't answer, her jaw stiff, her emotions a scalding whirlwind. She drove robotically, intensely, nearly running red lights and getting us out of the main area of downtown, before she found a spot she could pull over without getting honked at. Slamming the car into park, she smacked her palms on the steering wheel, letting out a long string of curse words that startled me. Without meaning to, still weakened and frail from whatever had happened to my mind just minutes before, I found myself caught up, swearing with her, smashing my fist into her car window hard enough that I knew I'd be bruised after.

Chloe watching me act out, swore quietly to herself once more, and then took a breath, using whatever meditative skill she'd pulled out earlier to calm herself as much as she was able.

"Sorry," she said, biting her lip as if she wanted to say more but needed to keep it inside. I sat with her, stewing in rage I didn't understand, feeling like maybe I needed get out and kick a stop sign or slam some doors until she leaned her head back, the anger boiling down to a tolerable simmer. "We definitely know this was Kincade."

"We do?" I asked, flexing my fingers to keep them from permanently cramping into fists. "What ... Did you see something? What happened back there?"

Chloe took her time answering and when she spoke, her voice was quiet, low, restrained. "Chiv is a memory fae. He can read and give and take memories from people or objects, or even the air around someone if they're powerful enough. He could probably read you, at least a little just because of your empathy."

"Great," I spat, feeling vaguely exploited.

"Oh, that's not the worst part. The nugget you had, it came from Kincade."

"Um. No, that one came from that kid, remember? Samuel ... something with eighteen last names."

"At first, yes, but Kincade is the reason you have it. After you were attacked by the Lofriska, she circled around—before they came back to rest, before Izzy and I found you, which is why none of us caught her. She used some potions, connected your gold to a piece she had and turned them both into—" Chloe cut off, her jaw tightening as rocky, tumbling, sharp irritation rumbled. "Communication devices, basically. Since then, you've been carrying the rock around, right? Taking it everywhere, having a hard time parting with it?"

"... Yeah."

"That's on her. She wanted to make sure it was useful, that she could check on you whenever she wanted. As a result, she's been spying on you here and there."

"What?" I yelped, horrified by the idea, feeling ten times as exploited as before. "Holy shit!"

"Yeah," Chloe said, wrinkling her nose. "It was strong stuff, too, the spells. I'm surprised they didn't wash away when you and Owen nearly drowned."

"Oh god," I whispered, realizing that not only had Kincade been able to dip into my life whenever she pleased for the last three months, but now

Chloe knew what I'd been up to as well. "So you could see … everything?"

"Everything you did when the coin was on you, yes."

"Uhhhhhh," I groaned, horrified, worried intensely about anything I may have said, done, obnoxiously sang, or broken since my birthday.

"You're not as interesting as you think," Chloe said, a smile tugging at her lips. "Though I do have to give you credit for getting Owen to do a striptease for you, I had no idea he was so playful."

I barked out a laugh, accidentally spraying spittle all over the dash of her car before clamping my hand over my mouth. "Oh my god," I mumbled muffled against my fingers. Chloe laughed, reaching out to pat my shoulder. "I won't tell him if you don't."

"No, if I tell him he may never do it again," I said, breaking before I could finish the sentence, laughing giddily at the memory. Chloe and I sat for a bit just laughing, enjoying the silliness, before she sobered, clearing her throat and taking a breath, sliding us both back to seriousness.

"I still don't know what Kincade did to Mel, but I could see her, here and there, when she peeked in on you and the most recent time was two days ago, at the office."

"Our office?"

"Yep. She was spying on you while you were eating lunch at your desk and Mel appeared before she disappeared. I can't tell if she meant to bother you and decided to mess with him instead, or if he was the goal the whole time."

"How do we find out?"

"We get his memory back."

"From Chiv?"

"I don't want Chiv anywhere near Mel, not in the state he's in. If his soul really is mostly gone, having someone as powerful as Chiv dig around in it could be dangerous. And, compared to the gold coin, the coat won't cut it anymore. I admit, I fucked up, tossing it out of the deal, but it's too late now."

"So how do we do it?"

"Watch and learn, grasshopper." Smiling, giving a confident wink, despite the worry and guilt jostling around in her guts, Chloe restarted the car, pulling away from the curb without explaining further.

Olivia R. Burton

Nine

"Mel?" Chloe called as we pushed into her apartment. When Mel didn't answer, Chloe stepped into her living area. Poopy was draped along the back of the couch, limbs stiff on either side. She barely moved when Chloe rubbed a hand along her spine. "Where's Mel?"

The cat didn't answer, but Chloe kept petting her anyway.

"He's probably raiding your stash of sex toys," I offered, though I could feel him off in the bathroom. Mel stepped out as I yanked open the fridge and went for the date balls that I'd erstwhile rejected. Any sugar in a storm.

"What'd you find out? Am I cured? Will I be cured?"

"We know Kincade's been tracking Gwen, which is probably how she found out about you being a werewolf."

"That's it? You didn't learn anything helpful?" Mel scoffed, stopping halfway between the bathroom and Chloe. Instead of arguing or explaining, she lifted her arm, snapped her fingers in my direction.

"Quick! Take your shirt off!"

Distracted from his frustration, Mel whipped around to face me. I wasn't stripping, of course, and when he found me cramming dates into my face he frowned, disappointment rumbling.

"I don't know why I fell for that."

Chloe chuckled. "Sorry, you're probably still a little high."

"Yeah, about that," Mel growled, closing in to loom over her as if he could intimidate her. I'd seen her best him in wolf form, though and, even if it was only because he was a good dude who hadn't wanted to hurt her, he still didn't stand a chance. "What the hell did you give me?"

"Happy juice," Chloe said, stepping around him, to set his coat on the counter, still in the bag. "Here's the plan: You're both going to stay here until things are settled. So, we're gonna go pick up some things, pack some overnight bags and pick up Sonny."

"Sonny?" I asked around a gooey mouthful of almond butter. Chloe nodded.

"Just so you're not worrying about him."

"He's gonna stay here?"

"No, with Lydia."

"Who's Lydia?" Mel asked.

"Don't worry, you'll find out." Proudly cagey, Chloe jerked her head at me. "Stow the snacks, Arthur. We've got places to be."

"Be quick," Chloe ordered, spanking Mel as she passed him, strolling into his kitchen. He snorted, grinning at her and winking, but there was no bump of lust like usual. I considered him intently, thinking how much less annoying he was as a human than as a werewolf. I'd always assumed everything about him that I found objectionable had sprung from Mel as a whole, but perhaps I was wrong and he could blame his endless lust, intolerable sex drive, and inability to stop eyeballing my rack on the fact that he was a werewolf.

Though, I had to admit to myself for the moment that I actually didn't mind when he eyeballed my rack. Sometimes it made me feel pretty and, honestly, it was only fair for how often I stare at his ass. And his abs. And his stupid, pretty face, dammit.

Chloe and I made ourselves comfy in his kitchen as Mel packed himself an overnight bag, her sliding onto a bar chair, me sliding into his pantry to search for the chocolate he'd given me earlier. As I munched on pilfered sweets, Chloe jerked her chin at me.

"So, you seeing him again?"

"Mel?" I asked. "I assume he won't be invisible once he's got his overnight bag, so yeah."

"Lance," she said with a grin and a wink. "If he's your ex and he's in town, it's only polite."

I scowled, stuffed an entire caramel cup into my mouth to prevent myself from cussing her out. Once I'd swallowed, I shook my head. "No, never. I don't even look at the cover of their third album if I can help it."

"Why? Their third, what's that, the …" Remembering the image on the cover, Chloe barked out a laugh. "That skinny waist and bulge is him?"

"Well, the bulge isn't, let me assure you, but it is him yeah."

"And you don't want to run right back on jump on that?"

In response, I chucked a peanut butter cup her way, making her laugh. She caught it, tossing it expertly back and hitting me in the brow. I winced, but picked it up off the floor and ate it anyway. Mel kept a pretty clean house, I reasoned, and wasting chocolate had to be a sin *somewhere*.

"I am gonna try to get dinner with the band at some point," I said, chocolate finished, pantry shut. "Rita made me promise and you don't say no to Rita."

"Man I love her," Chloe said, a wistful grin on her face.

"She'd love you too. You're just her type."

"Really?" Chloe beamed, doing a happy little wiggle with her shoulders as fizzy lust burbled through her. I felt my own body respond and it called me back to Mel's current state.

"Is Mel really only a horndog because he's a ... dog?"

"It's part of the werewolf physiology, yeah."

"Man. Here I was just thinking he was a shit all these years."

"You don't think he's a shit," Chloe chastised, rolling her eyes. "You love him. You secretly wanna get back in his pants and make half human, half-werewolf babies with him."

I wrinkled my nose at the thought of Mel's pants, and turned right around and went back for the chocolate again to soothe me.

"I think I'm ready," Mel said, hauling a rolling suitcase behind him. "Well, wait. I might want another jacket. And I didn't grab my toiletry bag. Should I bring extra shoes?"

"The ashtray, the paddle game, the remote control, and that's all I need," Chloe quipped, making me laugh. Mel wasn't listening as he turned to head back into his room, but I wasn't certain he'd have gotten the reference anyway. By the time we were all buckled into the car, I'd cleaned Mel out of his chocolate stash and I was starting to feel a little sick. Rare for me, but it had been a weird morning and all I'd had was sugar and caffeine.

"You've got to be quicker than Rapunzel here," Chloe said as we hit the main road.

"I'll just throw some stuff in a bag. You've got shampoo and everything right?" Chloe nodded, and I gestured loosely. "Yeah, I'll be fine."

"Why are you so fluffy today, Mel?" Chloe asked after a bit, reaching out to curl his longer-than-usual hair around her finger. He shrugged, unbothered by the question.

"I'm assuming Veronica liked me this way."

"You're assuming?" Chloe asked, a little bump of suspicion thumping me in the chest. "You don't remember?"

"I remember," Mel corrected, that panic fluttering his guts again. "She liked the shaggy look."

"She asked you specifically to go surfer?"

"Well," Mel said carefully, glancing over. "She must have."

"But you can't remember?"

"I remember fine."

"He's lying," I said, watching the two of them from the back seat. Chloe nodded.

"I know."

"I'm not lying, I remember everything fine."

"You keep saying that and yet you can't tell us anything about the date."

"I've told you a dozen times. We went out—"

"—we had sex, I came home, and went to bed," Chloe and I both said at the same time, silencing Mel. Embarrassment flapped at me like a flock of startled birds and I winced, even as I grinned at the accidental synergy Chloe and I had managed.

"Well," Mel said after a bit. "See? You know what happened, which means I already told you because I remember perfectly."

"You will, anyway," Chloe assured him, reaching out to pat his knee. "Just be patient."

Mel sauntered into my room as I was fighting viciously with the zipper on my duffle bag, swearing under my breath at the traitorous, metal son of a bitch.

"I've never been in your room before," Mel observed, stopping at the corner of my bed, looking around.

"You didn't slip in to creepily watch me sleep that one time?" I asked. He frowned at me.

"If I had, I would have been able to stop you from stumbling to the kitchen to eat ice cream on your ass at three in the morning."

I shuddered, hating the reminder of when I'd been psychically linked to a demon and the children she'd kidnapped. Mel looked around once again, considering me as I continued to zip and unzip the bag what little I could manage, trying to figure out what it was stuck on.

"Does your boyfriend stay over?"

"Why do you care?" I asked, finally getting the stupid thing to reach the end. "Yes!"

"I'm just curious."

"Why?" Slinging the bag over my shoulder, I grinned at him. "You jealous?"

"No," he assured me, though the faintest puff of dishonesty clouded out of him, surprising me. "I'm just … curious."

"About my sleeping arrangements with other men?"

"Maybe," he said, before clearing this throat.

"Why? You need tips?"

"On satisfying you? No, I'm beginning to think that's impossible."

"It's not impossible at all. I'm pretty easy to please, for the most part."

"And yet you insist I couldn't do it."

Careful, I told myself, feeling a little shard of hurt spear out of Mel and jab me right in the heart. He'd always been bothered by my insistence that I hadn't enjoyed our one sexual encounter, but suddenly, here in my bedroom, alone, with half his soul missing, he was genuinely hurt. I wasn't really sure how to respond. Swallowing hard, I dropped my bag on the bed, thinking we might need some time.

"I mean. Maybe with other women … But for me … You see—"

"Oh god," Mel growled, rolling his eyes, the spear of hurt widening into insult and outrage. "Don't pretend you feel sorry for me, don't pity me as if everything that went wrong—as you put it—in bed was my fault."

I laughed, annoyed that he would blame *me* for our disappointing encounter. "What the hell do you mean? How could it *not* be entirely your fault?"

"Forgive me if I'm wrong, but you were there too, right? I wasn't alone, doing everything by myself. You consented, which means you had a say in what was going on."

"I … did, but … but …" I didn't have a defense for that, really. I hadn't exactly shouted from the rooftops what I'd wanted out of him, if only because, yes, I had felt a fair amount of pity for him at the time.

"Plus, did you even consider everything that was going on around us?"

"We were alone in the house, what are you talking about?" Suddenly defensive, speared with guilt, I flailed my arms in frustration. "What was going on around us?"

"Everything! We weren't on vacation, Gwen, we were there on a job! I'd just recovered from having my soul sucked on by a succubus, and you weren't exactly acting like yourself, which was of some concern, considering the fact that we were investigating what seemed to be a mind-altering cult. And, don't forget, you'd already rejected me once."

"I hadn't rejected you at all!" I snapped. "*I'd* started making out with *you*, not the other way around! It wasn't my fault the damn spider waltzed in and threw me off my game."

"I—" Mel cut off, jaw going tight, realizing that he had no argument for that. "Well, I didn't know that! As far as I was concerned, kissing me had made you vomit."

"So that's why you were a two-pump chump?" I accused, my shitty attitude running away from me. Snapping my mouth shut, feeling remorse ride in on a wave of Mel's shame, I sucked in a breath, wanting instantly to take back what I'd said. Mel glared, snarling, and then turned around and stormed out.

"Fuck," I swore, dancing foot to foot, trying to decide if I wanted to chase him down and take back what I'd said or let him run away and sit with his thoughts. Chloe slipped in before I could decide, looking between me and Mel.

"What's Princess Jasmine mad about now?"

"Not mad," I corrected, feeling sick to my stomach and defeated. "I managed to throw our bad sex in his face once again. Mash it, even. Just really stuck it right up his nose with the full force of my own stupidity."

"He seems a little more bothered than usual," she said, closing in and opening my bag. "You have everything you need?"

"This isn't my first sleepover."

"Toothbrush? Underwear? Pajamas?"

"Yes, yes, and yes."

"Deodorant, socks?"

"Um."

Chloe laughed, stepping around me to head into my closet. "Did he explain his side of things this time?"

"His side?" I asked, before heading into the bathroom to get my deodorant.

"Yeah," she said when we met up at the bag again. "That he thought before things started that maybe you'd been drugged and he was still smarting from Norma's rejection, and the fact that you'd already rejected him once?"

"Have you two talked about this?" I demanded, somehow horrified at Mel and Chloe conspiring behind my back.

"Of course," Chloe said, zipping my stupid bag with no trouble at all. "That's what friends do. You and Mel should talk about it sometime. Then maybe you can cut his dick a little slack."

"I'm not doing anything with or to his dick ever again."

"You sure?" Chloe teased, grabbing my bag. "I bet you'd really enjoy it if you gave it a shot."

"Don't push it."

"I would never," Chloe said solemnly, even as puckish amusement bounced out of her to bonk against my chest. "Besides. I think men prefer if you pull it. Not all the way off, mind you—in fact, it's really more of a sliding motion."

"Oh jeez," I groaned.

"Like this, see?" When she lifted her hand to demonstrate, I fled.

Mel refused to acknowledge my existence as we drove and I let him stew. Chloe seemed fine with the silence, using it as an excuse to turn up her music to ear-bleeding decibels. Somewhere around the time I lost both eardrums, I reminded her we had a delicate bird in the back seat. Chloe relented, turning the music back down.

I peered at Sonny in his little travel cage, made kissy noises at him.

"You're sure he'll be okay?" I asked. Chloe gave a nod but didn't stop humming along to her music. When the song finished, she caught my eye in the mirror.

"Lydia will take good care of him. She knows Kincade, too. She may be able to help."

"Another assassin?" I asked. "And you guys all just hang out at, like, a clubhouse or something?"

"Oh sure," Chloe quipped. "We have potlucks and picnics. Occasionally a squabble breaks out over who gets to shoot the leader of Tezbulistan, but we can usually resolve our differences with a good, old fashioned arm wrestling competition."

I squinted up at her, setting Sonny's cage down on the seat next to me; he rocked on his little perch, adjusted himself to compensate. "Is that a real place?"

"No."

Chloe's friend lived over an hour away in Stanwood, but I was able to screw around on my phone as we drove and Sonny didn't make too much racket. Mel stayed silent and brooding the entire time. When we finally pulled up into a gravel driveway, Chloe unbuckled the seatbelt before she'd even turned the car off. She didn't look at either of us as she spoke.

"Gimme a sec, okay?" Chloe said, tossing the keys in the middle cup holder and heading up to the house. Mel glanced down at them and then intently out the front window, avoiding looking my way. I rolled my eyes, trying to ignore the hurt still broiling in his guts. I should have apologized, explained myself, eased the pain there but I didn't know how to broach the subject. Plus, he was feeling so unhappy about being human in the first place, so weak and useless, I was afraid to make it worse by trying to soothe his ego and accidentally bungling everything even worse.

So, I just set my gaze on the house ahead, staying mute.

It looked purposefully dated, built recently in an older style. There were incredible plants surrounding it, with pops of color here and there despite the weather. Chloe made her way through a perfect, white, picket gate and up a twisty walkway. She disappeared behind a trellis nearly covered in ivy and then it was just Mel, the bird, and me.

Eventually, as I cleared my throat, deciding to go against my instincts and try to smooth things over, Chloe appeared again with an absolutely beautiful woman in tow.

"Looks like we can—" Before I could finish, Mel was out of the car, striding toward the two women with a slight swagger to his step. As I climbed out after him, I watched him go, wondering why the show. I could detect no hint of actual arousal in him, which was odd, though perhaps it would be the new normal if Mel couldn't get his wolf back. He thought Chloe's friend was pretty, sure, but I was used to feeling a sting of excitement behind his emotions that just wasn't there. Usually Mel would have been attracted to her even if she looked like Daniel Craig in bad drag, all craggy and shiny, but now I could feel only a light appreciation emanating. As if he was admiring a particularly pretty flower and not the lovely woman we'd come to see.

I looked her over as Sonny and I closed in, considered her long, straight hair and big eyes. I couldn't see the color from where I was, but they looked light, maybe a pale blue or green. Immaculate cheekbones, a perfect jaw line, and a narrow nose made her a knockout. Mel approached her directly, held out a hand. Instead of shaking hers when she returned the gesture, he captured her fingers between his palms and spoke. By the time I got close enough to hear what he was saying, she was smiling, flattered but disinterested.

"Lydia," she said, sliding her hand gently out his grip, leaving a little contact at the end just to be polite. Then, spotting Sonny, she brightened, gleeful to be in his presence. Sonny felt similarly excited, which pricked my pride a bit. "Sonny!"

Sonny warbled excitedly, squawked when she held out her hands and I gave him over. He scooted to the edge of the small cage when she lifted it to make kissy sounds. Despite my jealous nature, I grinned, glad to see my little feathery son happy.

"Gwen, this is Lydia," Chloe said.

"Nice to meet you," I said. When I held out a hand to shake, she wrapped her fingers around mine, gave a tug.

"We should get inside; Conures don't take well to this weather. Come, come."

I felt the tug again, harder this time, and she pulled me toward the house. Chloe and Mel trailed behind, which was just as well, as I didn't have to look at Mel's face to be reminded that the was still bitter over our fight.

Ten

The inside of Lydia's house was just as alive as the outside. She had thriving plants in every corner, a macaw perched near the back wall of the living room, and a pudgy, grey-muzzled dog snoozing under the window. As we entered, Lydia lifted the cage, her fingers on the latch, before turning to me.

"Mind if I pull him out?"

"Well," I said, glancing around.

"There's no way out, don't worry."

"Oh, yeah. Sure," I said. Immediately, she unlatched the cage, reached in. Sonny was all too happy to see her, giving her face little beak-bump kisses as she turned her cheek to accept the nuzzles. "I guess he remembers you."

Lydia turned to grin at me, noticed we were all still standing around.

"Oh, sit down, please. Chloe said you'd be dropping him off here for awhile because Kincade's around?" Taking her own advice, Lydia sank into one of her cushy chairs, making sure to keep her hand stable so Sonny wouldn't topple. As she did, he made his way up her arm, chirping happily as he went.

I tried not to be jealous.

"Yeah, she's used some sort of spell on Mel, here." Chloe gestured to Mel as she took a seat on Lydia's matching sofa. Mel did the same, settling his hips next to Chloe's, despite the amount of space open to him. I took the chair opposite my bird and his new best friend.

"He looks fine to me," she said, winking at Mel.

"I'm normally a werewolf," Mel said, though he winked back. Lydia's brows went up and she gave him an appraising once-over before she nodded.

"That explains the physique."

69

Mel grinned, pleased at her assessment and I rolled my eyes.

"And how are you taking the change?" Lydia asked as Sonny weaved under her hair, nipping lightly at the pearl stud in her ear.

"He's burned himself on some coffee, gotten shot with a crossbow tipped with princess toxin, and Gwen sliced his hand open with a knife."

"Oh my," Lydia said, pity rolling out to gather around Mel, who sighed, annoyed at being outed. "You poor thing."

"It's been tough," Mel said breathily, laying on the dramatics a little thicker than I felt was necessary. Lydia's lips twitched as humor burbled inside her like a teapot about to go off.

"It must be different, having to adjust to not having the protections and skills of a werewolf,"

"It really is," Mel said, eyes downcast, playing up his misfortune.

"Tell me," Lydia cooed, teasing. "Is it like a whole new world?"

"I ... guess," Mel said, looking askance, sensing something was up but not sure what.

"A new ... fantastic point of view?" she finished with a grin.

Mel rolled his eyes, but smiled tightly, shaking his head. Refusing to answer, he watched her, jaw set. Chloe laughed, patting Mel's thigh, letting him know it was all in good fun.

"I'm sorry," Lydia said, though she only managed it through her own round of giggles. "Look, I'll put Sonny away and then we'll chat. You can tell me what happened and I'll see what I can do."

I got up as she did, figuring she'd want his cage, but she only gestured toward the hall.

"Come Gwen, see his room!"

"His room?" I asked, lost.

"Go on," Chloe said, wrapping her arm around Mel's shoulder as if he needed comforting.

Lydia and I passed three rooms, one of which looked to be hers, and ended in a large sunroom with the shades pulled back. A massive cage took up most of the far side, split down the middle by bars and a sheet of clear Plexiglas to keep any occupant birds physically separated. Perched sleepily in the left side was another Conure, this one much greener than Sonny, but just as beautiful.

Lydia went straight to a rolling kitchen cart tucked into a corner, spoke as she pulled open the door on the front to reveal that it contained a mini-fridge. "I'm so glad to have this little guy back, even just for a few days. He and my other Conure get along so well. It's adorable."

"I didn't know he'd even met other birds." Lydia stood up with a little ceramic bowl of sliced fruits and vegetables and gave me a happy nod.

"Oh yes. When he was here last time, I put him in his own cage for a while, figured I'd let them get to know each other slowly. They took to each other right away, though." Turning to the cage, she pulled open the door, made kissy sounds at the bird inside. It came right over, warbled out a tinny tune, and then happily accepted the chunk of apple she handed over. Scooping Sonny off her shoulder, she set him on the perch next to the other bird and gave him a little piece of carrot. They munched together happily, and I closed in.

"What's his name?"

"Harold," Lydia said with a grin. I snorted out a laugh, met her eyes despite the fact that it felt a bit awkward with us being so close.

"I love it."

"I think it's hilarious. The macaw? Theodore—I *always* say the full name—and the dog is Reginald."

We shared a giggle at the idea of animals with such crusty names often reserved for giant, old, white men with fat, bristly mustaches as Lydia loaded the birds up with snacks. When we were certain they were content, we headed back into the living room.

"Tell me what's happened," Lydia said, settling in once again, gesturing to Mel for him to go ahead. Confused for a moment, he perked up.

"Oh, me. Well. I'm human."

"Yes," she said with a laugh. "But how?"

"I assumed Chloe had told you."

"She did, but I'd like to hear it in your words."

"Oh. Well. I woke up human. And, um. I asked Gwen to help me. Chloe got—"

"No," Lydia interrupted gently. "How did you become human, what do you think happened?"

"I have no idea. That's why we're here."

"She says Kincade's involved, is that right?"

"I don't know Kincade, but I'd assume Chloe knows what she's talking about."

"What did the woman you met last night look like?"

Mel squirmed inside again, as had become the default response to all questions about his date. "Well. She was pretty."

"Did she look like me? Chloe? More like Gwen? None of the above?"

"She was … I mean, we went … We went on a date, and we had sex, and I came home and went to bed."

"That's his line," Chloe explained. "I'm thinking a rote potion?"

"Perhaps, perhaps," Lydia said, getting to her feet again and heading around the corner into the kitchen. Mel watched her go, curious, easing out of the usual panic that cropped up when he was expected to recall the date.

"Lydia will help," Chloe assured him. "Especially since it's likely Kincade used some sort of potion on you. If it was plant-based, she'll have the answer quick."

I hazarded a guess as to why, just trying to fill the silence. "Because she's vegan?"

Chloe looked to me, dead sober in her expression, even though she thought my suggestion was absurd. "Yes. Going vegan gives you special powers."

When I frowned, knowing she was messing with me she chuckled, gestured to the greenery lining the walls.

"No, she's a chloromancer, she can control and read plants. She makes her living making potions, selling them within the community."

"The same community that refers to it as, 'cheesecake?'"

Chloe laughed, unbothered by the bite in my sarcasm. "Perhaps, though I highly doubt Kincade has the compassion to consider veganism."

Lydia came back with a tray full of vials and bottles, some opaque, some clear; some contained brightly colored liquids, some had fresh or dried plants inside, and some looked to be empty. "What's the last thing you remember?"

"From what point?" Mel asked.

Lydia shook her head. "Sorry, stupid question. Give me a moment."

Kneeling, setting the tray on the coffee table, Lydia started rearranging the vials with one hand, patting Reginald with the other as he lumbered over. The dog snuffled up against her armpit, placated for a moment when she gave his butt a scratch, but huffed, annoyed when she stopped. Reaching out, I called quietly to him, waiting for him to amble over to me, delighted when he did. He let me pet his face gently but only twice before he abruptly turned, aiming his rump my way.

When I didn't immediately start scratching, he turned to eyeball me, impatience burbling. Solemn and chastised, I began to scratch.

"Sorry," I said, but all was forgiven. Already, his impatience had warped to bliss. Still mixing liquids, dried herbs, and fresh flowers, Lydia grinned at me, pleased that Reginald had found someone to scratch his ass.

"Try this," she said, finally pouring a light pink hued potion into a bar glass and holding it out toward Mel.

"What is it?"

"Jägermeister."

Mel frowned, knowing she was joking, and eyeballed her disapprovingly, but drank it anyway.

"Pay attention to the taste," Lydia urged. "Tell me if it's familiar."

Like a good little test subject, he dumped the liquid into his mouth and sealed his lips, swishing it around a bit. Chloe and I watched intently as he discerned the taste of the potion and then swallowed. Reginald the dog grunted at me, bumped his rear against my knees again, reminding me that I'd stopped scratching and this displeased him.

"It doesn't taste like anything," Mel said after swallowing.

"Not the culprit, then," Lydia said, reaching over. She snatched the cup away from him, mixed up another potion cocktail and handed it over. Mel sighed, took a long sip. This went on through three more potions before I felt a snap of shock. Mel swallowed immediately, gave the cup back.

"What was that?" he demanded, worry and excitement riding his psyche like a cowboy on a bronco.

"I should have trusted my gut and started with that," she said to herself, grabbing vials and mixing them speedily into a fresh cup. This time, she put a drop of red liquid into a drop of blue, paused to consider, and added a drop of orange. Mel watched eagerly, as she mixed, jolting twice when it seemed like she'd hand him the cup but continued mixing instead. Finally, she held it out. "Now, drink this before you pass out."

Panic at the prospect seized him and he grabbed the cup, tossing his head back and tapping the base of the cup to make sure he got all of the scant liquid she'd handed him. Eyes fixed on hers intently as he handed the cup back, anxiety crackling through him, he licked his lips.

"Did that fix it?"

Instead of answering, Lydia set the cup down, watched him askance as mischief built up inside her breast. When Mel's eyes rolled back and he collapsed across Chloe's lap, limp and unconscious, I understood why.

Frowning down at Mel, sighing and petting her hand over his head, Chloe asked. "What was that for?"

"A reset," Lydia said, organizing her potions again.

"That fixed him?" I asked watching Mel, worried his werewolf emotions were about to come roaring back to scald my skin and stab me in the eyeballs.

"Oh no, not completely. I can't give him his soul back, I can just help him remember everything that happened. He'll wake up a little foggy, but it should come back to him over the next few hours."

"Then what?" Chloe asked.

"Than you find a way to return his soul to his body."

"You can't do it?"

"She can't," Chloe said quietly, before shifting to slide out from under Mel to let him rest on the couch directly. "Can I speak with you for a moment?"

Lydia nodded, pushing to her feet. They left me alone with Reginald the dog, who didn't mind the abandonment so long as I kept scratching. Eventually, he grunted, yawned, and wandered off, leaving me to my own thoughts.

I watched Mel sleep, wondering what sorts of memories were in store for us once he woke up and recalled his night with Kincade. Chloe hadn't exactly led us to believe Lydia would fix everything, but she'd sort of inferred it. Or maybe I'd just been reading into things, wanting to be done with all this as soon as possible.

Sure, Mel was infinitely more tolerable as a human, but now things were weird between us, Kincade was out there, possibly with his soul, and I couldn't go home to my giant stash of candy and sweets. Chloe wouldn't let me have a kitchen full of sugar at her place and I wasn't looking forward to trying to placate Mel's ego on only date balls and fresh fruit.

"Ugh," I groaned, jolting when Reginald echoed me with a similar grunt. Turning to him, I found him staring sleepily at me from his place next to the fireplace. Huffing out an awkward sneeze, his brief disappointment at nothing fading into sleepiness, he lowered his head and passed out. "I hear you, dog."

Eleven

Chloe was pensive and silent as we drove, Mel was groggy and still pissy, and I was lost in my own thoughts about Sonny and how happy he'd been with Harold and Lydia. The drive back to Seattle was stoic until we hit Shoreline, when I realized that this particular rumble of my belly wasn't my belly at all, but my phone.

Digging it out of my jacket as fast as I could, I answered without looking. "Hello?"

"G-Spot! You up for dinner? Like, soon? We're all starved and missing you!"

"Rita, hey." I grinned, pleased for the emotional relief of Rita's outrageous attitude and absurd nicknames. Glancing at Chloe and Mel in the front seat, I considered that they could use the relief too. "Yeah, I'm game, as long as you don't mind me bringing some friends."

Chloe's psyche jumped with excitement a second later when she realized what I'd said, but Mel was still staring out the window like a depressed teen, disinterested in future food plans.

"Yeah, of course, the more the merrier!"

"Chloe's vegan, so we'll have to find some place she can eat."

"No worries, babe. J-Bird's been veg for like ten, D-Bag only eats fish, H-Jay's trying the plant-based, gluten-free deal, and Lance is an asshole so no one cares what he eats."

I laughed, an awful shriek of sound that came out like I'd been stabbed but was really just a delighted break from the bad mood I'd been stewing in for an hour. Mel glanced back, a bit of worry burbling, but I avoided his gaze.

"I'll find a place and text you, cool?"

"Yeah, that sounds fine. We're up in Shoreline right now, and we have to

75

drop some stuff off, but we can probably be there …" I glanced up at Chloe, who caught my eye in the mirror, mouthed an answer. "An hour."

"Perfection! We'll catch you."

"I hope you two are hungry," I said once I'd hung up.

"I could eat," Chloe said. Mel didn't speak, though the rumble of discomfort in him resembled hunger enough that I could assume he could too. Chloe gave him another few minutes, before she reached out to rub his shoulder. "Don't worry, Snow White; we'll steer you clear of any poisoned apples."

We got to Chloe's building in record time and she nodded to the kid who got off the elevator as if they were old friends. He looked barely legal, with headphones the size of basketballs on his ears, a skateboard in his hands, and the distinct feel of a non-human that I didn't recognize. The moment he was in the narrow lobby, he dropped the skateboard and hopped on. I could only assume, as the giant, former-freight elevator doors shut, that he'd opened the door he was careening toward, rather than slammed into it.

"You hit three," I pointed out as Chloe leaned back from the panel.

"I know."

"But you live on four."

"I know." Smiling over at me with a look I wasn't entirely sure I liked, I glanced at Mel, figuring we'd share a suspicious solidarity over her grin. He was studiously staring at the wall, so I just rolled my eyes.

"What are you up to?" I asked as the doors opened and Chloe gestured for us to step out into the hall. Instead of following us, she pointed to the door directly across from the maintenance closet.

"Head over, I forgot one thing."

Instead of bothering to ask again what Chloe was up to, I just did as she said, stepping out into the hall, sighing when Mel moved past me silently, ignoring me as if I didn't exist. Chloe headed up as Mel walked dutifully where she'd told us to go. I stayed halfway between the elevator and the apartment door, not wanting to disturb anyone or look like I was lurking. A few minutes passed, with Mel acting like he was the only person left in the world and me tapping my foot impatiently.

Finally the elevator descended again, Chloe stepped out into the strangling silence, and whispered, "Crickets."

I frowned at her, but my annoyance turned to panic when she pulled out a key and put it into the door of the apartment directly below hers.

"Whoa! What are you doing?"

"Letting you into your temporary home."

"Our what?" I asked, worried we were about to walk in on an older couple doing something I certainly didn't want to see older couples do. There wasn't anyone in there, but Chloe had talked so much about her downstairs neighbors I felt like they were a constant, a pair of sweet older people who didn't deserve an empath, an ex-werewolf, and an ex-fairy-executive-assistant barging in on them mid-dinner.

"There's no one here," Chloe assured me, gesturing for us to head in.

"Did they move out?"

"Who?"

"The Lennoxes! Gerta and William."

"They never lived here. Come on, get your stuff inside, we've got dinner plans."

"Chloe," I snapped when she grabbed my wrist and tugged me toward the door. Mel had already headed into the pitch darkness, unbothered by the intrigue and possibly unaware that we might be walking into the apartment where people had died peacefully in their sleep so recently Chloe hadn't even told me about it yet.

"The place is empty, Gwen. It's fine."

"Did they die?"

"They never lived here."

Giving up on dragging me in, Chloe followed Mel, strolling straight for a light switch I wouldn't have been able to locate on my own. Cautiously, still stuck on the idea that I was walking into someone else's home uninvited, I made it to the doorway, watching the place light up like an old bunker finally visited after a few decades of emptiness.

"We're supposed to stay here?" I asked. Chloe nodded, moved across the laminate floor to the little slice of kitchen at the far wall. It had a small refrigerator, a microwave mounted above an electric stove and a small, bucket sink. She pulled open the freezer, gestured to a bunch of boxed meals and then pointed at the narrow counter and the cabinet above it. "Food, plates, utensils. There's a bedroom with two beds, a bathroom. I think I've even got a TV here, somewhere."

"Internet?" I asked. Chloe shook her head. "Can I still connect to yours?"

"No signal in here, sorry."

"What is this place for?" Mel asked, passing me to inspect the bedroom she'd gestured to. Still stymied by the sudden change in my reality, however small, I continued to stand just inside the doorway, looking around. There was nothing of decoration to speak of in the long, skinny room; just a couch across from a closed cabinet, the kitchen, a two-seater table with folding chairs, and the doorway into a bedroom. On my second full sweep, I noticed pale gray symbols on the ceiling just in front of each visible door.

"It's a safe house, basically."

"What does it keep safe?" Mel glanced at her, concern rolling through him.

"For today, you two." Catching something in my face, she held up a finger.

"I'm not saying you have to spend all day and night down here. This is just for if I'm not around to protect you or if Kincade tries anything."

Mel moved back to the center of the room and did a three-sixty turn. When he paused to face Chloe, there was a sadness in him that got to me a little.

"You really think she's coming back for us?"

"It's not about what I may or may not think she's doing; I'm planning for the worst to make sure you guys are safe. Now." She clapped Mel on the arm just below his wound; he flinched. "Lets get dinner and hopefully your memory will come back before bedtime."

"What about the real Mr. and Mrs. Lennox," I asked as Chloe locked up the apartment. She looked back at me, confusion riding her face.

"What do you mean?" Turning, she hooked an arm through mine and tugged me toward the elevator. Mel followed. "They don't live here. I made them up. Well, I didn't invent fake people; they existed, but not in this building and not in the last few years."

"What? How—what?"

"I never lied to you, I just ... told you outdated stories about other neighbors."

"But I've seen them," I insisted. Chloe tipped her head, eyeballing me like a teacher waiting for her student to figure out the answer to a stupidly easy math question.

"Have you?"

"Yeah," I claimed, trying to picture exactly what I was talking about. I swore I'd seen an elderly couple in her building before. At the very least, I'd seen signs of life from their apartment. "I think."

Chloe smiled and we all shuffled onto the elevator. "It's a front. Anything you see from the outside of their apartment is faked. Lights, timers, shadows. It's like the *Home Alone* Christmas party."

Mel snorted out a laugh and Chloe grinned back at him. The elevator came to a stop and we moved out into the foyer. Looking around as if seeing the place with fresh eyes, Mel asked, "So you rent two apartments here?"

"Well," Chloe hedged. We hit the street and she steered us both toward her carport. Once we were settled inside with the heater blasting, Chloe cleared her throat. "I own the building."

"You do?" I asked. Mel turned to her, lifted a brow.

"No shit?" he asked. She shook her head, pulled into the street.

"None at all. I bought it when I moved into town. I wanted to have the freedom to make adjustments as necessary. Besides, it kind of pays for itself."

"This is crazy," I said. Mel twisted carefully in the seat, avoided aggravating his wound.

"Why? It's just a building." Oh, suddenly we were speaking again? I pushed forward as far as my seatbelt would allow.

"It's not just a building! It's got to cost … I literally have no idea how much it costs. That's how foreign the idea of owning an apartment building is to me."

"It's one of the smaller ones in the area," Chloe assured me. "I've gotten many offers to sell so someone can build a towering stack of apodments but I like my place. And I don't really need the money."

"Why the hell do you work for me, then?"

"For fun. It certainly isn't for the salary."

Scoffing, insulted, horrified, *guilty* that I was a terrible boss, when I'd thought I'd been a pretty decent one, I glanced at Mel, annoyed that he was grinning, amused at our exchange.

"Why are *you* laughing? What do you pay Betty?"

"I pay Betty more than she deserves. She's a saint and a Godsend, a whiz with billing. She may even be better at her job than Chloe is at hers."

"Careful," Chloe joked, sliding her gaze his way. Mel patted her on the shoulder lightly, still grinning, his mood much lifted from where it had been earlier.

"You have to understand, I say these things because I'm more scared of her than I am of you."

Chloe laughed. "Fair enough."

Rita attacked me with a hug as we stepped into the restaurant, squeezing a breathy laugh out of me as I did my best to hold my footing. She grinned at Chloe when she pulled away, snapped and pointed at Mel when she noticed him.

"Nice to see you again, big guy. You look sleepy, you cool?"

"I'm cool," Mel assured her, grinning because you can't help but grin around Rita.

"Cool," she said, turning to hold her hand out to Chloe. "Nice to meet you, friend. Rita."

"Oh, sorry," I said, realizing I had the manners of an ill-bred dingo. "This is Chloe, my best friend."

"Huge fan!" Chloe said, delighted when Rita jammed her into a hug as well. "Of both your bands."

"Oh man, thanks! I'll tell the gals you said so. You should come to our show."

"That would be fun," Chloe said. Rita grabbed my hand, yanked me through the restaurant to an open table near the bar. "The gang's all here!"

"Sorry we're late," I said once we got to the group. I studiously ignored Lance, taking a seat three away from his and hoping he would spontaneously cease to be, somehow.

"Not even," Rita assured me, plopping down next to me. "We're all out for the night, no more appointments or whatevs. We got all the time in the world."

"Indeed," Lance purred, making my eye twitch. The room was a swirl of emotion but the smug insecurity was unmistakably him. "I've carved out my evening just for you; it'll be just like college."

"So it's gonna last five minutes and then you'll ask me to get you a beer?" I snapped, refusing to look his way. Rita barked out a laugh, a quiet rumble of amused, second-hand embarrassment rumbled through the group, and silence took hold for a moment. Chloe rescued everyone, taking the hit and turning to distract Lance from bothering me or getting murdered by me, and I did my best to just enjoy my time with old friends.

I probably only enjoyed dinner so damned much because Rita and the band had no shortage of embarrassing stories about Lance. It seemed that ten years passing had stolen from me the chance to experience a bevy of examples of Lance humiliating himself. By the time I'd eaten my meal and two desserts, a bit of pity had started to creep in.

Though, one look at Lance's shaggy, dark hair, overdone eyeliner, and leather vest sucked it right out with the force of a hundred Hoovers.

Even Mel seemed to be enjoying himself, his ego boosted by the fact that the band was curious about his job. Chloe spent her second cocktail trying to get someone in the band to admit whether or not any of their early songs had been about me and I was trying to shut her up. She is squirrelly, though, and easily evaded my attacks.

"Fine. Fine!" Chloe relented with a laugh when I attempted to smother her with a wadded up cloth napkin. "I give in! I won't ask you about it anymore. Not here, anyway. Rita, you'll text me later?"

Rita winked, made an agreeable double click sound with the side of her tongue and I threw the napkin at her. She threw it back and Chloe caught it, kept it away from me as she gave me a faux glare. When Jason pushed to his feet and moved around us to head toward the exit, joint in hand, Rita took his seat, leaned over me and started chatting up Chloe about what she thought of the new album. Mel and Harvey were ensconced in a discussion about, of all things, the best place to get mani-pedis in the city, and Dennis was still buried in the latest Stanley Sneedley book, *The Floating Airship*. I considered asking him what he thought of it, so far, but I heard a hissing sound and felt a grab of emotion snag at my arm, a desperate curiosity that pulled my attention.

Glancing around, I realized Lance and I were the only two not busy. My human shields had abandoned me.

Before I could completely process what this might mean to my sanity, Lance leaned around the back of Chloe's chair, wiggling his finger at me in a come hither gesture. My eye started to twitch but I didn't get up and run out after Jason like I wanted to. No one gives me enough credit for the fully adult struggles I go through every damned day.

"Chloe told me about your blossoming."

"What?" I asked, wondering what bullshit he'd sifted out of some perfectly logical sentence Chloe could have said to him.

"She's told me about your realization, your coming in fully to your own truths. I really appreciate that you could finally see the desire in yourself and I'm happy you've found a partner who can satisfy the hole that I'm certain I left."

"*What?*" I repeated, thinking he sounded like someone satirizing one of his dumber songs.

"I'm just sad for the world at large that, truly, after me … no other man could satisfy you."

Realizing what Chloe had done, how she'd tried to protect me from Lance's advances, the lies she'd told him about my current sexuality, I held my tongue, watching him with as blank an expression as I could manage. Finally, swallowing the insults I wanted to hurl like grenades right at his ego, I leaned in closer to be heard over the din. It was awkward, but Chloe and Rita were too into their discussion to notice when I sighed dramatically, pushing my chair back and twisting to face him enough that my spine was no longer screaming obscenities.

"Ah, yeah. Chloe and I are very happy together." I gave a brief nod, let my gaze roam to the table in an attempt to locate any other verbal port in this douche storm. I felt Lance's fingers wrap around mine and I jerked my gaze back to him. To my surprise, he didn't look like he was about to invite me to regain my heterosexuality by having a quickie with him in the bathroom. I squinted suspiciously at the soft smile on his face.

"I'm glad you're finally happy, Gwen."

"You're … glad?" I asked, my voice flat with disbelief. He gave a chuckle like he was reluctantly accepting a compliment about his magnanimous spirit. I considered hitting him.

"You were such a lost soul when we were together, unhappy in your former life with Stanfield."

"*Stanley,*" I corrected, though he ignored me and kept proselytizing on his own virtues.

"I did my best to fill you with affection and satiate your need, but you … you still had a yen for more. You came to me with such a *longing* to be loved and, yet, no matter how much love I gave, you were never quite satisfied."

"Well, that's true," I agreed, certain he didn't realize we were now talking about our disappointing sex life. Lance squeezed my fingers, making me feel like they'd been dipped in some sort of radioactive sludge intent on dissolving my phalanges right through my skin.

"It's just so good you finally found what makes you happy. I'd like to think I played some small role in helping you to truly learn to appreciate your sensuality, to really come into your own as a woman. At the very least, I hope that you consider me somewhat of a sexual Sherpa to you in your younger days."

"Uh," I grunted, staring at him with my jaw hanging open. He was dead serious; his ego had really convinced him that I was a happy lesbian because he'd stuck it to me good ten years ago.

For once in my life, I found myself thankful for the burn of werewolf emotions as they crept up behind me.

Twelve

My arm started jumping, which I immediately assumed was because I had developed a spontaneous and completely understandable allergy to touching Lance. When the burning started along my skin, I pulled my hand away from his, sat up to rub the back of my neck and looked around to see what waiter had brought a scalding plate too close. When my gaze landed on Kincade, I froze, my eyes widening in stunned fear.

"Chloe," I whispered, smacking her roughly in the shoulder repeatedly and spastically.

"Yes, sugar?"

"Kincade's a werewolf," I whispered.

I saw Chloe's long, confused blink in my peripheral vision, felt a slight drift of amusement lap at me before it dissipated in horrified anger and, unless I was mistaken, the barest minuscule sliver of envy. Chloe pushed to her feet, stepped around the chair to face Kincade full on. Kincade stopped just outside Chloe's reach, ran her eyes over the group.

She looked about the same as the last time I'd seen her, though with fewer bruises and a different color tipping her short, expertly styled mohawk. She was a little shorter than me, with twice my muscle, a strong face dominated by a self-satisfied grin. Her outfit was comfortable, casual, made for easy movement, but it didn't lack style. When she'd threatened my life just months before she'd dressed much the same. Really, other than the red in her hair, she was exactly the same, except that now she was a werewolf instead of just a nasty, selfish mercenary.

"Heard you found my note and thought you might be looking for me," Kincade said. Dishonesty draped itself over us both, nearly suffocating me so intensely I flailed my arms around, trying to throw it off before I realized it was an emotion and not a heavy blanket.

"I decided it's time I collect my things," Chloe said, shifting her weight slightly. As her hand close in on her hip pack, Kincade tilted her head.

"Didn't you hear your little empath? You've been out of the game too long if you think you stand a chance against me now."

"Who's your friend?" Rita asked from the back of the table, concern a thick shell across her skin. She had no way of knowing the history between Kincade and Chloe, or even the much more recent history between Kincade and Mel, but she knew something was up. In typical Rita style, she wanted to fix it, to make everything chill and everyone happy. "Introduce us."

Kincade's eyes lit as she closed in, stepping around Chloe as if she trusted her not to attack in front of witnesses. I tensed, expecting Chloe to do exactly that, but nothing happened and, before I knew it, Kincade was reaching a hand toward Rita.

"Veronica. It's very nice to meet you, Ms. Stemple. I love the band."

The moment a compliment was on offer, Lance pushed to his feet, eager to get right in its path. I watched in fascinated horror as he practically threw his shiny, stupid self right into harm's way.

"A fan of the band is always a friend of mine. Nice to meet you, Veronica." Gliding like he was on the lead float in the asshole parade, Lance stepped around Chloe and me, holding a hand out toward Kincade. I wasn't sure if he expected her to shake it or kiss one of his many, tacky rings, but she only stared, derisive confusion arching one perfectly plucked eyebrow.

"Who the hell are you?" she asked flatly, pulling a shocked, nervous laugh out of my throat. Harvey gave me a look to match the nervous amusement wobbling in his chest, Dennis stuffed a pot sticker into his mouth, and Rita let out a teeny, tiny snort.

"I'm … I'm *Lance*." Baffled by the fact that Kincade wasn't falling at his feet or trying to tear his clothes off, my idiot ex pushed his hand further toward her. Kincade just looked at it as he explained, exasperation squeaking out with his words. "I'm the lead singer. *Of Eye Masters*."

Kincade turned her gaze back to Rita, her brow still up.

"My other band," Rita explained. Chloe, still and quiet between me and Kincade, reached out to grab our uninvited guest. I noted she'd pulled three metal bands out of her pocket, slipped them over her thumb, middle, and ring fingers. They weren't rings, exactly, too wide and plain to be considered decorative, but they covered the space between her knuckles and palm like armor. Unflappably unbothered by the idea of Chloe getting a grip on her, Kincade let Chloe think she had an edge.

At first.

Grinning, she looked over, meeting Chloe's eyes for just long enough to wink. Then, with the speed of a cheetah on PCP, she twisted, twirling Chloe into her arms like a dance, breaking the grip. Rage jumped out of Chloe, crowding around me like angry porcupines, making me wince and groan. Hugging Chloe's back to her chest, Kincade kissed her cheek, whispering condescendingly into her ear.

"You're unusually ill-prepared, Gavel."

There was another blur of motion as Kincade grabbed Chloe's wrist and spun her out, twisting the joint as if she'd break it. Despite the fact that Chloe's hand was being bent almost completely back against her wrist, she didn't cry out. Pain was stabbing out of her, making me nauseated and I stumbled against the table. Mel shoved to his feet, a storm of impotent anger whirling inside him as he stepped around the table. Before he could get far, Kincade pointed his way, wagged a finger at him.

"Stay. Don't get any ideas pretty boy, you know I could snap your wrist and hers in one hand. Now." Taking a deep breath grinning brilliantly around the table again, Kincade spared a wink for Rita, before changing tactics. Adjusting her grip on Chloe, forcing her back a step, she let go. Despite the pain I knew Chloe was in, she didn't try to baby her wrist; she just stepped to place herself slightly between Kincade and me. Kincade only watched her, delighted by her priorities.

"Man, you need a Xanax or something, Veronica," Rita suggested, closing carefully around the table as if she could still remedy the tension. "Come on, sit down and I'll buy you a beer. You two can talk this out."

Kincade shook her head. "The Gavel and I have much too much history to bother talking. This sort of relationship requires action." Without warning, she popped Chloe in the face with her fist. I yelped but Chloe only grunted at the impact, staggered back a step. I considered that we must have a god or fate or Satan himself on our side for her not to have killed Chloe outright.

"That's enough!" Harvey ordered, his voice booming. We had half the restaurant looking at us, now, and the panic from the guy behind the bar was just the tip of the terror iceberg. I knew that, if we didn't get out of here soon—and leave a sizable tip—we were going to have police-type problems on our hands.

Kincade lifted her arms, palms out, and took a step back from Chloe, her gaze sliding, joyous and proud toward Harvey. He paused halfway around the table, possibly reconsidering his attempt to use his mass to muscle Kincade out of the restaurant. He was twice her size but it wouldn't matter and, while he couldn't have known that, I could feel the little flap of anxiety in his chest telling him to just stay the fuck back.

"I didn't come here to pick a fight," she explained after a bit, her gaze going to the blood dripping down Chloe's chin. Mel's werewolf lust jumped within her, screaming heated, bloody need at the sight of it and I felt disgust swamp me. Mel had never liked blood or pain, not from what I'd seen. He was a lover *and* a fighter, sure, but the years I'd known him had taught me that his lust was … pure, for lack of a better word.

No, I realized as Kincade's libido heated and boiled, this was all her.

"I just came to say hi to an old friend, to give you the chance to back off before you get yourself hurt. I've got business here, and your beautiful friend—" Kincade winked at Mel and her libido practically purred. "—here had something that could help. Don't worry Fido, you'll be back to your old self ... later. I don't intend on keeping what I took. I'm not a greedy, selfish *shit,* after all."

Gaze sliding to Chloe, writing volumes I couldn't read, Kincade took another step back, eyeballed the group.

"No one else wants to be the hero? We're all done? No more trouble?"

"There's going to be trouble," Chloe said so quietly I was sure no one but me and Kincade could have heard it, though she made no move to make good on the threat. "I'll promise you that."

Harvey, sensing that the conflict was on its way to a close, grabbed a cloth napkin from the table and closed in to press it against Chloe's face. She jerked when he did, annoyance whipping through her, but she let him do what he could to care for her.

As Kincade started to back toward the door, she pointed at Rita.

"Looking forward to the next album, love. Ta!" Giving one quick wave, Kincade turned, rounded the corner and disappeared. I could still feel the burn of her emotions, but they were secondary to the shamed, sick animosity screaming through Chloe.

"I'm gonna—"

Before she could move, everyone within touching distance grabbed for her, but Mel managed to close in first. He merely stood in front of her, wide as a barn, intimidating as a kitten, but he stopped her anyway.

"Don't," he murmured, pain fused like copper along his words. "I know what I can do and if she can do any of it, you need to stay here."

Chloe aimed a bloody snarl his way and then grabbed the cloth from Harvey, jerking away from the men surrounding her. Harvey put his hands up just like Kincade had done and then immediately seemed to realize what he was doing. Dropping his hands at his side, he stepped deliberately back.

"You should get that checked out," he said after a moment, feeling lost and worried for her. "That's a lot of blood."

"What a bitch," Rita said. Dennis squeaked out a laugh, watching us. His emotions were a discomfort sundae with a heap of whipped confusion sliding awkwardly down the side. I remembered him as a bit of a Sneed so it wasn't a surprise to me that he had responded to the situation like other admirers of my ex-husband might have. Fans of Stanley Sneedley do not jump into fights or threaten to call the cops. They stand by and try not to be noticed. Like panicked bunnies.

"Are you okay?" I asked Chloe, once I could speak. One of the waiters came over to us but kept peering backward as if he wanted to make sure he had an exit strategy if things got hairy again. Chloe ignored us both.

"You'll have to leave," he said. Chloe turned sharply to him and he visibly flinched. Despite the fact that Lance was standing closer, Mel slid in, wrapped an arm around the man's shoulder and led him back toward the bar.

"I am so sorry about that, sir. Please, I'll take the bill and …" His quiet voice trailed off as they moved further away.

"Chloe?" I asked, hauling myself to my feet to put my hand on her arm. She didn't push me away but I could feel that it was an effort of will. She probably wanted to be out tearing Kincade a few new assholes instead of being coddled but we both knew she couldn't, not at the moment. "Do you want some ice?"

Taking a deep breath, Chloe turned back to face the table, forcing herself to visibly relax. She was still keyed up, but you couldn't have seen it in her face. Speaking through the napkin, she apologized.

"I'm sorry, guys. I … really hope this doesn't … go viral or something."

"Oh!" Lance wailed suddenly, making Dennis jolt. I glared his way, already annoyed, even though I didn't know what the fuck he was about to say. "I had not even thought about what the public would think of this! I must get our social media handler to diffuse the situation. Excuse me, my friends. I need to make sure that our side of this story gets out before there's a rash of inappropriate headlines insisting we had anything to do with this little scuffle. Gwen, it was nice to see you. Give me a call later, if you need any further, you know, *guidance*."

Swinging his coat off the back of his chair, Lance swept toward the front of the restaurant, holding his hand over his eyes as if a thousand flashbulbs were going off in his face. Truthfully, I think we were the only ones in the restaurant who had any idea who the hell he was.

"Why does he say things like that," Rita demanded with a roll of her eyes. "*He's* the only one who even has our Twitter password!"

I couldn't tell you how Mel got us all out of there without causing a scene or costing a fortune, but he managed. Jason, who had missed the whole thing, had to be filled in, but he was of the same mind as Rita: Kincade sounded like a shithead.

I said a quick goodbye to the band, shared a moment with Harvey over Lance's melodramatics, and we filed out of the restaurant.

"Mel, I need you to drive," I said as we closed in on Chloe's car. Mel glanced at me, a puff of curiosity escaping him, but he nodded and diverted at the last moment to cut Chloe off from the driver's side. She stopped abruptly, glared up at him, still holding a wad of bloody napkins against her face. Mel gave her a quick eyebrow waggle and a wink, and then reached down to gently take the keys from her fingers. She didn't let go at first, but

Mel just kept peeling her fingers away, speaking gently.

"You probably shouldn't be driving with that wound. Come on, give 'em over." Chloe fought through what, to me, felt like the urge to give him a matching broken nose, but let the keys go, moving stiffly around the car to the passenger's seat. I gave Mel a small nod of thanks and then climbed into the back seat. Once we were on our way back to her place, I reached forward, set my hand on Chloe's shoulder, as close as I dared to the bare skin of her neck.

"You okay?" I asked. She didn't answer but I could feel that she wasn't. Taking a deep, courage-boosting breath, I shifted in my seat. "This is for your own good!"

Before she could argue or attempt to stop me I moved my hand, slapped it against the side of her neck, shoving my empathy inside her. She let out a sound of shocked, mindless anger as she lifted her free hand and grabbed at my wrist, trying to pry me off. I was fueled by panic, though, and worry for her state of mind. I found the anger inside her, used my powers like a vacuum and sucked it out.

Her snarling tapered off into a relaxed sigh as her shoulders slumped and her hand dropped back into her lap.

Chloe's anger was *alive,* thrashing and pounding against the inside of my ribs like my heart was taking a baseball bat to my sternum. As her rage soared through my veins, I felt my fingers clench on the bare skin of her delicate throat. I considered reaching my other hand forward, gripping her tightly under her chin and choking the life out of her. Chloe's anger wanted to draw blood, break bones, and tear skin. Some small part of my brain pointed out that this wasn't me; I didn't want to hurt Chloe.

She buys you cookies and saves your damn life, it pointed out. *Think about the cookies! You love cookies!*

I grabbed onto that logical, sugar-loving part of my brain, used it as a sword to fight off the anger. I closed my eyes, easing my breath out slowly, and pulled my hand away from her skin. Tucking my fist against my chest, I leaned back in the seat, tried to ignore the fact that I was shaking. I needed to concentrate, to use the tools and techniques my father had tried to teach me over the last few months.

While it didn't make Chloe's anger dissipate any faster, I was able to unclench my jaw and overcome the urge to start screaming wordlessly. When I opened my eyes, Mel glanced at me in the rearview mirror, worry tightening his features. That too bothered me, though I couldn't tell you why, and I crossed my arms tightly over my chest, fisting both hands around my coat at my ribs.

"Gwen?" Chloe said, her voice slow. I didn't answer, but she pressed on. "I'm sorry. You okay back there? You want some cake? I got some cake at home."

I couldn't risk opening my mouth to speak so I just gave a single nod, despite the fact that she couldn't actually see me. When no one spoke for a moment, Mel leaned slightly closer to Chloe as he took a turn.

"She nodded. I think she wants cake."

"Gwen always wants cake. She'll do anything for cake, won't'cha?"

I didn't nod this time, because her calmness was making the anger slippery, hard to hold down. The fact that I wanted to pin her to the ground and punch her in the throat until my hands went numb was now more important than the fact that I had done this to myself. I couldn't uncross my arms because that small, logical part of me that was watching the rest of my body from a safe distance knew it was a bad idea.

When we finally pulled into Chloe's carport, I tore at the seatbelt, yanked it off and shoved out of the car. I slammed the door hard enough that I hoped it would break, and took a stomping walk toward the far edge of the building. When I felt I was far enough away that no one had followed me, I let out a screech. I railed at the bare cement wall, turned and kicked it three times before I realized I did *not* have the shoes for this.

The pain of my bruised toes only made the rage worse and I twisted back to the street, seeing red. Chloe strolled over, her form loose and calm. She smiled at me, lifted her chin in greeting rather than waving or speaking. She gave me some time to pace, to shudder, to consider jumping on her and tackling her to the cement before she spoke.

"Come on, hit me," she offered. My entire body jerked, intending to do just that. I was able to stop myself at the last minute and she shook her head. "It's okay, do your worst."

"No," I growled. Chloe grinned crookedly and I felt humor well up in her.

"I want you to hit me as hard as you can," she intoned. I bared my teeth, clenched my fists. The fact that she was joking only made me angrier.

"Go away!"

"It'll be fine," she insisted, tucking the bloody napkin into her hip pack. "I've seen you hit. You couldn't knock over a three-legged stool."

Insult sparked and that time I wasn't able to stop myself. I shifted my weight, shoved my fist forward, aiming for her bruised and swollen nose. Chloe countered, batting away my attack easily, dancing back out of reach. Freshly enraged that I'd missed—that she'd *dodged me*—I cried out again, caught my footing and twisted to attack. She parried several more of my pathetic punches before I felt the anger start to recede. It was hard work failing to beat someone up and my body was starting to insist I wind down.

Chloe kept up her guard as she waited to make sure I was done, as she watched me pant and deflate, and then stepped forward, wrapping an arm around my shoulders.

"Let's go upstairs, Sugar Ray. You can fight the cat."

"That sounds mean," I croaked, letting her lead me toward the door. Mel was standing just inside the landing, nervous energy cracking around him. He was worried, though I couldn't discern if it was for me or Chloe.

"You're right," Chloe cooed as we hit the door. "I wouldn't do that to you. Poopy's got quite a left hook."

Thirteen

Mel and I sat next to each other on the couch while Chloe cleaned up. Neither one of us had said anything since coming inside and neither one of us had wanted to displace the cat from her seat in Chloe's big red lounge chair.

So, there we sat, silent, staring at the television mounted to the brick wall across from us. It was off, but you couldn't have told that just from watching us; we were pretty attentive to its blackness. Once my stolen anger had completely dissipated, I turned, caught his eye.

"Sorry. About earlier."

"The fight?" he asked. I nodded and he gave a lazy shrug. "It's fine."

"No," I said, biting my lip. Lowering my gaze, I let out a breath, tried to keep myself from mumbling incoherently. "I should've realized that it takes two to tango. I didn't think about what was going on. I just … wanted to get laid and you were there, and … yeah."

Mel seemed to consider my words for a moment and I looked up to see the expression that would go with the little thread of embarrassment running through him. He was giving me a crooked smile, which he followed up with a nod when our eyes met.

"It's okay, really. I know I wasn't at my best, considering how—ah—out of practice I was. I'm not usually … a sleepy slug, I swear," he insisted. I smiled, hoped the conversation would end there. Mel continued on, straightening his posture like he was taking on a heavy burden. "I'm sorry, too. I shouldn't have taken such umbrage to your disappointment. I didn't mean to pick a fight."

"You don't—You didn't." I said, swallowing thickly, surprised he was taking credit for the tiff and feeling guilty for not already admitting that, really,

I had been just as big of a dick. We sat quietly for a bit and I bit my lip, suddenly very aware that we were touching, leg to leg, bare arms pressed together. Mel noticed too and a thread of affection grew inside him, something I'd never felt from him, not in this way. It was serious, deep, similar to what I'd felt once upon a time from my ex-husband. Fear demanded I shift, pulling away and putting a stop to it.

"Umbrage?" I asked, making it painfully clear I was trying to tease him. "Like Professor?"

"What?" Mel asked, confused at the turn of events.

"Mel! Are you into Harry Potter?"

"I—" Cutting himself short, he considered me for a moment, a little tense, but unbothered. Swallowing thickly, he turned slightly, like he couldn't quite meet my eyes. Rolling with my teasing, he continued. "Look. I like to be prepared for all manner of discussion and certain ladies like those books." He corrected when I gave him a cynical glare. "*Adult* ladies!"

Glad we were back on even-footing, I laughed. "You just don't seem like the type."

"To read Harry Potter?"

"To be literate," I clarified. Mel rolled his eyes, but humor still burbled. He was enjoying the teasing and, in fact, I realized the affection I'd been trying to chase off was still there, still thick and serious and scary. My laughter trailed off and we sat there, eyes locked, still close enough to kiss. We both realized at about the same time that at some point, I'd dropped my hand to rest on his thigh. Our gazes fell together to my hand, before both of us looked up again, our eyes meeting. Mel let the silence go for a beat before ruining it.

"You wanna make out?" he asked.

"What?" I breathed, barely able to get the word out.

"You heard me," Mel purred, amping up, suddenly turning aggressive, as if he was challenging me. Somewhere in him a tiny flap of panic had started, wiggling like a flag in a storm. He pressed on and I realized that he was just as scared of our sudden closeness as I'd been.

Thank god!

"I'm human now," he continued, his voice a low growl. "No burning emotions. I won't even need the necklace this time. Come on." He set his hand on my thigh, as I'd done to him. "Take your pants off."

Chloe walked out, saved me from having to take myself out in a messy murder-suicide scenario. "Down boy."

Mel twisted in his seat to see her and I fought my first urge, which was to gasp or yelp in surprise. Despite the fact that she had bandaged up her face and covered her nose completely, I could see bruising along her eyes. I got up, stepped around the couch as if I could help.

"I'm fine," she said, waving me off. "I took a painkiller, cleaned up. I'll just look like an idiot for awhile."

Mel lifted his hand to point as if he were threatening her. "If anyone asks, you walked into a door."

Chloe rolled her eyes, frowning at his distasteful joke. Instead of going with it or chastising him, she turned to me, rubbing a hand down my shoulder.

"How're you?"

"Me? I'm fine. I didn't get socked in the face by a werewolf."

"She *isn't* a werewolf," Chloe insisted, that small seed of rage sprouting again. Collecting herself, she gestured to the couch and then stepped around it toward her big, red chair. Despite the cat's whining, half-asleep protesting, Chloe lifted her up and took her seat. Settled into Chloe's lap, Poopy sat up crookedly, looked Mel and me over with one half-closed eye. She reminded me of an angry, sleepy pirate, though her anger was already fizzling back into sleepy contentment.

"Werewolves are born, not made. She's just … stolen Mel's wolf," Chloe explained, giving Poopy's head a quick scratch. "She can't actually shift."

"Will I really be back to normal soon?" Mel asked.

Chloe's gaze drifted downward, something seizing her that was much deeper than a simple distaste. It seemed to dry her out, to turn her insides to stone and threatened to crack open a fissure in her, but she kept it under control.

I moved back around the couch and sat down, pressing my back to the armrest so I could face them both. Chloe shifted in her seat, which apparently irritated Poopy enough that she moved to the edge of the chair, jumped across the gap between it and the couch. Mel ignored her as she crawled into his lap.

"You don't do this," Chloe mumbled quietly, guilt and despair swamping through her, splashing against the wall of discomfort and depression deep in her core.

"What?" I asked quietly.

Chloe lifted her gaze, seemed to come into herself. Swallowing hard, pushing back the emotions deep inside, she shook her head.

"It's late, but I need to go out."

"Where?" I asked.

"To get something to fix me?" Mel asked. Chloe smiled, but it was small and tight.

"Like she said, you'll be fine. Probably. If she truly doesn't intend to … You'll be fine in a few weeks."

Chloe stood and Mel followed suit, but before his stunned silence could be overcome by his need to argue, Chloe rushed into her bedroom.

"I can't stay human for a *week*," he insisted, turning to me. I lifted a brow, wondered if I wanted to risk my sanity again by taking his panic for him. I decided I didn't, but that I knew another way to distract him.

"You're sure?" I asked.

"Would you wanna lose your empathy for a week?"

"I mean," I said, as if truly considering it. The idea wasn't wholly unappealing but I could see his point. "Weren't you just the one saying that now's the perfect time for us to have sex?"

Mel blinked at me, surprise creeping up the back of his panic to wrap a garrote around its neck. The panic struggled against the assault but Mel's surprise called lust in as back-up and the panic went to the mat.

"Are you flirting with me?" Mel asked, shifting his stance. I just shrugged, found us making intense eye contact.

"I'm just saying words."

Mel and I sat there, eyes locked, grins tugging at our lips, but neither of us made a move. Chloe strolled back out into the room before we could actually make anything happen.

"Come on, downstairs you go."

"What?" Mel asked.

"I'm not leaving you two here alone, unprotected. Come on. I won't be gone long and then we can all sleep up here with the cat."

Leaning down to scratch Poopy on the head, she jerked her thumb at the door.

"Do we have to?" I asked, not looking forward to the dim, windowless prison again.

"Scoot," Chloe said, before throwing a sugar grenade my way to get me moving. "There's cake down there. Get going."

The cake in Chloe's safe house was, in fact, a single Twinkie, but it counted. One can never be disappointed by Twinkies, at least not if one is an empath who wants nothing more than to eat one form of sugar stuffed inside another. Mel and I watched TV from opposite ends of couch, carefully not touching each other. Mel was pretty delighted to discover reruns of an old soap opera from the eighties, and I just went with it. The fashion was all pastels, the hair was all massive, and America's incredible overabundance of shoulder pads was on ample display.

I didn't ask if he'd watched the show before, partly because I didn't want to risk talking to him and partly because I liked my own idea that Mel had learned all he knew about seduction from this ridiculous farce of a show. If he told me he wasn't secretly yearning to impregnate his own evil twin and then fling himself down an elevator shaft, I would have been crushed. I couldn't risk it.

Chloe came and got us a couple hours later and we all trudged back upstairs to her place. I only noticed once we got to her door that my lack of signal down in her supposed safe house had kept me safe from a series of texts from Owen.

"Oh!"

"What?"

"Owen." I paused outside the door, while Mel headed in as if the whole situation didn't concern him. Chloe leaned on the jamb, watching me but not intruding as I scanned the texts. "He couldn't find anyone to come help but he'll try to be here as soon as he can finish his job and get a flight."

"Tell him I'm dealing with it."

I started to text and felt a little jolt of regret in Chloe. She didn't speak but I could tell she wanted to. "What?"

"Actually, do you … mind if I tell him?"

"You wanna text him?"

"On your phone, as you, but yes."

"Why?"

Dishonesty started to cloud around her, obscuring the regret and making me tense. In the end, after a long pause, it dissipated and she shrugged, shaking her head. "Never mind. Just tell him … Say it's all under control."

"Like, those exact words?"

"Sure," Chloe said, keeping her tone casual, while her psyche clearly wasn't.

"What's wrong?"

She took a deep breath, her eyes downcast for another long moment before her jaw locked tight for a moment and a small, bitter smile curved her lips. When she spoke again, she was very, very careful with her words.

"Owen and I have a history with Kincade. Due to the … nature of what she's done, I'd rather keep him out of it."

Something wasn't right there but I couldn't pick up on why or what. She wasn't lying, everything she'd said was completely true but I didn't like it all the same. I watched her stare at the ground for awhile before realizing that I didn't have to like it. I'd seen both of them deal with Kincade just a few months ago, had felt the hatred Kincade had for Owen and the distaste Owen had for Kincade. If Chloe wanted to keep them separated, I had to trust her.

"Okay."

She met my eyes and a little spasm of surprise wriggled through her, as if she had expected me to argue or fight her. I smiled, reached briefly out to rub her shoulder, and then got back to texting.

It's under control. Apparently Mel's gonna be fine wthin a week, if he doesn't get himself killed as a human first.

Leaving it at that, because it was later than I'd stayed up in ages, I trudged in after Chloe. She gestured to a charging bank with extra phone plugs, and then moved to a skinny closet across the living room to make up the couch.

It wasn't the first time I'd slept with Chloe and that was the exact reason it was four in the morning and I was the one of us who was still awake. She was still next to me, stretched out on her back, arms across her belly. Even though her nose was bandaged, her breathing was slow, unlabored. I was terrified that, if I fell asleep, my tendency to thrash and kick would only injure her further.

I wasn't sure why I'd insisted Mel get the couch.

Doing my best not to disturb her, I rolled out of the covers without lifting them, and tiptoed out to the living room. I closed the door as far as I dared and made my way as silently as I could to the couch.

"Mel," I breathed into the darkness. I could feel that he wasn't asleep; he was worried about something. He shifted as I came around the edge of the couch, snorted out a quiet laugh when I stubbed my toe on an end table. I got one awkward, pained hop in before Mel shifted, grabbing me around the waist and tugging me down onto the couch.

"Sit down before you kill yourself."

"I can't sleep," I grumbled, lifting my foot to inspect it in what little light was streaming in from the street. I heard Mel feeling around in the blankets for something, before the light from his phone flashed on, blinding us both. We shared twin jolts of discomfort before he aimed the light away from his face, fiddled with its settings to turn the brightness down. Setting it on the table as a nightlight, he turned to me.

"What's wrong?"

"I'm scared I'm going to beat Chloe up in my sleep." Mel nodded, watching me set my throbbing foot on the ground before looking back to my face.

"You do sleep like a jackhammer."

"Exactly. She's injured and went to bed grumpy and I don't want to hurt her face or have her … like, do some sort of crazy Jujitsu on me and break *my* nose if I accidentally whack her." Mel chuckled at the image but his amusement was shallow, a thin layer atop a cauldron of unpleasant emotions.

"How's she really doing?" he asked after a bit.

"Ah," I said with a sigh, as if I didn't know how to explain exactly. There was too much there, too many things to bring up, not the least of which was our recent encounter with Kincade. Mel gave me a moment, before pressing on.

"I usually consider myself a master of body language—a real cunning linguist of the female form, if you will—"

"I won't," I interrupted. Mel grinned but continued.

"But she's better than most at hiding what she's really feeling. Without my wolf senses, I can't hear her heartbeat or—well." He waved a hand to explain away whatever else he might've meant and I got the feeling he expected me to know exactly all his tricks for detecting lies and emotions. "I'm worried about her."

"She's … pissed," I settled on. "Unusually so. She and Kincade have a history and, while I don't know the extent of what happened between them, I know it's really, really getting to Chloe. It's weird, man. I'm not used to her being so mad she can't think straight."

"No," Mel agreed, turning to look toward Chloe's bedroom. I considered his profile in the low light of his phone, as silence settled and we both thought about Chloe. A few moments passed before I realized I was admiring his pretty face and thinking that, hey maybe his earlier suggestion of making out wouldn't be such a chore.

Snapping myself out of it, I shifted in my seat, moving away from him as delicately as I could without making it obvious. Mel finally came back to the conversation, unhappiness simmering.

"I was really worried, back at dinner, that she was just gonna shove me down and go after Veron—Kincade. It scared me." His voice quieted even more as he admitted to the fear and I felt a swell of affection for him that I wasn't sure I'd ever felt before. Lust, friendship, a general appreciation of his ability to banter but this was deeper and it … actually felt pretty nice. "I don't want her to get herself killed trying to make me a wolf any sooner. If it's gonna happen, I can wait. I can take a few days off work or stick to cases that don't require any, you know, heavy lifting. I can deal with the inconvenience for a few days if it means she'll be safe."

"You're a good dude," I said without really thinking. Mel considered me, a teeny, tiny bit of suspicion clouding.

"Am I?"

"Less so when you're trying to get into my pants, but yeah." He chuckled and we sat there in the dark, eyes locked, alone in the early morning dark. He'd brought a loose pair of sleep pants and a long-sleeved thermal shirt than managed to mold to his chest in a way that I was sure he'd planned. I would not have been surprised to learn that he'd had it tailored to display the maximum amount of contoured muscle possible.

He looked good. Hell, he smelled good.

Something heavy and needy swelled between us, an intense connection that tingled right through the center of me and before I knew it, I was reaching out, tucking a curl of his dark hair behind his ear. Arousal swamped through him but when his gaze rolled gently to my lifted arm, it was gobbled up by guilt so caustic I gasped at the burn.

I jolted away, shocked by the change in him, clutching my arm to my chest, hissing and swearing.

"What?" he demanded, worry electrifying the guilt and making me jump to my feet just to move away. I knew what had happened, of course, and the fact that, nearly a year after the fact, Mel was still being an ass about the scars he'd accidentally carved into my arm sparked rage in my chest.

"Goddammit, Mel," I growled, stomping quickly to the end of the living room and back before I leaned down and poked him hard in the chest. "Stop it."

"Stop what?" he demanded, his own annoyance trying to combat the guilt.

"Stop being a bitch."

"What the hell are you talking about?" Mel demanded, jumping to his feet as if we needed to be on even footing.

"My scars! Every time you see them you get *weird.*"

"I don't get *weird!*"

"The hell you don't! You can't lie to me, remember?" I poked him hard in the heart. "I know what you're feeling. Even when I really, *really* don't want to!"

"I didn't make you an empath, that's not my fault!"

"But acting like a baby every time you catch a glimpse at my forearm does! I've told you a hundred times I'm not mad!"

"Oh sure, it's all about you. Everything's always about Gwen and what *she* wants."

We were still trying to be quiet but both of us were on the edge of failing and I could tell we both knew it. I wanted to end the fight, if only so we didn't start screaming at each other and wake Chloe up. Now more than ever, she needed her beauty sleep. Fists clenched, annoyance burbling, I did the only thing I could think of doing and punched Mel's arm, just below his arrow wound.

"Hey!" he chastised, just barely failing to whisper.

"Is *this* Chloe's fault?"

"What? No. Of course not."

"It's the same thing with me," I insisted, poking him again. I wasn't entirely sure what my argument was, but I was damned well going to make something out of it. Mel let out small sound of panic when I went in for a third and grabbed my wrist. His hand was warm, and I noticed he tugged a little, as if he wanted me just a step closer.

"You didn't know that you were attacking me, Kincade didn't know she was attacking you, and her goal was to go after Chloe in some way."

"Are you comparing me to Kincade?"

"Uh—I'm—I just mean that Chloe's who the arrow was meant for, right? And you're the one who got shot. Well. The … spider thing was who was— Look, you didn't know what you were doing. I don't blame you. And, fuck, Mel they're just scars. I still have full use of my arm and I don't even notice them anymore. They're just part of me. I don't understand why you keep beating yourself up over this."

"You don't have to understand," he said, pulling me in close as a greedy ache that I couldn't discern slammed through him. It was so quick and turned to panic so fast that I couldn't read it in the instant before he dropped my arm, dancing back, and pacing away just as I had done. When he got back to me, he stood close—but didn't touch me—and whispered, "You're not the one who has to live with the mistake."

"I'm the only one who has to live with the mistake. It's *my* arm."

Mel and I stared at each other in the dim light as he fought off a fresh wave of guilt. It wasn't as strong, which was a good sign, and it seemed to settle quicker than it ever had before. His expression softened and, as a relaxed sort of defeat overtook him, he dropped onto the couch, his head falling back against the cushions.

"You really … don't hate me at all?"

"Well," I said, finding his question funny, considering our history and how hard I found being around him when he was wolfy. "Not for this."

Mel laughed, which felt nice, a good relief to the tension that had been crackling between us. I settled down to sit next to him, turning to lean my shoulder against the cushions, and rested my head on the back of the couch as well.

He was oh so quiet when he said, without looking my way, "You should just sleep with me."

"Excuse me?" I asked, though I knew he didn't mean it the way it sounded. Mel laughed, rolling his head so he could see me.

"You know what I mean. Neither of us wants to disturb Chloe, and we've done it before."

"True," I said, nodding as if it was only good sense. "But did you forget the part about me sleeping like a jackhammer?"

"I've survived worse."

"As a human?"

Mel was quiet, considering the danger of my thrashing and flailing. "Maybe if I wrap you up real tight in the blanket I'll be safe."

"There you go. Just roll me up in a rug like Cleopatra."

Fourteen

I woke alone on the couch to the smell of food cooking. While it hadn't taken Mel and I long to find a comfortable position, I had evidently rejected the warmth of being wrapped and spooned. I was now stretched out on my stomach, arm draped off the side of the couch, face buried against the back. I pushed up to scan the room, wondering when Mel had gotten up.

Turned out he hadn't; I'd just forced him onto the floor at some point.

"You hungry?" Chloe asked from the kitchen. I yawned, wiped the drool off my chin, and forced my body to cooperate until I was sitting up. Mel was slumped on his uninjured side on the floor, covered in blankets.

"That's my secret. I'm always hungry," I said. Chloe paused in her stirring and pan-shaking to look up at me with a wink.

"What were you *hungry* for last night?"

"It—nothing—I didn't want to beat you up and Mel wouldn't leave the couch."

"So you performed a hostile takeover?"

"Damn straight."

Careful not to step on Mel's hand, I got up, padded toward the bathroom. By the time I was back at the bar chairs feeling slightly more awake and aware, Mel had woken up, too, and reclaimed the couch. He was rubbing the back of his neck, irritation crackling around him. I decided I didn't have to feel guilty that he was sore because it had been his idea for us to sleep together.

"Order up," Chloe announced. Mel pushed to his feet too, crossed the living room to the bar. Chloe winked as he took a seat but set a plate down in front of me. It was a mound of vegetables mixed in with carbs and tofu. I would have normally done my best to eat around the vegetables, but she'd done a damn good job of making sure they were fully integrated with the carbs.

Rats.

"What's on the agenda for today?" I asked, immediately before shoveling food into my mouth.

"Mel's gonna make some calls to his clients and ours and you and I are going to see Merrin."

"Why do I have to stay and make the calls?" Mel asked. Chloe slid a plate across the counter in front of him and I noted with some jealousy that she'd given him double the portion I'd gotten.

"Because Evadne doesn't like you. And someone has to do it."

Mel sighed but didn't argue, though I could tell some petulant part of him wanted to. We ate in silence for a bit before I felt I'd satisfied my great and terrible hunger just enough to continue questioning her.

"Why are we seeing Merrin?"

"Because this—Because. Okay." Chloe paused, a rare seesaw of indecisiveness wobbling in her guts for a moment before she bit her lip, and then pressed on. "What's been done to Mel, taking part of his soul, it requires a witch."

"You think Merrin stole my wolf?"

"I don't know, but I doubt it. I don't think Evadne likes Kincade any more than she likes you."

"Small blessings, I guess," Mel said, before shoveling another forkful of food into his mouth. I jabbed my fork into three huge chunks of potato on his plate and he glared but didn't fight me.

"But you think she might know who did?"

"She could probably give some tips, yes. Did Owen ever get back to you?"

I blinked at the change of subject and then looked over at the charging station at the end of her counter. "I hadn't even thought to check." Chloe grabbed my phone, handing it over face down, nerves crackling as if she really didn't want to read what he might have said. I unlocked the phone with one hand, still eating with the other, and snorted at the response.

"What?"

"He says to keep Mel locked in a tower and order him not to let his hair down for anyone but us."

Mel rolled his eyes, weary of the princess jokes, but he said nothing.

"Then that's what we'll do. We'll drop you by the office."

"No getting locked in the safe house?"

"It's midday and I've let Madeline know Kincade's up to something. She'll keep an eye on him."

"Could she stop Kincade all together?" I suggested, liking the idea of Kincade trapped in a sexless swirl of succubus-induced desire. "Like, permanently, even?"

"She ... could. She won't, but—actually, that's something to think about."

"Siccing a succubus on the bitch?" Mel sneered, frustration and impotence swamping through his chest.

Without thinking, I reached out, rubbing Mel's back, sliding my hand up to touch the back of his neck, taking on just a little of the dread brought up by the talk of a creature that had snacked on him once upon a time. Cramming tasty food into my face to stop the stolen emotions from overwhelming me, I slid my hand back down his back once I'd taken on what I felt to be enough, but didn't break contact. Mel glanced at me, curiously, but I didn't look over, unwilling to take any gratitude.

"No," Chloe said, looking off into the distance. "We don't know where she is or what she's up to, but we really should find out. I can probably find someone who will tell us where she'll be once or twice but being able to actually track her would be real handy."

Chloe drummed her fingers on the counter as a giddiness burst in her guts. Mel and I kept eating, him ignoring my hand on his back, me ignoring the emotions I'd sucked out of him. Eventually, after she'd dumped her plate in the dishwasher and run a sponge over the counters real quick, Chloe skirted the counter toward the bathroom.

"I'm gonna clean up, get ready. I wanna get out of here as soon as possible."

Mel didn't put up too much of a fuss at being asked to call and email our clients, though I was certain mine wouldn't be thrilled—yet again—at being asked to skip sessions because of the nebulous and all-purpose, "personal emergency" excuse, but we didn't really have much of a choice.

We drove in silence for awhile and, when my thoughts about my busy life led me to once again think about how much happier Sonny seemed with Lydia than he did at my house, I cleared my throat and started talking, just to keep my head on straight.

"So, Kincade needed a witch?"

"Yep," Chloe said, a bit of discomfort oozing along her calculating seriousness.

"But you don't think it was Merrin?"

"Highly unlikely, but we'll ask."

"And you want to track Kincade?"

"I want to try. Whatever she stole Mel's wolf for, it must be serious. It's—it just has to be something really big."

"You don't like talking about this, do you?"

"No," Chloe admitted immediately, anxiety seizing her for a moment. I didn't press, hating the fear in her, especially since she so rarely displayed it. Chloe was chill, rolling with all punches, able to leap empath tantrums in a single bound, a superwoman who seemed to be up for handling just about anything. The fact that this scared her made me worry and sort of made me want to just call the whole thing off.

"But you said if we do nothing, that Mel will go back to his old self?"

"He … could."

"I thought you said he *would*."

"Ultimately it's up to Kincade."

"That's not what you told him," I thought, trying to remember if there had been any hint of deception when she'd phrased it that way to ease his mind.

"If we can find the witch who's involved with all this, we'll know for sure."

"And she'll help us track Kincade?"

"A witch can give us the tools to track Kincade, assuming we can get those tools onto her person."

"And how do we do that?"

"We have to know where she'll be so we can be there first and get the jump on her."

"But then couldn't we just stop her then and there?"

"Ideally yes, but if not, we need a backup plan."

"This all sounds very dangerous. I think I'd rather just hide under my desk and eat cake."

"Yes, but that's your solution to everything."

"It's a perfectly valid life decision sometimes!" I insisted, liking that her worry was easing.

"When has it ever done anything positive?"

"Uh. I'm certain it would help in the event of an earthquake."

"Okay, I'll give you that."

"I found Izzy under my desk once," I said, shaking my head with annoyance before jolting and realizing that, Eureka, I'd solved it! "Izzy!"

"Here?" Chloe asked, looking around as if she expected to spot him.

"No! He can fix this!"

"I—well, maybe he could, but that's not what he does."

"Well, no. What he does is eat all my candy and have a lot of sex with you, often where I can hear it." I shifted in my seat, trying not to think of the fact that my psychic shielding is not great and I would often soak up the sexual desire and satisfaction from their lunchtime encounters. Chloe just waggled her brows, knowing exactly what was on my mind.

"Look," she said after a bit, catching my expression and laughing as she spoke. "Just because Izzy is powerful doesn't mean he's my cosmic solution vending machine. Though, I'll admit, sometimes I wish I could just shake him real hard until something useful falls out. He's actually around for a purpose and, while he can sometimes … bend that purpose to include tossing a little help our way, there are limits to his bendiness."

"So, call him, see how far he bends this time."

"He doesn't have a phone."

"Really?" I could have sworn I'd seen him with one once or twice, but I guess it could have been Chloe's. Or a toy phone filled with candy. "How do you get ahold of him?"

Chloe threw me a lascivious wink and purred, "Usually quite enthusiastically, and with both hands."

"Oh jeez," I spat, shaking my head as if I could rattle the naughty visual of her words right out of my brain. Generally I do not have any problem with hearing all the sweaty, fluid details of what she does with her partners but with Izzy it was another story. Something about him made my brain reject all notions of sexuality. It wasn't that I found his skinny form and impressive angles unattractive; I just could not picture him as anything other than a clumsy weapon of mass sugar-consumption, and nor did I care to.

Desperate to get as far away from talk of sex as I could, I pressed on.

"There has to be something he's good for. Could he track down Kincade so you can snipe her with a silver bullet and we can be done with this?"

"Werewolves are a type of fae; they don't have a silver allergy, they have an iron allergy. And consider how well it worked out last time Izzy thought he could lead us to Kincade, how did that work out?"

"I mean. He kept her from kicking your leg in and he figured out the tree thing." Thinking about some of the other shit he'd done while in Montana with us, I made a gagging sound. "And he licked me."

"He … What?"

"I had ice cream on my face and he wanted it."

"Ah. Yeah, he does that." Chloe nodded, her confusion dissipating, lust oozing gently through her, grossing me out before she even spoke. "He's all tongue."

Evadne refused to let us see exactly where their new home was located, but she did agree to bring Merrin to a local coffeehouse and meet us there. Chloe didn't press the issue, though I was curious how we would discuss such sensitive subjects in a crowd of Capitol Hill coffee nuts. I was told not to worry and promised a cookie so I stopped arguing.

"I want that one," I said as we entered the café. The display case held all manner of delightful pastries, but the one with the sprinkles caught my eye. Chloe scanned the angular bottom floor and then leaned back in an attempt to see over the railing to the second level. I pointed vaguely to the back corner of the mezzanine where I could feel the wintery breeze of fae emotions. "Up there, at the back."

"Here," Chloe stuffed a ten dollar bill in my hand and headed immediately toward the staircase near the wall of books. Taking my place in line, I let her go. I didn't feel it prudent to point out to Chloe that she'd given me significantly more money than I would need to get just one cookie.

Clearly this meant she wanted me to buy three or four.

By the time I got upstairs and to the table, they were already deep in discussion. Evadne, slim and pale with short blue hair pinned in forties-style bumps above her ears, glanced up at me, gave a small smile. You would definitely mistake her for human if you didn't know an alternative existed, but she was inhumanly lovely, skinny without looking bony or underfed, and dressed in a hyper stylish mix of vintage and modern clothing. Despite the chilly weather she hadn't bothered with a coat or even sleeves, and her skin showed no sign of goosebumps or frostbite. She seemed somewhat fond of me, though Chloe had cautioned me many times not to trust it when a Fairy is nice to you.

I took a seat across from Merrin, setting some of my treats on the table on front of me. She looked good, filled out some and cleaned up. No longer was her hair scraggly and limp; Evadne had gotten her to brush it and pull it back, at least from her face. She was wearing a nice coat, too, though she'd pinned enough colorful buttons and pins to it that, when she reached out to break a chunk off of one of my cookies, she jingled and clacked.

"What'd I miss?" I asked into the silence. Chloe drummed her fingers across the tabletop twice and then leaned back in her seat. Evadne lifted a brow, watching me take my seat and get my snacks settled. I felt her emotions breeze toward me like a sudden January wind, though they weren't unpleasant. She thought of me like one thinks of a cute but dumb animal and, really, I couldn't blame her. She'd only really seen me at my worst.

I shivered against her inspection but didn't say anything. Merrin reached out and grabbed the rest of the cookie I'd left on a napkin in front of me, but didn't contribute anything to the conversation. I let her have it, no fight, both because I'm scared of Evadne and because I genuinely like Merrin. I may be six-years-old at heart, but I can still share.

"Pet will help you with a tracker, though you'll need someone to apply it," Evadne said, watching Merrin nibble.

"I can find someone," Chloe assured us.

"Pretty hair," Merrin said, setting a single bite of cookie down on the napkin and looking off into the distance. She seemed to watch something intently for a moment before she wrinkled her nose. "He smells of skunk."

Gently, Evadne reached out, tucked Merrin's hair over her shoulder and patted her back. "What's this?"

"Big ice, tiny tables. The history, though. It has weight." Reaching across the table, Merrin set her hand on the table, turning to face me with an unusual focus. I smiled at her.

"Hey," I said, figuring she'd just caught on to the fact that I was even there. Evidently, the more powerful the witch the less connected she was to the real world. Merrin often lived in her own mind, unaware of what was going on right in front of her. It wasn't unusual to have entire conversations with her before she realized I was even in the room.

She lowered her gaze to the table, mouthed something I couldn't catch and then reached out for Evadne's hand. Evadne took it without hesitation and Merrin's breath came out foggy despite the warmth of the coffee shop.

"I think Pet has a suggestion for you, someone who may be able to help."

"I have contacts," Chloe assured Merrin, though Merrin continued to watch the nothing she was focused on, which seemed to have moved just behind my head. She winced, turning slightly away as if she'd seen something unpleasant, and then squeezed my hand.

"It's already passed, but it must be done," she said with a sad sigh.

"What—" I jolted, nausea swamping me as the world around me rocked, narrowed, and shot down a tunnel of darkness, slamming to a halt in the evening air, leaving me facing a wall I didn't recognize. I stumbled, turning in a panic, trying to figure out where the fuck I was and what the fuck had just happened.

Olivia R. Burton

Fifteen

"Jason?" I asked, looking at my old friend as he stared off into the distance, taking a drag off a joint. It was quiet out, though I could hear familiar music inside the building we were standing near. He didn't answer me. I called again, reaching out to grab him, but my hand swiped through him. I froze.

"Holy shit," I breathed, as he lifted his head and blew a few trick smoke rings into the night. Digging his phone out of his pocket with his free hand, he skimmed his text messages, grinned, particularly pleased at one of them, and then responded with a few heart emojis. I turned to look around, still curious and confused what the hell I was doing spying on Jason … in the evening, I realized. It had been light outside, mid-morning back where I'd been before getting sucked through space and time to be there.

Jason took another drag, walking further out from the restaurant, just strolling casually, staring up at the city sky but I stayed back, morbidly curious about why I'd been brought there. I heard a yell, a booming, familiar voice so quiet I wasn't sure at first I'd heard it at all. My empathy had fled, leaving me blind in a way, and I couldn't tell where it had come from, but I've been around for thirty years and could at least take an uneducated guess.

Circling the building, I found a side door propped open and grabbed for it. I couldn't actually make contact, of course, which was disconcerting, but it did give me an idea. Swallowing hard, deciding that the worst that could happen was that I'd look like an idiot to any ghosts in the area, I closed my eyes and walked right through.

I made it! I thought, much too eagerly when I opened my eyes and saw the inside of the restaurant I'd been at just the night before. My excitement crashed and burned immediately, though; I'd made it through a solid door, back to a scene I'd really hoped to never relive. There, across the way was Kincade taunting Chloe, the band looking stunned and confused, and Chloe bleeding down the front of her own shirt.

"No one else wants to be the hero? " Kincade asked with that same shitty grin from before. "We're all done? No more trouble?"

"There's going to be trouble. I'll promise you that."

"Whoa," I mumbled, closing in slowly, skirting the bar and tables out of habit, watching the rest of the evening play out. It seemed to go quicker this time, though I wasn't sure if that was magic or just the benefit of hindsight. Kincade left, Mel played the hero and, much to my surprise, Jason walked right through me to stop near the table and look around.

"What the hell happened?"

Rita turned, just as I remembered, grabbing his arm gently. As she began to explain, the world fizzed upward like the opening to a Bond film, dizziness overtaking me once again. After a long, confusing moment, I opened my eyes to find that I was back in the cafe, seated next to Chloe, my eyes boring onto Merrin's. She looked intensely lucid, her expression serious, her jaw locked. In fact, I realized as my empathy seemed to wake up in my brain, she was *very* unhappy with me.

"This is going to cost you."

"What's she mean?" Chloe asked, a thrum of nervous energy vibrating along my skin. I groaned a little, feeling sick emotionally and physically, and crammed my last cookie into my mouth. "What happened?"

Merrin's expression relaxed, her gaze drifted to the crumbs on the table, and she let go of my hand, murmuring something I couldn't understand. Evadne looked between us, settling on me. When I didn't respond, she lifted a brow, an icicle of irritation jabbing me between the eyes.

"You've understood, I assume?"

"Understood—Oh, the—Um." I couldn't figure out what she meant, my brain still foggy, my sudden glaringly intense empathy making me feel like I was standing too close to a speaker, with Chloe's metallic, hard concern rubbing up against me. I swallowed, wished I had gotten another cookie, and tried to concentrate. It only took a moment to realize that, oh hey, what she'd been trying to show me was actually pretty obvious.

"Jason!" I cried, immediately embarrassed by my volume. "Jason. He wasn't there when Kincade was. She doesn't know what he looks like!"

Chloe's expression stayed serious, but a small curl of intrigue twisted in her. "He … *is* just her type, soft and quiet. It could work." Meeting Evadne's eyes, she continued. "When can you have the tracker ready?"

"There are some supplies to acquire, at your future expense, but it should not take long."

"Slater still has a debt to me on his books, please remind him of it," Chloe said. Evadne's lips split and her harsh smile was blinding.

"Gladly," she purred.

Mel was stretched out as far as he was able on the visitor's couch when we got back to my office. Rupert was sprawled along his body, taking up as much of him as she could with her considerable, fuzzy bulk. Both her front and back legs were extended, the tips of her white toes pressed to the underside of his neck as if threatening to strangle him.

I could tell by the low throb of emotions in the room that both of them were asleep. Chloe and I paused to look over the scene as we stepped inside and she paired a little pop of affectionate delight with a grin. Doing her best to shut the door silently, she took one step closer. I jolted, grabbing her arm and holding her back.

"You'll wake the cat," I said, my voice barely above a whisper. Chloe blinked at me, lifted a brow.

"So?"

"She gets mad when you wake her," I cautioned.

"She'll be fine," Chloe said, moving further across the small waiting room. I felt my shoulders tense as she dropped down to balance half a butt cheek on what little couch was available to her. Neither creature stirred, so Chloe reached out to run a hand down Rupert's striated, orange back.

As Chloe's hand reached the base of her flaccid tale, Rupert's spine fur twitched twice and she lifted her mustachioed face to turn and deliver a crushing glare. To my surprise, Chloe didn't wither or grab her face and scream as her skin melted off. I could tell, even from where I'd backed up to nearly cower in the corner, that Rupert felt this lack of melting and screaming was a disappointment.

"How's my baby?" Chloe purred at the cat, reaching up to scratch Rupert roughly at the back of her neck. Rupert yawned, her eyes somehow landing directly on me when she opened them. Pleasure at being attended to swamped her but I still felt like maybe I should hide under the desk and hope she didn't see where I went.

"I'm fine," Mel said, eyes still closed. "Security pinned me to the couch, wouldn't let me up. She may have roofied me."

"She's good at that," Chloe said, sliding her hands under Rupert's belly to heft the great beast into her arms. Rupert let out a loud wail and I backed up another step. Mel and Chloe both turned to look at me with identical looks of amusement on their faces.

Sensing my terror, Rupert stretched a leg out of the cage of Chloe's arms to scoop sharpened claws at my face, even though she was across the room.

"That cat has it out for me," I told them. "She hacked up that hairball right in my seat, left it there for me to sit on. She probably hid in the corner, waiting to watch me sit in her sick so she could cackle madly."

"She was more likely already sleeping there, trying to warm the seat for you when she had to hork," Chloe explained. I shook my head.

"No. No. Just keep her away from me."

"What time is it?" Mel asked, pushing into a sitting position. He bent forward, rubbed a hand over his face and then back through his hair. The action made him look attractively tousled and, threats on my life aside, I had to admit to myself I appreciated how he looked in his snug sweater and jeans.

"It's just after noon," Chloe answered, carrying Rupert past me to the hall that led to the records room and the bathroom.

"I slept pretty good on this couch with Rupert," he said, catching my eye. I frowned, pushing away from the desk and closing in a few feet.

"I'm surprised she didn't slash your throat or slice off your thumbs," I said, keeping my empathy out to make sure she didn't sneak up on me. "I'm convinced the only reason she hasn't taken over the city and recruited minions is that she can't get the office door open."

Mel snorted, pressing his elbows back to stretch, drawing my eyes and hormones right to his chest as he flexed and shifted.

"Evadne and Merrin have an idea of how we can get a tracker on Kincade so we really just need to find a way to locate her," Chloe said, strolling out into the main office, standing between Mel and me. "I've got some feelers out but so far no one's gotten back to me. She's probably laying low."

"Kincade?' I snorted, shaking my head. "You must be thinking of some other asshole mercenary with too much power and an insanely revved up libido. I'm surprised we haven't seen her on the news leaping building to building like the Hulk just to show off."

A bubble of surprise popped in Chloe and she sighed, her surprise souring into regret in an instant.

"What?" Mel asked. Chloe shook her head, jaw tight, and put her hands on her hips.

"I didn't even think about it that way."

"About what, what way?"

"About Kincade being … Kincade. She's just gotten werewolf powers, feelings, *needs*, and somehow she's not showing up on any—well, I mean, I have a few people in the area who would tell me if they saw her or saw evidence of her. Yet, there's been none, other than her showing up at the restaurant to mess with me. And how did she know I was there in the first place?"

Abruptly, Chloe jolted, twisting and disappearing back into the records room. It wasn't really the shelf-lined warehouse my label makes it seem, but we did have a few file cabinets in there, along with a fridge, a tiny kitchen and, now, the cat's things. I glanced at Mel, both of us lost, but before I could call to ask Chloe what had happened, she reappeared, intense and determined.

I noticed, as she was advancing on me, that she had a strange, lovely metal accessory on her right hand. It looked like five rings made of gold filigree, with delicate chains stretching down to the equally exquisite band around her wrist. Then, her hands were grabbing me, digging into my pockets, undoing my jacket and feeling along my body outside my clothes before I could stop her. Despite Mel's newfound humanness having tamped down his usual sexual desire up until then, I did feel a wisp of lust start to curl as Chloe felt me up. Torn between telling him to stuff it and asking Chloe what the hell she was doing, I only stammered for a second.

Finally, as I got out, "What are—" she abandoned me, turned and grabbed Mel by the front of his sweater, hauling him up.

He let her, pushing to his feet and holding his arms out to the side, letting her pat him down. The lust clouded a little thicker and our eyes met over Chloe's head, locked and held as she felt him up. The eye contact only made things worse, but before either of us could cross the room to grope at each other and make out, Chloe stepped back, shaking her head in frustration.

"Nothing. Shit."

"What? What was that for?" I asked.

"And what do I owe you," Mel purred, smiling down at her as if they'd just shared a special night together. She glanced at him, did a double-take, and then relaxed into amusement. He winked at her and she calmed a little more.

"Sorry," she said. "I thought maybe she'd gotten another tracker on one of you. So, either she's bribed someone to keep her apprised of our movements and keep hers secret from me or last night was a fluke."

"A fluke?" Mel asked, anger starting to simmer. "You think she punched you in the face on a fluke?"

"I think she could have found us by accident, figured she might as well fuck with us while she had the chance."

"It's possible," I thought, thinking back to when she'd shown up, when she'd claimed she'd come deliberately and I'd felt her lie like it was a weighted blanket thrown over my head. "She was straight up fibbing when she said she'd come to say hi, when she said she'd heard you'd gotten her note."

"So what was she doing there before she realized we were also there?"

"Getting dinner?" I suggested. Chloe rolled her gaze to me, calculating, determination steeling her psyche. After a bit she shook her head.

"I don't think so. If she's in town, she's staying somewhere. We can't really run hotel to hotel asking for her—who knows what alias she's using now? Though ..." Chloe trailed off, intrigue blossoming. "I do know her pretty well and I think I have an idea of who might have spotted her in the area but not felt it ... prudent to tell me about it."

"Chloe," Mel said after a thoughtful pause.

"What?" she asked. Mel reached out, gripping her shoulders gently, holding her eye.

"Why do you want to do this?"

"Why do I want to stop Kincade? She has your wolf. I thought that's what the whole point of this was, to make you whole again."

"But didn't you say that I'd go back to normal anyway? We don't have to hunt her down. You don't have to get involved."

"What—Where is this coming from?"

"You said, when we met for the first time after you were off the job that you were done with this, that you needed to be done with this. I don't—" Mel's psyche shifted, groaning like tectonic plates suddenly feeling the need to relieve pressure. "Um. I don't really—I don't …" Abruptly, Mel stepped back, dizziness warping his expression as he grabbed for his head. "What's— Oh Jesus."

He collapsed back, right into the embrace of the couch, groaning like he might vomit. Chloe leaned over him, pressing her hand to his cheek, easing him to lie down.

"What happened?" I demanded, rushing closer.

"Looks like his memory's finally coming back," she said, tipping her head to watch him as he squeezed his eyes shut, grabbing for his head. "Though, I guess it's kind of moot at this point, since we know who attacked him and what exactly she did."

"You know *exactly* what she did?" I asked, curious at the intense disgust that accompanied Chloe's explanation. It wasn't solid sickness, though. That dominated, but it wasn't entirely genuine, not fully an expression of horror and anger at a revolting action taken. There was jealousy there, a tiny gelatinous ooze of envy coating the outside of it, as if she wished she could have done whatever this horrible thing had turned out to be.

Chloe glanced at me, shame creeping along her spine like spindly fingers, but she didn't speak. Leaving her to her secrets, we both leaned over Mel, watching him relive whatever had happened that had ruined his weekend.

Sixteen

When it was over, Mel was exhausted all over again, as if he hadn't slept on the floor next to me or the couch under Rupert. His face was pinched, his mood sour, and I could only do so much to relieve it. I slurped out as much of the grumpiness and intense offense as I could, but it seemed boundless and, by one o'clock, I wasn't sure how much more I could take.

"Why don't you get out of here," Chloe said, stepping into my office to regard me across my desk. I frowned up at her, slightly offended, if only because Mel's mood had fermented my entire outlook into something rancid.

"Why?"

"Because Mel's going to need some more time to process before he can tell me exactly what happened and I have an errand for you to run, something that might cheer you up."

"You've found a bakery that needs all six-hundred-eighty-four types of its pastries taste-tested?"

Chloe laughed. "No, I need you to go talk to Jason, to see if he'd be willing to plant a tracker on Kincade."

"Oh. Oh, yeah," I said, frowning, remembering that was a thing we were gonna do. "I'm not really sure how to ask him that, though."

"It is a pickle, isn't it? But I think you're exactly who could do it. You know that little sucking trick you just did on Mel?"

"Don't phrase it like that," I said, feeling my cheeks go red. "Don't—I didn't suck—I mean."

Laughing again at my discomfort, Chloe leaned across the desk, patting my hand. Her mirth bled into me, cheering me some, easing my embarrassment at everything to do with Mel and sucking.

"Look, just tell him we need him to do us a favor, ask him how he knows

115

the preternatural world, and—"

"How he knows what?" I demanded, shaking my head. "He's not going to know what to do with that."

"He will, Merrin wouldn't have suggested him if he didn't have some sort of experience with this sort of thing."

"Jason's human, he won't know what I'm talking about."

"He will," Chloe repeated, frustrated with me. "And, if he doesn't, use your empathy."

"How? Once I start mentioning fairies and werewolves, I can't exactly just banish the notions of throwing me in a loony bin. Those'll be stuck fast."

"No, but you can take his confusion and discomfort. Then, why wouldn't he do it? It's like eating cow versus chowing down on a giraffe."

"*How* is it like that?" I argued, horrified by the idea of eating something that could peek in a second-story window without a ladder.

"You'll eat a beef burger, right? Even though I've told you how cruel it is, yeah? You have no emotional problem with doing something even though, when you really *think* about what you're doing you're grossed out. *But if* someone told you to eat a *giraffe*, which is basically the same thing, you'd *really* be bothered. So, try it."

"Try to make Jason eat a giraffe?" I asked, though I knew I was being willfully obtuse. Cows and giraffes couldn't possibly be the same thing, I told myself, desperate to argue against her point for no reason I could identify.

"You know what I mean," Chloe said, before stepping back to watch me stew in contemplative silence.

It made a weird sort of sense, I could admit. I could clean up baby vomit but the few times I'd been faced with adult barf I'd been overwhelmed with disgust. Functionally they were no different, but emotionally one was way worse than the other. Maybe I could change Jason's, "what the hell? No!" to a simple, "what the hell?" and a casual agreement if I could get my feelers in there.

"I guess I can try," I agreed. Chloe brightened.

"But try the magic angle first. He could have an empath cousin or a werewolf aunt or something."

"Wouldn't he be a werewolf, then?"

"Not necessarily. Just ask."

"I'll … figure something out," I agreed, getting to my feet. Chloe headed back out to check on Mel, while I went to the filing cabinet next to my desk, digging to the bottom to grab a candy bar I'd hidden there from Chloe. Finding it had been eaten—possibly by me, but more likely by Izzy—I left in a grump, telling myself I'd stop by a Starbucks on the way and buy myself the frothiest, ten-pumps-of-syrup mocha piled high with whipped cream and sugar sprinkles I could possibly afford.

Rita met me in the lobby, though I had to wait for her to detach herself from a small gaggle of teen girls. She wasn't much taller than them, even in her fat platforms, and she managed to match them with every excited squeal. By the time their parents finally pulled them away and she spotted me, she'd given away her scarf, her sparkly hair clip, and her purple and red striped gloves.

Just seeing her cheered me up considerably.

"Hey G-Spot!" she called, bouncing closer and hooking her arm through mine. I smiled over at her, wrapped an arm around her back, and hugged her against me.

"So good to see you," I said. Rita tilted her head, frowned my way.

"What's wrong?

"It's just been a hard morning. The rest of the band upstairs?"

"Mostly. Lance ran off with some groupie—of age. I made sure to check because he's not that bright—Dennis is probably off buying half a bookstore somewhere. It's just me, Harv, and Jason. What's going on? You sounded like a sack on the phone."

"Sack?" I asked as we stepped into the elevator.

"Sad sack. Depressed." Rita hit the button for the top floor, which I was sure had to do with Lance being a demanding prima donna, and shook my head.

"I'm having an issue right now. I need to talk to Jason about something sort of important, and it's also kind of private."

"Ah, okay." Rita nodded, gave a small smile. "If there's anything I can do, let me know?"

"I will." I smiled, pulled her into a spontaneous hug that she returned so enthusiastically I thought my ribs might crack. "I've missed you," I wheezed out.

"We need to get back in touch. I don't do much social networking, but I am a textaholic. Sometimes it even gets a little dirty if I'm feelin' saucy."

Laughing at her candor, I thought about my mostly phone-based relationship with Owen, about some of the saucy texts we'd exchanged. Poking me in the chest, Rita squinted my way, mischievous curiosity groping out of her to grab at all my parts.

"What's that face? It looks like a happy sex face."

"You're not wrong, but what makes you think that?" I asked. Rita winked, steered me down the hall to the right.

"Because you never once made it when you were dating Lance."

I cackled as we made it to her door and Rita dipped her key into the lock. We stepped into the living area to find Jason was sprawled out on the one of the beds watching TV. Harvey was spread-eagle across the other bed, head tucked under a pillow, sleeping so hard I wouldn't have been shocked to learn he'd been drugged or knocked unconscious. Jason glanced over, jerked his head at me in greeting.

"Hey J-Bird, G-Spot wanted to ask you something," Rita explained, sweeping in to throw herself on the bed next to him. He bounced but ignored her.

"What's up?"

"Is there actually somewhere we can talk in private?" I asked.

"We could use Lance and Dennis' room. It's right across the way and I think we've got a key here somewhere."

Rita dug a hand into her pocket, produced a key packet, and handed it over without looking. Her other hand grabbed the remote off the nightstand and Jason sighed.

"Don't change it," Jason begged. Rita just winked at him and did so anyway. He rolled his eyes but it was mostly for show. I was quiet as he and I headed back out into the hall and paused in front of a door diagonal to the room they were in.

"Whoa," I mumbled, stopping dead as I entered the darkened cave. "It smells just like him." Jason snorted, nudged me gently until I moved far enough in so he could follow me. He shut the door, moved straight to the window, and yanked open the heavy curtains.

"I get flashbacks to college every time we go on tour. I think the bastard gave me PTSD."

"I don't blame you, but at least you never had to see him naked."

"What do you think scarred me for life?" He tossed his hands loosely away from his body as if gesturing to an entire room full of people. "I've seen his bony ass more times than I care to count."

"Okay, fine, but at least you never had to touch it."

"You got me there." Jason shrugged, toed a leather vest off the couch, and then dropped into it. "So what's up?"

"This is … gonna be weird," I warned, closing in to plop down next to him. I needed an in, I thought, a way of tossing out insane ideas and facts and making them sound perfectly normal and believable. Jason watched me calmly as I tried to figure out how to say what I needed. Finally just deciding to press on and see what the hell came of it, I blurted. "I'm an empath."

Jason blinked, thoroughly perplexed, but didn't jump straight to terror or worry at my state of mind. Small favors.

"Okay. Like … Well, aren't you a psychologist? Isn't that good?"

"Not—No, I'm not that educated. I'm a therapist. And, I don't just mean I listen and empathize well. I actually feel other people's emotions, like I'm feeling them myself. It's … magic."

A stony, nervous sort of realization chilled Jason, widening his eyes and straightening his spine just a touch. "Magic?" he asked, before his gaze dropped to the ground.

"Yeah. How ... does that make you feel?"

Jason swallowed hard, tiny wiggles of nervous energy crawling through him. "I don't ... Magic?"

"Yeah. I can't, like, saw a woman in half or anything, but I could tell you what anyone around me is feeling. Or where they are, even if I can't see them. Or if there are, like, gophers running around."

"Gophers?"

"Underground, you know?"

He was watching me, head cocked, but his discomfort was easing, his curiosity blooming. I gave him a few moments, reaching out gently to grab his hand in case he changed his mind and decided to jump up, terrified of me, and try to run away.

Instead, after making a low, resigned sound he said, "My uncle can read minds."

It was my turn to be curious, surprised, and a little scared. "Wha—really?"

"I didn't think so. I mean, he would do it when we were kids, you know, but I ... just kinda told myself once I got older that he was fucking with us. But, like, he *knew* what we were thinking. Is it like that?"

"No, I can't read thoughts, just emotions."

"That seems like a step down," he said, before guilt throbbed. "Sorry, that—was that rude?"

I laughed, shaking my head. "No, you're totally right. I think reading thoughts would be pretty damn handy. As it is, I can just, like, tell when some asshole's about to tell me off."

"That could be handy too."

"It mostly just gives me a headache."

Jason chuckled, relaxed into the idea of me and his uncle being just a little bit different. "Was that it? You just wanted to tell me you have magical powers?"

"Actually, I was hoping you could do me a favor."

"Yeah, sure. Probably. As long as it doesn't interfere with the show or cause me to see Lance naked or something."

Snorting out an awkward sound of horror, I shook my head. "Oh man, no. Nothing like that. Um. Okay, so you know how last night at dinner—well, you weren't there until after, but this asshole Kincade showed up and punched Chloe in the face and—Okay, it's hard to explain. Um. Well. So, she stole something from a friend. From Mel! You know Mel. Well, she stole something. From Mel."

"What a bitch."

"Yeah, right? Well, she stole something and we need to get it back. But obviously she's not going to just let us—Oh! Okay. I know—" I cut off, lifting my hands to flail them madly, the explanation coming fully formed into my brain as if I'd magically summoned it. "We need to put a tracker on her so we can see where she goes so we can get the thing back, right? But we can't put one on her without her knowing because *she* has powers too, right? So, we need someone who, like, knows what's up—" I gestured to him. "—to put the thing on her. And you're just her type so she'll let you get close, and you can put it on her and we can get the thing back. Is that cool?"

"It sounds … Sorry, why me?"

I swallowed, lost, not actually sure how to answer his question. "Uh."

"I could do it, I guess, but it just seems weird."

"Well. She knows the rest of us. And she hates some of us. So. Well, I guess she has a thing for foxy blond dudes and you're a foxy blond dude." Jason blushed, pleased embarrassment clouding around him. I grinned, nudging him. "You are, man. And we're not asking you to sleep with her or anything. Just flirt a bit and get the tracker on, and … I don't know. I'll buy you a beer as thanks."

"You don't have to do that. If she stole something and you need help getting it back, that's cool. I can do it."

"Oh my god, you're the best." I leaned in, hugged him quickly, and then backed up taking a deep, relieved breath. He gave it a few moments before looking around.

"Did you wanna go soon, or …"

"Oh! I'm not actually … sure. I'll have to ask Chloe when she's gonna get the tracker."

"Oh. Cool, okay. Well. Gimme your phone and I'll pass along my number and you can just let me know when you're ready and we can get together. We have a rental but if Lance is still out squirming around on some poor girl, I can catch a Lyft."

"Ugh," I said, disgusted at the idea of Lance in general, but especially in a sexual sense. Jason laughed at my reaction, shaking his head.

"Hey, just remember you never have to touch his ass again," he said, trying to ease my disgust.

"I appreciate that," I said solemnly, clapping him on the shoulder. "You're a good man."

Chloe had given me her car and taken Mel in his car from the office back to her place. I left Jason with instructions not to tell anyone what we'd talked about, explained that, even though he had already agreed, it would probably take awhile to get the tracker together. He still had time to back out if he wanted.

I'd barely walked in when Chloe approached, shooing me back toward the door. "Good, you're back. I've got to go out and get the spell components. You two are—"

"I thought Merrin and Evadne were getting them," I said. Chloe paused, a little bubble of surprise popping in her head before she squinted and leaned in close.

"Were you actually *listening* yesterday? With cookies in front of you?"

Sensing she was teasing, I frowned. "So?"

"Just makes me think maybe you really do like Mel after all."

"Oh my god," I rolled my eyes, hoping she wasn't going so far as to suggest I liked Mel *that way*. "I just—you seemed—whatever."

Chloe laughed. "There are some things she needs that I'm in a better place to procure. You two will hang out downstairs. Eat, take a nap, make out, I don't care what you do as long as you stay down there."

I threw Mel a look that shut him up before he could speak but I could tell by looking at him that he wasn't up for teasing.

"You're the boss," he said, getting to his feet and coming over.

"Actually, I'm the boss," I corrected. Chloe just patted me on the head.

"If you'd been any later I would have left a trail of treats to lure you down like Hansel and Gretal."

"Didn't they end up in an oven?"

"You need to catch up on your fairy tales," Chloe said, before quirking her head and frowning. "Actually, I guess it depends on who's telling the story. I've met a fair few Crones who like the story ending with a tasty teenager pot roast."

Disgusted, I let her lead me downstairs without arguing further.

Olivia R. Burton

Seventeen

"I might take a nap," I said when thirty agonizing, silent, awkward minutes had passed and my lack of internet connection was really starting to get to me. Mel didn't say anything or look away from the TV, even though it was off. Wondering for the hundredth time if he'd told Chloe about his recovered memory, I changed tactics. "Or have a snack. Are you hungry?"

Mel took a second to answer, but then looked over, surprise lifting his brows for a moment before he shook his head. "I'm good."

"Are you?" I asked, closing in, looking him over from behind the couch. He took a deep breath, shook his head shallowly, and let out a bitter, breathy laugh.

"No."

Skirting the couch, I took a seat on the arm, reaching out to pat his ankle. Even though I'd only meant it comfortingly, he pulled his legs back to leave room for me to sit, so I did.

"What's going on in that pretty head of yours?" I asked. He was still for a bit before shoving his hand through his hair and shaking his head.

"I don't know. Everything feels surreal and wrong. Even though nothing really came to mind that was—I mean, it was just a date, just sex, I don't remember the actual … I don't remember everything. The part where she—um. Where my soul … I don't remember it all, but I feel weird."

"How so? You want to talk about it?"

Mel eyeballed me, suspicious for a moment, before his gaze dropped and he seemed to reconsider his assessment of me. "I guess."

"I do this sort of thing for a living, you know."

"Counsel people after bad dates?"

"Yes, precisely, that and only that, so don't get derailed talking about your mommy issues."

Mel chuckled, shaking his head, and then cleared his throat as if he was about to drop a verbal bomb. He didn't speak for a long time, though, and I waited patiently. He was a tiny tempest of emotions, none of them too extreme, but it was chaotic all the same. Finally, he rubbed at his face, sat up a little straighter, and began.

"Uh. Well. We went—I picked her up at the hotel, and we went out to dinner. We had fun, she was fun. She had a lot of personality, and was in a really good mood the whole time. I actually—when I told you how we met at the office, that was sort of fuzzy too. I knew that's what happened but I couldn't really remember it clearly until it all came back. We didn't meet in the elevator, she was waiting at the elevator, hanging out at the door on her phone until I showed up. She was aggressive, flirting instantly, but it's not the first time a woman has really been into me so I didn't think anything of it." I wanted to roll my eyes, just out of habit and bitchiness but I kept my face blank and non-judgmental.

"She asked me out, told me the name of her hotel, and told me to pick her up at eight, which I did. We didn't text or anything, though I do remember looking up the name of her company—Maiden Consulting— and finding nothing. Anyway. We got dinner and she invited me back to the hotel; we did sleep together, she mixed us some drinks, but then it just goes blank for awhile. I don't have any idea what went on before my memory sort of … clouds?" Mel frowned, as if that wasn't quite the right word and its inadequacy was offensive. "Fuzzes? I don't know how to explain it, but it's like I can remember … feelings, very human feelings, but not sights or sounds."

"What were the feelings?" I asked, setting my hand on his ankle, tucking it under his pant leg to press against bare skin in case I needed to ease his mind at all. He was quiet for awhile, considering, before he looked up and met my eyes. He was more confused than bothered, but I kept my hand where it was, just in case.

"I felt really awful. Sick and weak, thirsty, sad. Everything felt wrong, but I was driving. I was alone and driving … home. I got home and I showered and went to bed as if nothing had happened. But I knew something had happened. I remember I couldn't sleep but I wasn't sure why. I just felt like something had gone wrong, or like I was supposed to be doing something but I'd forgotten what. Or like … I don't know. It was really miserable, but eventually I fell asleep for a few hours. Then, when I woke up, I didn't really remember anything, but it was like I didn't have to."

"You just knew you were human and that's all?"

"Sort of. I woke up feeling tired, like I hadn't slept enough. I hadn't, it had only been about two hours, but it felt off. I was going to go for a run, to get my fur on and wake up that way but I couldn't. When I realized the extent of what was going on, I panicked and … thought of you."

"Of me specifically? You didn't run through anyone else?"

"I guess it was you. I just knew I wanted someone to help me. It was sort of like being drunk, you know? Where you know your brain should be focusing on something but it keeps drifting away or getting distracted by something else. Usually I focus on sex if I've been drinking, so maybe that's why I thought of you."

I could tell he was flirting a little, that it didn't go any deeper than him wanting to ease the tension, so I rolled my eyes good-naturedly, and shook my head.

"What has the memory coming back thrown you off so much?"

"I don't know," Mel admitted, shrugging helplessly. "I just feel really down, like someone just died."

"Perhaps it's like realizing anew what you've lost. You're just dealing with the loss all over. It sounds like you didn't really have time to mourn it when it first happened, possibly because of whatever she did to you to make you forget in the first place. Have you eaten? What usually makes you feel better?"

"Chloe suggested I eat but I'm really not in the mood."

I frowned at him, askance. "I don't understand. You're not in the mood to eat? Is there a mood for eating? As far as I'm concerned, eating is an all-the-time necessity."

"Funny, that's how I feel about sex."

"Well, I can't help you there," I said, subtly removing my hand from his ankle so the contact didn't give him any ideas. "But we should find something to ease your mind. Something *else*."

Mel chuckled and I felt his mood lighten a little, the cloud of uncertain unhappiness thinned out a bit. Hoping he'd follow my example, I got to my feet.

"I'm gonna nap, and I think I spotted two beds in there, if you want to join me. I don't know how long Chloe's going to be, but even fifteen or twenty minutes would help. I didn't sleep well last night."

"Oh, *you* didn't sleep well? You, who got the comfy couch didn't sleep last night, lording your soft cushions over me while I slept on the hard floor?"

"Keep your mind off my soft cushions, mister," I warned. Mel barked out a laugh, amusement sparking through him, burning away more bits of sadness. I backed up a few steps, watching him sternly, before I turned and headed into the bedroom. I heard him get up and follow me as I hit the door. I warned him off without looking his way. "No funny business."

"Am I really that amusing?" Mel asked as I dropped my hips onto one bed and bounced a few times to test the springiness.

"What do you mean?" Finding the bed lacking, I rolled off the other side to repeat the gesture on the far bed. Mel stood in the doorway watching me.

"You're always saying that."

"Am not," I argued, stretching out on the bed. The pillows were lacking, so I snapped and pointed at the ones on the other bed. Mel, understanding what I was rudely demanding, closed in, grabbing one and handing it over. I tucked it under my head and changed the subject. "Did you see a heater anywhere? A thermostat? It's chilly."

Mel's lip curled and I realized my mistake too late to stop him from purring, "I'll warm you up."

"That would qualify as funny business."

"See? Am I really that entertaining?"

"Are you really that irritating?" I asked, tilting my head as if I hadn't heard him correctly. "Yes, yes you are."

Mel rolled his eyes, but he was grinning. "Can't be that irritating if we keep ending up in these situations."

"What—" I cut off as he shifted, toeing off his shoes while his hands went to his waist. "What are you doing?"

Undoing his belt, Mel looked up, caught my eye innocently. There was a low throb of desire in him, not full on lust, but it was dangerous just the same. "I thought we were napping."

"Yes, fully clothed."

"These are very expensive pants," Mel said, as if offended by the notion that he be expected to keep them on. "I don't want them to wrinkle."

"You slept in your pants earlier just fine!"

"Are you really that bothered," Mel said, sliding his stupid pants off, "by being in the same room as a man who isn't wearing pants? Are you worried something might happen?"

"No," I insisted, turning my gaze to the ceiling as Mel continued to strip down to just boxers. He folded his clothes nicely, setting them on a dresser along the far wall, and then turned to consider me for a moment. He looked stupid good, even with all the bandages and the bruising he'd gained since becoming human—most of which were from me, I thought. I swallowed hard, determined to keep my eyes on his face.

"It is chilly, isn't it?" he said after a bit.

"So put your clothes back on."

Mel only grinned, leaving the room. I sighed, suddenly antsy, though I couldn't identify why. I rolled up into a sitting position, drumming my fingers on the bed, my brain running over all the things that could possibly happen when he came back to the room. I bit my lip, feeling him move around out in the living room with curiosity and confusion. Finally, a blip of relief bumped me and I felt him approaching. The moment before he was visible, I called out.

"So why are you so funny?"

"You tell me," Mel said, stepping around the bed to sit on it facing me. A heater kicked on. "You're the one who's always accusing me of being so."

"No, I mean, when have I ever done that?"

"Any time we … spend time together, really."

"Like?"

"Well." He seemed to think about it seriously, his attention drifting off while my own drifted downward to his sculpted torso. I had to force my eyes back to his face when he spoke. "The first time you spent the night at my place, after we'd eaten and had a good evening. You got drunk, warned, 'no funny business,' and then proceeded to sniff me."

"That makes me sound like a creep," I argued, through a laugh. Mel chuckled, pressing on.

"Then, after I'd—I mean, when you …" He swallowed, discomfort rumbling through him before he pressed on and owned it. "After I bit you, when I came to see how you were."

"When you came to beg for sex, you mean."

"I was not!" he argued, though I knew he hadn't been. "I was being a fine, upstanding fake husband, offering comfort to my fake wife in her time of need."

"Oh sure," I said, shaking my head. "And if your fake wife, high on painkillers, had just so happened to try to shove her hand down your pants, you wouldn't have objected."

"Is that what you wanted to do at the time?" he asked, pretending to be scandalized. "Because that, my friend, would have qualified as funny business."

I had no come-back for that, perhaps because my hormones had been derailed instantly at the idea of putting my hand down his pants. We watched each other intensely, lust building between us, as it had a bad habit of doing, and I realized that I really needed to get the hell out of there or risk something happening.

I stood up, my jaw working, trying to get out some plausible explanation for why I was fleeing but I couldn't come up with anything. We were just two people in a bedroom, staring at each other. The outside world had melted away, taken with it the issues that had landed us alone in a dimly lit room with not one but *two* beds. Finally, forced awkwardly through my lips came the words, "I'm not tired anymore."

As I attempted to flee, Mel grabbed my hand. It was gentle, but it stopped me, sent lightning up my arm and back down my body to my warm and slightly throbby center.

"Stay," he said quietly. My heart was thudding and I couldn't look at him because we were near enough that I worried if I did I might just fling myself into his arms and finish undressing him.

Slowly, Mel pushed to his feet, pulling me in closer. I pressed my hand against his chest and realized as I did that he wasn't a werewolf anymore. Of course I *knew* this already, as it had been the focal point of our interactions

127

over the last day and a half. But suddenly it came very sharply into focus, the reminder that this would just be like sleeping with any normal human man. I could feel everything he felt, enjoy him through my empathy without his werewolf emotions burning a hole in my brain. Maybe Mel as a human would be a whole different experience than Mel as a werewolf had been.

Or, I thought, maybe Mel as a human would be *worse* than Mel as a werewolf and my ultimate boredom at his performance would crush his sad, human psyche.

"You're … not yourself anymore. It's not safe to sleep in the same bed with me in your … weakened state."

"So we won't sleep," he murmured.

I was staring at his chest, convinced that, if I looked up, he would kiss me. I like being kissed by Mel. It's an altogether pleasant experience. The man knows how to use his tongue, his hands. He knows how to make it seem like it's just the two of you, like nothing else will intrude. I also knew that, if he kissed me, it wouldn't end there.

Biting my lip, I looked up to meet his eyes but leaned back enough that I made it clear I had more to say.

"Does that sort of line work on other women?" I teased, trying to lighten the mood, to grab it in a chokehold and drag it away from the serious, sexy cliff it was teetering over. Mel smiled and I felt something blossom inside of him, something heady and thick, warm and inviting. As he leaned in, he whispered.

"Other women don't matter, Gwen."

I felt Chloe outside the door at about the same time something else in Mel overtook the blossoming affection. Her emotions were a mix of eagerness and worry, whereas his own words had caused in Mel a surprisingly pure embarrassment. The front door to the apartment opened and Mel jerked back, his gaze jumping to the bedroom doorway. I felt myself stumble, not realizing I'd been leaning into him.

"You guys around?" Chloe called, just before she peered in to bedroom. Shock puffed around her when she saw us, Mel in his boxers, me undoubtedly looking just as confused as I felt. She gave a knowing grin. "What's … going on *here?*"

"Nothing," Mel insisted, like a kid with his hand caught in the cookie jar, rushing to grab his pants. I watched him, my mouth hanging open as I tried to figure out exactly what was going on. His lust wasn't completely gone but the embarrassment and irritation had risen up, beaten it into submission. Now, instead of a hungry jungle cat, it was a cowering kitten in the corner.

"Yeah, nothing," I said. Chloe caught something in Mel that she understood all too well, and smiled my way.

"I got the stuff, dropped it off with Merrin so we should be able to pick up the tracker soon. In the meantime, we're gonna go visit a friend who I believe will be able to get us to Kincade so we can plant the tracker or—if we get lucky, stop her altogether."

"And how are you going to stop her?" Mel asked, yanking his sweater over his head, muffling the last bit of his question.

"I'm working on that. First we need to see if she's even going to be where I hope she'll be."

"And where is that?" I asked, stepping wide around Mel to close in on Chloe and keep my back to him.

"Once Mel's decent, I'll show you."

We hit a dingy part of SoDo, parked next to a vacant lot, and headed down the street to a massive warehouse labeled with currently unlit, jagged writing proclaiming it to be Frigid. Posters outside spoke of bands and shows and a sign next to the entrance announced that no one under twenty-one was allowed. It was too early for the club to be open, but that didn't stop Chloe from pushing in and acting like she owned the place. The front door was unlocked, possibly to let employees in, or maybe it just sensed Chloe coming and didn't want to risk her ripping it off its hinges.

"Should we be—" I started. Chloe waved me off, paused at the bar.

"Vier!" she called, scanning the room. It was giant, a modern design made to look like a futuristic warehouse. The ceiling was high, criss-crossed with shiny chrome pipes that likely had no function at all. In the very center of the room was a round bar made up of two half-circle counters dressed with blue lighting in various shades. High tables with no chairs dotted the empty landscape and a VIP area at the back held a blue couch with tables made to look like giant ice cubes.

A sense of cold dread shot down my spine as I thought of Merrin's words from earlier. My frigid spine aside, the temperature inside matched the décor, though I was guessing that would be appreciated once hundreds of writhing bodies were heating the place up.

Mel stepped up next to me, hands tucked in his pockets, and watched Chloe. I glanced at him, but he continued to pretend I didn't exist, as he'd been doing since Chloe had shown up and we'd blown apart like shrapnel. When I poked at his psyche, I found a skinny, wiggly thread of embarrassment running through the center.

I wasn't terribly bothered by Chloe realizing he and I had been moments from sucking face. She wasn't teasing me about it and it wasn't like he and I hadn't done it before. Mel, on the other hand, seemed more bothered than if she'd caught him dressed in a frilly dress announcing that he was Queen Victoria and trying to assert some sort of royal decree about cockroaches.

"Vier!" Chloe called again, when we remained alone in the chilly warehouse. After a second, she smirked, twisted to step around the curved bar, and grabbed a martini glass from the hanging shelf above her. Turning to Mel and me, she smiled. "You guys want a drink?"

"Is that allowed?" I asked. Chloe shrugged, dropping down below the line of the bar, and called out loud enough that I knew she didn't mean it just for me.

"I'm sure Vier won't mind me helping myself to refreshments while he keeps me waiting."

I let out a nervous laugh and it came out foggy. The temperature in the room had dropped quite steeply quite suddenly and I felt like I needed to blink my eyes a few times to keep them from freezing over. When Chloe got to her feet, she was holding a bottle of blue liquor in one hand and vodka in the other. Smiling, she looked around as if she could see the change in temperature, and set the bottles down. She twisted to face the far corner.

A man was standing there in an impeccable suit. He wasn't human, but he was pulling it off pretty damn well. He was about my height, with wavy black hair, piercing blue eyes, and cheekbones to kill for. The skinny blue lines running down the fabric of his pale grey suit matched his tie and shoes perfectly. He was across the giant room from me and I felt like I'd been picked up and dunked into a tub of ice water.

Everyone ignored my teeth chattering while Chloe lifted the blue booze, jerked her chin at the man. "You want a drink?"

Vier smiled, strolled over with a spring in his step that reminded me of a con man who had just pulled something over on a particularly observant mark. When he reached the bar, I was shaking so hard I wasn't sure I could stand up anymore.

"Elise," Vier said with a smile. I rolled my creaking eyeballs around looking for another person, but it seemed he was addressing Chloe. It shouldn't have surprised me that she hadn't given him her real name.

Leaning an elbow on the edge of the bar, he scanned Mel and me, lifted a brow. "Who have you brought me, today?"

Ignoring his question, Chloe said simply, "I've come to call in my favor."

Eighteen

"I don't know what you mean," Vier said, watching as Chloe continued to mix a drink like a professional. She glanced at us, then back to the Fairy.

"Shall I explain to these two humans what exactly it was you *needed* my help with?"

"Hmm," Vier considered, the temperature around us plummeting so fast I hissed at the burning pain in my fingers. Mel glanced sharply at me, his curiosity warping to worry right before my empathy seemed to freeze solid. "You know, it's all coming back to me now."

"Good," Chloe said, lifting the shaker and mixing her drink. "Has the Battle Maiden been in recently?"

"Is this all you're after?" Vier asked, before his gaze slid to me and he frowned. "Empath?"

Chloe nodded, dismissive of my suffering. "Answer the question; we'll discuss the terms of my favor redemption once I know where we stand."

"Are you okay?" Mel asked, leaning in. I realized that he'd put his hand on my back but I couldn't feel anything except the burning, freezing pain of standing near this damned, beautiful, frigid asshole. I wanted to answer but all that came out was a sigh of tiny icicles. Mel jolted, sweeping his arms around me and hefting me like a prince rescuing a princess. "I'm taking Gwen outside."

Chloe waved apathetically, like a queen who doesn't give a single shit what some lowly servant chooses to do with his time, and pressed Vier again. "Battle Maiden, have you seen her?"

"Oh yes," I heard Vier say, as Mel rushed me back toward the door. "She's quite enthusiastic."

Distantly, despite the fact that I thought my empathy had frozen into uselessness, I could feel a scalding spear of triumph from Chloe.

Mel hustled me back out the front door and, somehow, the winter temperatures felt three or four times warmer than the inside. When he hit the corner of building, Mel set me on my feet, unzipping his jacket in a surprisingly selfless act of bravery, wrapped my arms around his waist, and pulled the jacket around me as much as he could. I breathed out a shaky sigh of relief, feeling the heat of his body start to make a dent in whatever the Fairy's powers had done to me.

We stood there, silent, sharing his jacket, as he rubbed vigorously at my back with his one good hand, holding me as close as he could manage with the other. Finally, after what felt like ages, he set his warm palms on my face, turning it up so he could look intently into my eyes. Seeing something that pleased him, he grinned.

"Good," he mumbled almost to himself.

"What?" I managed breathily.

"Your lips had turned purple," Mel said quietly, his brow furrowing at the memory. I winced at the idea, but knew it was no longer an issue. Glacially, my empathy was coming back, waking up from its hibernation, grasping onto Mel's heat. I realized, as we stood there, eyes locked, that his hands were cradling my face as if we might start kissing and, even more mortifying, that the lust from earlier was back.

We pulled apart at the same moment, Mel turning to shake off whatever feelings he'd been having, me crossing my arms over my chest and turning my attention absolutely anywhere else.

"Thanks!" I said, not looking his way, scared to death he'd notice my reaction and get insulted. I knew I wouldn't be able to explain myself, not in any way that wouldn't hurt his stupid, human feelings even worse. I didn't stop to consider why *he* was so bothered, despite the fact that riding the edge of his embarrassment and panic was a thin, greasy ooze of regret.

"Yep," Mel said, tucking his hands desperately into his pockets. "No problem."

We stayed separate and quiet for another few minutes, neither of us sure where to go or what to say. When I finally felt Chloe approaching again, I breathed a sigh of relief.

"Thank god," I mumbled. Mel glanced at me, confused, but knew what I'd been relieved about when Chloe emerged.

"We're all set for tonight."

"That soon?" Mel asked.

Chloe nodded, before doing a double-take, catching something in our behavior that she recognized and could very clearly read. Amusement at our stupidity tugged at her lips but she didn't give in and laugh at us.

"Yeah. Apparently she was here last night, and told the bartender to leave her tab open for the week, so he assumes she'll be back again tonight."

"What if she skips tonight and doesn't show up for a few days?"

"We'll just have to hope she wants to get laid enough that she doesn't."

I called Jason when we got back to the apartment, explained that we needed him that evening, and he agreed without hesitation. Chloe had me ask him to shower fresh, to make sure that no lingering scent of my earlier hugs remained for Kincade to sniff out, and left him the tracker and an earpiece in the club.

"He must think this is so weird," I said, shaking my head as I hung up. "Not being allowed to get within, like, fifty feet of any of us before meeting some stranger to stick a computer chip in her pocket."

"Computer chip?" Chloe asked. My phone buzzed in my pocket, and I shrugged.

"I'm guessing that's what it looks like. Hold on." Seeing Owen's name on the screen, I paused, gestured for them to head inside. "You guys go on, I'll be right up."

Chloe looked around as if she half-expected Kincade to leap out of the bushes and tackle me, but I just waved her off. Trusting that I'd be able to sense Kincade coming, she nodded and headed inside.

"Hey you," I said, putting the phone to my ear.

"I had some time, so I thought I'd call to see how things are going. Is Mel better yet?"

"Ah, apparently he won't be for awhile."

"Intrigue," Owen purred, and I heard a door shut behind him. "You found out what took his soul?"

I was quiet, not sure how much I should reveal. Chloe hadn't wanted me to tell him about Kincade, but he hadn't wanted me to tell Chloe about Mel, and that hadn't worked out so bad.

"Apparently it was Kincade. She's a werewolf now."

Owen went silent again, that scary, intense sort of quiet that speaks volumes. Nearly a full minute passed before he said, "And Chloe knows."

"I—yeah, how did you know?"

"I know Kincade and can only assume that, if she didn't orchestrate Chloe finding out, someone else would. Is she …" He went quiet for long enough that I could feel my spine twist into a tense knot. Then, he sucked in a small breath and asked, "Has she come up with a plan to get Mel whole again?"

"Sort of. She's going to try to grab Kincade tonight and if that doesn't work, we're going to put a tracker on her so we can trap her some other way."

"And then what?"

"I … guess we wait and keep her on ice until things go back to normal? I don't know how long that'll be, though."

"Chloe hasn't told you?"

"How long? No. Why?"

"She's not planning anything else, is she?"

"Like invading Poland?" I joked, not sure why he sounded so serious. "I don't think so. Why?"

"Like I said, this isn't something she's really … good to deal with anymore. Has she any idea how she's going to keep Kincade under wraps?"

"I didn't ask."

"Ask. Let me know what she says. I've already made plans to come by after I'm done here."

"Ooh, a treat!" I said.

"I won't be able to stay more than a day, but I assume that's not a problem."

"Nope, we can do a lot of damage in a day."

"Indeed," he said. "Should be another few days at most, but I'll let you know."

"I look forward to it. Be careful."

"Am I ever not?"

"Touché."

Chloe was in the shower when I got up to her place, and I couldn't ask her much of anything, so I raided the fridge instead. I realized, as I was reaching for the last of the date balls, that I hadn't really had anything healthy in over a day. Reconsidering, I grabbed a pear off the counter and bit in, dribbling juice down my front.

"Dammit," I mumbled around the sweet fruit. Mel approached from the bedroom, leaning across the bar counter to judge me.

"You've gotten juice all down the front of you," Mel said, leaving me waiting for some sort of come-on. When nothing came, I swallowed, nodding, and turned to grab a paper towel. It was weird not constantly being hit on and I honestly couldn't discern if the change was from him being human or just because suddenly things were rubber-banding back and forth between flirty and antagonistic much quicker than was our habit.

Before I could investigate, Mel jolted, something coming to mind. "I almost forgot, Chloe wanted me to give you her phone, said she got something you'd want to see."

"Did she order me a comically large cake out of which many other cakes will burst like the tastiest strippers ever?"

Mel side-eyed me but didn't indulge my suggestion, grabbing Chloe's phone off the charging station instead. He handed it over unlocked, and I found a series of pictures of Sonny, happy and cuddled up to his new friend, or snoozing and cuddled up, or just eating next to his new friend. Something stabbed me in the heart and I wasn't sure if it was happiness or sadness.

I wanted my feathery son to be happy and well-adjusted, to get everything he could need in life and thrive but I also selfishly wanted him to myself. I wondered for a bit if I should get a second bird, but the shard in my heart shoved harder in and something told me that was the wrong direction to steer my thinking.

"You okay?" Mel asked. I set the phone down, reconsidered and turned it face-down, and then went back to my pear, chomping instead of speaking. "You sure?"

I frowned, lacking an answer, wanting to be mad at him for asking but knowing it was just me being petulant. I finished my snack as Chloe rushed out in a towel with a fresh bandage over her nose, rounding the corner into her room.

"Five minutes!" she called. Mel followed her in and, in his wolf days I would have assumed it was to shamelessly ogle her, but now I wasn't sure. Chloe wouldn't have minded the ogling, probably would have encouraged it, but I wasn't getting any sense of lust from him. Sighing, feeling for a moment like my entire world was off-kilter, I tossed my pear in Chloe's compost bin, and set out trying to get pear juice out of my jacket.

"He'll be okay, right?" I asked for the third time. Chloe ignored me like she had the last time I'd asked and continued to watch the front door of the club. We'd parked a few spaces away from Jason, waited until he was on his way, and then stood across the street and down a few buildings. Chloe was listening intently to whatever was coming out of the earbud, but so far she hadn't made any comments or suggestions to our boy. When I realized she wasn't going to answer, I twisted to face Mel.

"You think he'll be okay, right?"

"I hope so. I don't think Eye Masters can replace a guitarist as good as him," Mel said, sadness at the idea of losing a good band tinging the edges of his nervous psyche. I wasn't sure why he was nervous, since it was Jason we were sending into the lion's den, but I didn't ask. "And, you know, I don't want him to be hurt."

"Yeah, I gotcha," I said, patting his shoulder. Mel leaned subtly away from me, making it seem like he was just shifting his footing but a small bloom of embarrassment had started in his guts, a discomfort at contact that he'd never had before, not when it came to me or any woman. I frowned up at him, bothered by the change but almost scared to address it, lest it open another can of worms I didn't want to get into.

I mean, I want nothing to do with any can of worms but somehow Mel's worms were extra frustratingly wriggly.

I jolted and yelped when something wiggled up my spine through my jacket, like a dozen tiny animals scampering from the base of my spine up to the back of my head. Mel exploded with shock, tensing and lifting his hands as if he'd fight something off for me, but Chloe just whirled around, determination and annoyance changing in an instant to glee and lust when she saw who'd been teasing me.

"Pumpkin-cheeks!" she cooed, reaching past me to grab Izzy and pull him into a hug. "I thought you were here next week."

"I am here next week," Izzy said, wobbling through my empathy like the happiest Jell-o mold in the county at Chloe's touch. "What're you guys doing this week?"

"Waiting for Kincade," I said, still trying to shake off the phantom memory of his weird, wormy touching. Mel was watching Izzy peculiarly, uncomfortable confusion clouding out of him like acrid smoke. I side-stepped away from him, trying to avoid it, though I knew it wasn't possible.

"Oh." Izzy's mood plummeted, his expression going dour, locking his eyes to mine. "I thought we'd skipped this one."

"This one?"

"I thought we were in the one with the bunnies."

"The what with the bunnies?" I asked, noting Chloe had turned her attention back to the club while I dealt with her weird boyfriend.

"You're the girl … from The Internets," Mel mumbled at Izzy, his tone nearly an accusation.

"You just realized?" Izzy asked, before grinning. "You're doing better, all things considered. Though, I guess this is kind of another sort of bad."

"Didn't I … hit on you?" Mel asked, still lost. Izzy nodded as if agreeing to something casual that went on every day.

"Oh sure, every time." Izzy's gaze drifted suddenly, his attention shifting off of us like a beagle who's scented a squirrel. Abruptly, mumbling, "no, no," he darted off toward a gaggle of girls strolling up the street. They were glammed up for the evening in high heels, shiny dresses, makeup, and perfectly styled hair. I felt confusion and insult as Izzy approached, but couldn't hear what he was saying. Within moments, he'd lowered their collective guard and they were gathered around him as if he held the secrets to the achieving the perfect liquid line.

Hell, maybe he did, I didn't know.

"I had no idea Izzy was a man," Mel mumbled, still stuck on his previous mistake. Leaning over to Chloe he asked, "Is Izzy trans?"

"He's not human, Mel. Technically he doesn't really have a gender."

"Oh yeah," Mel said, relaxing somewhat. "I've been there."

"Not having a gender?" I asked. Mel scowled at me, though there wasn't any real annoyance behind it. Chuckling to myself, so focused on Mel that didn't even notice when Chloe suddenly took off across the street, dodging cars like a stunt coordinator had set them up just for her.

"Where is she going?" Mel asked. I twisted to see her book it past an oncoming sedan, hop the curb, and run through the open front door of the club. She weaved around the bouncer so effectively that he just blinked after her and, apparently, assumed she knew what she was doing and that he shouldn't interfere.

"Ohhhhh," I moaned. "That can't be good."

Olivia R. Burton

Nineteen

"Izzy!" I yelled, but he was still ensconced in the hugging and flailing of the girls down the street and he didn't hear me. Knowing he wouldn't be any help, I turned, waited for an opening in traffic, and took off after her.

Mel swore, "shit," before I heard his footfalls behind me.

The bouncer at the door held out an arm as if he would stop me but I decided I didn't *want* to be stopped. I hunched, covered my head with my arms at the last second, and ducked under his arm. I heard Mel slow down behind me a second before he started trying to talk his way in, frustration sparking from the both of them.

The club was freezing. Even with what looked like scores of writhing, grinding, passionate, warm bodies, it was icy. The emotional din on the other hand, was scalding. Lust, excitement, arousal, discomfort, glee, annoyance, and disappointment popped and sparked, jabbed and groped. I felt myself twitching, swatting at invisible sensations as I pushed through the people, trying to peer over the throng to find Chloe. On top of it all was my least favorite thing about lusty crowds: a low level electric vibration that made the hairs on my arms stand straight up.

It took me two minutes of searching visually before I realized I wasn't limited to such mundane investigation techniques. Closing my eyes, I tried to tear through the stifling cobwebs of emotions to locate what I was looking for: werewolf.

The cacophony of humanity was like a boiling soup and I was drowning in it. I tipped my head back before I realized that I could not surface for air. This wasn't something I could swim out of. Not only was this not a physical sensation, but I also couldn't just leave Chloe and Jason to Kincade's whims.

As I thought of her, pictured her in my mind, I felt the burn of the stolen wolf. It beat at me like a drumming in my head, smashing into my psyche with a hammer straight out of the forge. I grunted, took a steadying breath and turned to face the action.

I had to elbow a few strangers, growl a few threats, and almost trip someone to get there but, when I finally came upon the scene in the corner of the freezing club, I could barely feel the cold air anymore. Kincade was smiling at Chloe, standing across a table that was roughly chest-height. She had an arm around Jason's neck and I could feel his panic even through Kincade's emotions and those of the dozens of people around us. Chloe had a gun aimed at Kincade under the table and her psyche was crackling with anger. Kincade rolled her gaze to me as I closed in, shook her head as she let out a knowing sigh.

"I should've known the Scooby gang would be here soon. Did you invite Owen out, too?"

"I don't need him to kick your ass, Kincade. Let the boy go," Chloe ordered. She kept her tone as bored as she could, despite the volume she needed in order to be heard. Her emotions spoke another story.

"I'd rather see what happens when you shoot me," Kincade mused. She managed to make it sound thoughtful even though she, too, practically had to scream over the noise. Jason jerked, but Kincade had a grip on his neck, keeping his face nearly pressed into her impressive cleavage. "It'll really get the place jumping."

"Goddammit," Chloe said. I couldn't help notice her finger twitch over the trigger. Since a riot in the club would be exactly the last thing we needed, I stepped forward, smiled at each person in turn.

"So. What seems to be the problem here?" I asked. Kincade kept her eyes on Chloe for a moment before rolling them back to me.

"Hey lover, glad you could join us. I forgot to mention last we met, but your neck looks good."

"So does your nose," I commented. Kincade chuckled, reached up to pet Jason gently on the head, as if stroking a jumpy cat.

"He was a good pick, just my type," she purred. Feeling Chloe's irritation grow, I reached under the table, grabbed her wrist with my hand. Kincade darted her gaze down enough to frown for a microsecond at the motion she couldn't entirely see. Chloe threw me a warning look but didn't shake me off or put the gun away.

"How'd you figure out what we had planned?" I asked Kincade.

"I haven't yet," Kincade said. Leaning in close to my ear, she forced Jason to follow, still pressed to her chest. His arm flailed upward as if he would try to push her away, but it was a futile effort. I felt a snap of irritation out of him but I met his eyes, tried to promise with my expression that everything would be okay.

"A fan recognized him, mentioned they loved his stupid band," Kincade said loudly into my ear. I felt Chloe's aim shift to match her new position. "You guys did a good job though. I didn't smell any of you on him at all.

Kudos. Now."

Standing upright abruptly, she flicked her eyes around, before twisting, socking Jason in the stomach and knocking his head into the table all in one move. I felt a jolt of shock from him before pain overtook his psyche and he dropped to the floor. Knowing exactly what Chloe was about to do just from the outrage surging through her, I swallowed, prepared myself and squeezed her wrist.

Panic spurred me on, allowing my empathy to shove in and out in a second, carrying the anger away from her psyche and into me. Chloe stood, shocked for a moment, but what counted was that she wasn't shooting. She did turn to blink at me, frowning as I felt a bit of pain leak out of her. I was squeezing her wrist harder than I wanted and it was a physical effort to unclamp my fingers and take a step back. I noticed Kincade, then, standing just past Chloe, her head tipped in curiosity.

"What just happened *here*?" she asked. Chloe turned to her, lifted her hand as if she would strike Kincade. The wolf was faster. In less time than it would have taken a hummingbird to brush Chloe's cheek with its wing, Kincade had grabbed Chloe by the throat, caught her wrist and lifted her slightly off the ground. So far, under the neon, flashing lights, in the cascading shadows and amongst the grinding, intoxicated bodies, no one had noticed that anything was going on.

Chloe jabbed her knee into Kincade's stomach, which made her stumble, but I could tell it didn't hurt. She just smiled, squeezed Chloe's wrist until I felt an explosion of pain that made me groan and step forward as if I could help.

Even the stolen anger inside of me could not win out over the worry I felt for my best friend. Chloe was wincing, struggling against the hand at her throat and the grip Kincade had on her wrist. Somehow, Chloe had managed to keep her head enough to hold the gun at her thigh instead of waving it around or trying to use it. Abruptly, Kincade dropped Chloe to her knees, bent over her. She picked the gun up, pulled it apart enough to inspect it, and then gave Chloe an impressed nod.

"I applaud the effort, wasted as it was." Kincade hunched and twisted to knee Chloe in the chin hard enough that Chloe's head snapped back and she dropped to the ground. Standing tall, gun whole in her hand, Kincade glanced over to where Jason was huddled on the ground holding his bloodied face. Then, she turned to me.

"She didn't take my warning," Kincade said, looming close. I felt a ball of worry approach from my right and, when Kincade lifted her hand as if she would reach for me, I noticed Mel step in and try to stop her. She was, of course, quicker and slid easily out of his path, managing to grab his forearm instead. Mel tried to shake free but she stood calm, held him in place. When he swung at her with his other arm, Kincade rolled her eyes, ducked it, and moved in close. She spoke to him as she jabbed her fist into his kidney.

"Can't damage that pretty face, now can I? This will have to do." As if the shot to his side wasn't enough, Kincade kneed him right in the balls.

Mel cried out, his eyes going wide before squeezing shut. He dropped to the ground, hand clutching at his crotch, and Kincade moved toward me again. I took a step back, bumped against a woman who gave me a dirty look before she seemed to notice the three people on the ground around the table.

"Are they okay?" she screamed at me. Kincade threw her a look that scared her enough that she grabbed her girlfriend and they scurried off. Grabbing my jacket above my heart, fisting her hands in the fabric hard enough that it tore, Kincade pulled me close.

"I knew you were more interesting than you let on."

"Not really," I said, lifting my hands to grab at her wrist as if I would try to get her to let go of me. I didn't bother moving my gaze from hers as I noticed Chloe pushing to her feet. Kincade pushed in close, putting her lips to my ear. I moved my grip so I was touching bare skin.

"Don't sell yourself short, little empath."

"You're one to talk, with your six-inch heels," I said. Kincade laughed, pulling back to grin at my stupid comment, even as Chloe pulled a large syringe from her thigh pack. I expected her to make fun of me, but instead she tilted her head, her gaze darting to the side to let me know she sensed Chloe's actions.

"Our poor, stupid Gavel has never known when to give up."

I felt the surge of anger, the explosion of malice from Chloe just before I felt Kincade's grip on my jacket loosen. Squeezing my eyes shut, having already clamped both hands as tightly around her wrist as I could manage, I held on as well as I could. This, of course, meant that I moved with her as she tried to turn toward Chloe. Despite the fact that it nearly burned to do so, I paid attention to the emotions swirling within Kincade, twitching as a wave of frustration crashed over her at my surprise ride-along. She let out a rumble of a growl, trying to shake me off. Chloe dropped down, tried to jab the needle between Kincade's legs. Werewolves are nearly invulnerable in all but one spot; the idea of having a needle jammed into my lady bits made me wince, but Kincade reacted much differently than I would have.

Instead of crying and squeezing her legs shut and trying to stumble away, knees mashed together, Kincade roared in anger. Stepping back, wrenching one of her wrists out of my grip, she swatted at Chloe with her free hand. The needle arced through the air, skidded across the ground. Someone stepped on it, stumbled and laughed, too drunk to notice the liquid they'd spilled out from cracked plastic. I was still holding onto Kincade as she moved again and tried to grab for Chloe.

"No, no!" I called. I really, really did not want to, but I risked my sanity and shoved my empathy inside the tempest.

For a minute I was blind and deaf, naked and burning to death in a rocky desert. Distantly, I knew I was whimpering, that what I was attempting was a Bad Idea with a capital everything. But, on the edge of the scalding world, I could feel worry, pain, panic. I knew my friends were in danger and that pushed me back into myself. I had a hold on Kincade's emotions and I dragged them kicking and screaming and clawing and biting into my body.

I probably could have more easily lassoed the sun and pulled it out of the sky.

When I opened my eyes, I was staring at Kincade's face and her brown eyes were clear, confused. We were frozen together in the middle of a mass of moving bodies, staring blankly. I was shaking.

"What …" Kincade began, trailing off. Confusion tried to surface in her, but I grabbed it, held onto it, and tore it away from her. Worry tried to make an appearance but I ripped it out too.

I could feel myself losing the battle against her emotions. They were rioting inside me, fighting each other, tearing apart my insides. On the outside, she and I were calm, my hands on her wrist, her body relaxed as we stood across from each other.

"Gwen," Mel croaked, stumbling to his feet. A woman turned to watch him, made a comment about him drinking too much. Her boyfriend agreed, tugged her away.

"Mel," I said, swallowing back the sudden rage that wanted to come screaming out of my throat. My voice was uneven, my hands vibrating on Kincade's wrist. "Get Chloe and Jason and get out."

"But—"

"Do it," I said. I felt my grip on Kincade's wrist tighten so much that it hurt my fingers. She is slighter than I am and my fingers went entirely around her skin, the nail of my middle finger digging into my thumb. She wasn't bothered.

"What …" Kincade began to ask again. She was still a void. She had no emotions left to give and I had taken too many. I felt my eyes flutter as the werewolf emotions seemed to realize that I was not a suitable host. I didn't have the biology of an actual wolf, nor did I have stolen magic. I groaned as it felt like something inside of me was hooking claws into my ribcage and tugging inward. Kincade's head tipped in curiosity, but she didn't intervene.

I passed out somewhere between my heart being crushed and my head exploding.

This wasn't the first time I'd woken up to Izzy's hazel eyes and candy breath in my face and it probably wouldn't be the last.

Concerned and disappointed, he hovered over me, nose nearly pressed to mine. The lights were still strobing, the music was still beating against my skin. Kincade's emotions were gone, as were the pain and worry from Mel, Jason, and Chloe. I blinked, tried to kickstart my brain. Izzy smiled crookedly, stuffed a lollipop into his mouth.

"Y'awri?" he asked around the sucker. I squinted at him, tried to figure out what he was asking. Slurping his own saliva off the candy, he yanked it out of his mouth, spoke again. "Gwen, are you all right? That was pretty stupid. You've got your whole brain; you can't handle that. Come on." I felt his arm slip under my back before he yanked me upward. Somehow, even though I wasn't even sure I knew how to work my limbs, Izzy got me on my feet. Shuffling around me, he brushed at my clothes as if I'd gotten covered with dirt and then stood in front of me, sucker in his mouth.

"Come on, we've got places to be."

"Chloe?" I asked. Izzy cocked his head and, for a second I thought he was about to explain what was going on. Instead, he turned slightly, hopped and twirled up next to a young man making eyes at a taller man. Izzy shook his head, pointed at the taller guy, mumbled something to the young man, and then came back over to me. The young man looked confused but what little bit of lust had been percolating disappeared completely.

"They're cousins," Izzy explained, reaching to wrap his fingers in mine. "Parents are estranged, but they should *not* be dating."

"What?" I asked. I twisted to look back at the boys, who had moved a respectable distance apart. They did kind of look alike. Swinging our clasped hands like we were taking a stroll through the idyllic nineteen-fifties, Izzy turned to grin at me.

"Come on, let's go."

"What happened?" I asked. Izzy just smiled and started heading toward the door. I followed, keeping up surprisingly well for the amount of people in the club. Izzy weaved and dodged, foreseeing openings in the crowd that allowed us to move unmolested to the front door. As we passed by the bouncer, Izzy held up a hand.

"Congrats on the baby, Biff!"

The bouncer frowned at the smaller man, lifted his hand hesitantly. I could feel the confusion in him but it didn't stop him from meeting Izzy's high-five with one of his own. As soon as Izzy got what he wanted, we moved along. I turned as we shuffled down the street, trying to catch sight of Biff the bouncer as if he would have answers. I was still trying to figure out what was going on and where we were. I had vague memories of a scuffle and I knew I probably should have been worried or at least concerned, but I was having trouble keeping any thought from sliding right out my ears and onto the ground.

"Izzy?" I asked as we hit the end of the block.

"Yo."

"What's going on? Where's Chloe? Why does my head hurt?"

"Oh, I got that." Izzy reached up, flicked me in the forehead. I yelped and slammed to a halt. The pain from the miniature assault faded and, sure enough, my headache was gone. Izzy just squinted, inspected my eyes and then nodded. "You're good. That was stupid though."

"What was stupid?" I asked, rubbing my forehead.

"Slurping up all the werewolf mojo. You're just lucky you passed out instead of going stark-raving bonkers. I've been to that party and it is not fun." Izzy waved his hand dismissively as he turned to walk. "For the other partiers, that is. You and I had a blast."

Since we were still holding hands, I had no choice but to walk with him.

"I don't remember anything … I don't think."

"Well, think and then you'll remember."

Trusting Izzy to not guide me in front of a bus, I lowered my gaze, watched the ground pass beneath us as I tried to put the pieces of my memory back together. I was sure the inside of my head looked like someone had opened a thousand-piece jigsaw puzzle and just started flinging pieces into every corner. Deciding to talk it out, I turned to look at Izzy.

"I know Mel's human. I know he tried to make out with me and then he got weird."

Izzy scrunched up his face and I felt the bulk of his gelatinous brain landscape shift toward irritation. I didn't bother asking why. For all I knew, he'd just tripped over an angry hobo in some alternate timeline and he was reacting to that. With Izzy, you can trust that what you see is not what he's getting.

"I remember Jason … I know we were at the club. Then Chloe ran away."

"What's she running away from? She's not!" Izzy speared a finger into the air. "She's running to!"

"She's running to … to …" I trailed off. I almost had the puzzle together. There were just a few more pieces, tucked under the couch of my mind. I just had to dig around in the dust and clean them off before I could use them. As I finally mashed them into place it all came back to me, from sucking Chloe's anger to using my empathy on Kincade. I was suddenly aware of the agony of having every one of Kincade's emotions fighting over my insides like wolves over scraps of meat. "Oh, that *was* stupid."

"See?" Izzy said as we stopped next to a yellow VW Beetle. "Now get in. We're going sparkling."

"I don't know what that means," I said. Izzy had already let go of my hand and was making his way around to the driver's side. Jabbing a finger downward as if gesturing over the hood, he gave me as angry a face as I figured he could muster.

Shaking my head, I rolled my eyes, yanked open the door, and climbed into what was likely the least comfortable car seat I'd ever had the misfortune of smelling.

Olivia R. Burton

Twenty

"Is this your car?" I asked after we'd been driving for a while. Izzy had the radio up and he was head-banging—while still driving, mind you—to what sounded like ancient monk chants. I couldn't determine any sort of musical quality to the sound, let alone a raucous pattern to match the shaking of one's head. Combined with the occasional pops and grinding gears from the car, I was having trouble seeing why Izzy seemed to be enjoying himself so much.

I allowed him two more nods before I reached out and tried to turn the radio off. I hit three buttons that did nothing before the sound stopped. Izzy nodded twice more and then blinked over at me.

"What?"

"Is this your car?"

"Not yet," Izzy said, taking a sudden sharp turn. I gripped the door as well as I could, yelped when the motion slid my butt into a loose spring in the seat.

"Well, if you're leasing it, you need to reconsider. It's a piece of shit."

"Do you want me to tell you what happened while you were out, or what?"

Shifting away from the metal jabbing me in the asscheek, I turned to him, nodded. "Please do."

"Previously, while your brain was offline, Mel got Chloe and Jason out, Kincade stared at you for awhile, and then Vier asked her to leave. She was struck pretty dumb and she just toddled out. Like—" To demonstrate, Izzy wiggled his torso back and forth like a penguin waddling. "Luckily, the clubbers had no idea what was even going down. That's partly booze and partly glamour. Mostly booze; humans are dumb."

"Where are Mel and Chloe now? Are they okay? Is Jason okay?"

"How's Owen?" Izzy countered. I blinked at him, confused by the sudden

147

change in subject.

"He's fine, I guess?" Shaking my head, I frowned. "Why, what do you know?"

"Oh, he got shot. I thought you might've nursed him back to health with your boobs."

"He got what?" I demanded, sitting up straighter. "How do you know?"

"It's a thing I do. Actually, what time is it? Four?"

"I don't have a watch but I'm guessing ... like ten?"

"Oh, then not yet. But perk up, he's gonna need—oh wait, hold on." He swerved around another corner and I slammed against the door, grunting with the impact. Almost immediately, I felt the road under the car change. The tires bumped and growled over dirt, the undercarriage of the car pinging with stray pebbles. I squinted out into the dark and realized I couldn't locate a single building, road, or house. There were trees with patches of open land and, unless I was mistaken, we were driving along a coast.

"Where are we?" I asked. "I don't recognize this area. I didn't think Seattle had this much open space."

"We're not in Seattle, we're in Scotland." Izzy looked over at me and, even though I couldn't see the expression on his face, I could feel the irritation in his psyche, jiggling alongside excitement. "Duh."

Throwing him an annoyed glance before my brain completely processed what he'd just said, I turned back to to squint out at the landscape. Then, as Izzy made a sudden swerve to miss a tree and slammed on the breaks, I caught sight of crumbled ruins ahead of us.

"Did you just say *Scotland*?" I asked, finally catching up. Izzy didn't answer. I heard the door open before the car had come to a complete stop and, by the time I looked over, Izzy had exited the vehicle and was tucking the keys into his pocket. I was still trying to kickstart my brain.

"You coming?" Izzy yelled, pausing to twist to look at me. He grabbed the jacket zipper at his belly button, yanked it up to his neck, and then shrugged. "Okay, then."

When he twisted to start walking again, a little spike of fear screamed at me to get the hell out and follow him.

"Don't leave me!" I yelped, pushing at the car door until I could find a handle to yank. Izzy kept walking as I practically fell face first onto the grass, stumbled to my feet, and ran after him. He was smiling when I got close, staring at the shadows of the ruins in front of us.

"Did you say Scotland?" I asked again. He nodded, pointed ahead.

"Yep. Come on, let's keep going. I turned too late and the sun's gonna be up soon."

"So?"

"So, we'll be seen if that happens."

"Seen by who?" I asked.

"Seen by *what*, you mean." Izzy turned to wiggle his fingers at me and make spooky noises.

"Oh god," I groaned. Izzy snorted, shook his head over a laugh.

"I'm fucking with you. We don't have much time, though. Chop chop!"

"What are we doing?" I yelled after him as he took off at a run. Instead of answering, he teetered forward, extending his arms at the last second to roll into an impressive cartwheel. From there, he dropped into a roll over the grass, pushing to his feet as he came out of it.

When he threw up his arm to mime claiming the gold in some sort of gymnastics competition in which he was the only contestant, I jogged forward and grabbed the back of his collar. He made a surprised choking sound, flailed his limbs in a spastic, uncoordinated fashion. Even though I wasn't even sure he needed to breathe, the action seemed to shock him.

"Explain!" I demanded.

"Jeez," he grumbled, hopping back to keep himself from strangling. After a second he twisted, tried to face me, batting at my grip as best he could. I let go of his jacket and put my hands to my hips, hoping my angry teacher stance would entice him to talk. Blinking at me, he rolled his eyes and sighed.

"We need a bribe. Chloe's still out and Mel's no use, so I figured you and I could come get it. Plus, who doesn't want to see Scotland?"

"A bribe for what?"

"For Chloe. Come on, we need to keep moving. She'll be awake before long and if you're not there, she's going to raise hell." Jerking his thumb toward the ruins again, he took a step. "Although, you and Belial might get along pretty well, actually."

"Who?" I asked. Izzy grinned.

"Prince of Hell. Nice guy."

"Uh," I grunted, shaking my head. "I'll take your word for it."

"You don't have you. You've already met." Perplexed by his own words, Izzy shook his head. "Wait, that might be later, after you've done the stupid."

"Done—what?"

We traveled the rest of the way across the grass in silence and I inspected what we were getting ourselves into. At one point, the separate, dilapidated brick structures may have formed one impressive castle, but as it was, they were nothing more than a curious tourist attraction. Izzy bounced down a short set of stairs that had clearly been installed in more modern times and moved to the first building, leaning in close as if he was trying to intimidate it into giving up government secrets. When the building didn't throw up its arms and confess or burst into tears, Izzy shrugged, stepped back and twisted to face another one of the piles of old bricks.

"Not that one," he mumbled. I stepped up to the building, poked at it to see what he'd seen that I hadn't. I detected nothing except stone and moss. Izzy continued his inspection, moving from building to building until I felt his excitement jerk to the front of his psyche. Grabbing a hunk of brick from the wall as if it had been loosened just for him, Izzy held his arm aloft, grinning at me in the moonlight. I lifted a brow and closed in.

"You found something?" I asked. Izzy nodded gleefully, holding the brick out. I took it, looked it over. It just looked like a chunk of rock to me. "This is what we came here for?"

"Yup," Izzy said, grabbing it back from me. "Now, let's go. We don't have long." As he took off back toward the car at a skip, I hustled to keep up.

"Why do we need that?"

"I told you, as a bribe."

"But why that?"

"Because this has the most memories and because I'll add something of my own, just to make it more enticing."

As we moved up the steps, I considered his words, tried to figure out why we would need to bribe Chloe with memories from an old Scottish castle. We were halfway to the car before I realized what he was talking about.

"That's for Chiv!" I announced. Izzy threw me a look that clearly said he was disappointed in my stupidity and then nodded, looking forward again.

"Yeah, dude."

"Why Chiv?"

"How else do you think Chloe's gonna stop Kincade from being such a dick?"

"I …" I trailed off, shrugged as I climbed into the uncomfortable car seat again. "I don't know. I have no idea what he's capable of."

"Well, Chloe can explain it, don't worry. Buckle up."

"There's no seatbelt," I said after a second of searching. The car lurched forward, made a sputtering sound before Izzy grinned at me and gunned it.

Izzy pulled up in front of Chloe's apartment building and idled. I looked over at him, lifted a brow.

"You can't park here."

"I'm not parking," he explained. Flailing his hand behind him into the rear footwell, he grabbed the hunk of castle, handed it over. "Tell her I love her."

I took the rock, lost. "You're not coming in?"

"Naw," he said, his tone casual, his mood the opposite.

"What's wrong?" I asked. Izzy shrugged a shoulder, leaned across me. The car rolled forward slightly as he grabbed the handle, yanked it, and then shoved the door open.

"You'd better hurry." I stared at him, curious, but I couldn't make heads or tails of his emotions; I had no idea why he wasn't coming upstairs to canoodle his girlfriend in the most saccharine, disgusting manner possible. This was usually exactly their bag. It didn't matter if they were in public, in private, in danger, or completely safe. Not even the threat of imminent death would stop Izzy and Chloe from necking like tangled giraffes.

"Are you fighting?" I asked. They'd seemed fine at the club, but Chloe had been pretty distracted. Izzy shook his head.

"Go on. She'll be awake in a—now." Izzy shoved at my shoulder and I had to windmill my arms to catch myself on the door to keep from cracking my skull open on the curb. "Tell Badar I say hey! And that my face isn't on fire anymore."

I was able to push to my feet just as Izzy yanked the door shut and jerked the flatulent Beetle out into the street. I caught his wave through the rear window, but I didn't have a chance to ask who Badar was or why Izzy's face may have been on fire. Sighing in annoyance, I turned to the building, headed for the front door. I went straight for the elevator, shared it with a head-bobbing twenty-something girl with streaks of bright red through her dark hair. She didn't seem to notice me at all, even when I stepped off on Chloe's floor. I heard my best friend's voice explode through her front door as my hand touched the knob.

"You just *left her there?*" Chloe demanded. I peeked nervously through the ajar door and found her standing in front of Mel, pushing up into his face. Her left wrist was swollen, covered in bruises that matched the mottled purple and red along her chin. I wasn't sure how she was talking through the obvious pain she was in, but she was managing it. "You didn't even think to try—"

Chloe and Mel both looked over as I walked in and I felt surprise and confusion jump out of both of them, grappling at me like a pouncing tiger. It made me stagger and almost drop the brick.

"Gwen!" Mel breathed, taking a step toward me. Chloe got there first, approaching me as fast as she could hobble over. I caught sight of Jason in the far corner of the couch, a giant ice pack covering most of his face. He was just as surprised to see me, though he didn't seem to have anything to say about it.

When she was close enough, Chloe grabbed my hand, yanking me close into a hug against her soft and bruised body. Immediately, relief flooded through her as I held her. Chloe grunted when I gave her a squeeze.

"Sorry," I said, loosening my grip immediately.

"No," she said, pulling back to smile into my face. The smile was hesitant, like her voice. I was betting it was due to the fact that her jaw was, if not broken, then at least very badly sprained. "When Mel told me he left you alone with Kincade, I panicked. I thought she'd have killed you, or at least roughed you up. How are you?"

"I'm not the one who got socked in the face—again—by a werewolf. Why aren't you all at a hospital?"

"Mel's fine, Jason needs medical attention but nothing I can't hand—"

"No, you don't need to handle it. You need to get help. You—I'm taking you all to a hospital, let's go."

"I'm not," Chloe insisted, fighting against me surprisingly well for someone who looked like she'd been dismantled and poorly put back together with glue and busted parts. "Mel, you can take Jason to get help but I'm not going anywhere."

"The hell you're not!" I flailed, realizing I was still holding the brick. Dancing, lost, foot to foot for a moment, I finally settled on setting it down on the table where Chloe put her keys and stuff she didn't want to forget to bring with her. "You're badly hurt, you're probably concussed and not thinking straight!"

"Gwen," she said, going calm in a way I'd seen her do when I'd lost my mind many times before. "I'm not." Turning away, she moved toward Jason, standing close, guilt roiling in her as she addressed him. "You should let Mel take you to get your face checked out. Not to an actual hospital, though." Glancing over at Mel, she watched him until he seemed to get what she was inferring.

"Oh, yeah, got it. I don't know—"

"I know of one."

"Right."

"What's right?" I demanded, angry that I was out of the loop. "What the hell is happening?"

"Everything's going to be fine," Chloe assured me, though it just made me want to hit her myself. "I'm so sorry, Jason. I didn't think—I was an idiot. I shouldn't have let this happen."

"Not your fault," he said, muffled by the ice pack. "I should have worn a disguise or something."

"No," Chloe insisted, her own shame and guilt swamping through her. "You're not at fault at all, and I'm going to make it right. Don't worry."

I watched her, trying to fathom how it could possibly be okay, considering everything that had happened. She looked awful, freshly bruised, her eyes purple, her bandage having disappeared at some point to reveal the black and blue spreading across her face. I winced, wanting to cry at the state she was in, at how lost I felt, and how fucking *guilty* I was for having gotten her involved. Sensing I was losing it, Chloe closed in, hugged me again, refusing to let me push her away when I tried.

"No," I mumbled, my cheeks damp, my voice hiccuping. "I should have listened to Izzy and Owen and not let you get involved. I should have figured some other way to help Mel, to have just waited for Owen to come by."

Hurt pricked at Chloe and she pulled away, meeting my eyes. "Izzy told you not to let me help?"

"Yeah. When Mel got the arrow to the arm, he said I wasn't allowed to tell you. Owen said it too, they both knew this would happen."

"That's not why," Chloe said, sighing heavily.

"What's not why?"

"Slight change of plans," Chloe said, turning to head toward her bedroom. Something was curdling in her, some sort of warped determination that I didn't like and wanted to stop. Chloe's not the type to be stopped, though, which is usually why I adore her so much. Sure, I wish she'd stop making me run on treadmills and eat healthy, but even that I appreciate on some level. I am a danger to myself and others and usually Chloe's greatest asset is standing in my way or heading me off at the pass when I'm about to careen into some destructive situation.

Suddenly, though, the idea of her being unstoppable scared me, bringing me into some new reality I had never contemplated and wasn't sure I liked the idea of.

Olivia R. Burton

Twenty-One

"This can't be the right place," Jason said as we climbed out of Chloe's car in front of a Christian elementary school tucked into a Newcastle neighborhood. Dawn had hit and the sun was still sleeping, but I could smell morning on the chilly air. I gave a nod as I pushed out of the car and ran around to help Chloe before she could stumble face-first into the concrete. "This is a school. It doesn't even look like it's in use."

"It's supposed to look that way," Chloe insisted. She tried to push me away but when she couldn't quite stand on her own, she reluctantly accepted my help. Mel, who was as frustrated with her as I was, swept in, bent abruptly, and picked her up like he had me when Vier had turned me to ice. Chloe glared up at him but she didn't have the energy to be truly angry.

"So, we just walk right in?" Mel asked. I shook my head.

"We should go," I said. "It looks empty, like we'll get in trouble if we go in."

Jason was already climbing back in the car, nodding rapidly. Mel and Chloe shared a look of mild amusement, before she nodded toward a chain link fence that couldn't quite manage to keep itself upright.

"Past the fence, toward the third classroom on the right."

"Gotcha," Mel said.

"Guys," I insisted as they walked away. This was a bad idea and I really wanted to get back in the car and drive away. A woman approached along the sidewalk and the wiggly-tailed chocolate lab she was walking didn't even look our way. It made me pause to consider the scene. The dog wasn't even interested in peeing on any of the trees lining the sidewalk in front of the

155

school. Both he and the woman just booked it on past. By the time I looked back, Mel and Chloe had disappeared.

"We should go, Gwen," Jason insisted. I wanted to agree with him, to climb in the car and drive us both to a real hospital, but I knew Chloe was worth trusting. I shook my head, ignoring Jason's fluttering panic and jerked my head toward the building.

"Come on, we should follow them in."

"I don't want to," Jason said. I couldn't blame him. My skin was crawling with nervous energy. While my brain hadn't exactly conjured up images of being eaten by something with sharp nails and jagged teeth, my body was just as unhappy with the prospect of going in as if it had. Sighing, I stepped to him, wrapped my fingers around his hand. Swallowing, I grabbed hold of his panic, sucked it into myself. Physically shaken, I turned wide eyes on him,

"Come on," I squeaked, doing my best to overcome both his worry and mine. "Let's go."

"Yeah, okay," he said agreeably. He had to tug me to get me moving again, but we both managed to make our way to the faded, olive green classroom door with a taped and torn sign.

Pushing past the threshold was almost enough to make me throw up my hands, turn around, and run screaming off the property. Something inside did not want me here, and I was inclined to agree with whatever it was. Jason was making an uncomfortable keening sound as we stepped into the darkened room. Hadn't I sucked that panic out?

Desks, faded posters, discarded jackets, and chalky, unanswered math problems surrounded us.

"Are they here?" Jason whispered. "We should go."

"No," I insisted. Somewhere at the edge of my consciousness I could feel Chloe in pain and Mel's very human anxiety. "They're here. Keep moving."

"But—" I tugged on his arm, forcing myself to wade through the terror in my insides until we had crossed three rows of desks and made it halfway across the room.

Abruptly the scene changed.

The room lit up, the desks transformed from child-sized learning vehicles to adult-sized waiting chairs. Several of them were filled with what looked like extras from a particularly well-funded episode of Star Trek. I saw forehead ridges, gills, bright blue skin and one creature that was so shiny it was almost reflective. One wide-faced fae, which looked especially slimy, turned its bulbous eyes my way, opened its fat mouth to reveal a swollen, purple tongue. I let out a small wail and hopped to the side, plowing into Jason.

The soupy energy in the room was stifling but I could still feel human emotions ahead of us.

"Keep walking," I hissed at Jason. He nodded, his grip on my hand getting tighter.

"Definitely."

We crossed the waiting room, made our way out into the hallway where several fae who were more traditional in appearance crossed from room to room. A redhead turned golden eyes on us, slunk closer in a column of fabric that seemed to be made of light itself. It sparkled and shifted, bleeding from color to color until she came to a halt in front of us. It settled on the same golden hue as her eyes and she looked us both over.

"You're here with the Gavel?"

"Yes," I said. She reached out, grabbed Jason's hand and turned to tug him toward where I could feel Chloe. He cried out, tried to fight her off, but she ignored his effort.

"It's okay," I assured him, following them toward one of the classrooms. I found it had been converted into a triage center, filled with cots and beds. The redhead pushed Jason down to sit on one of the lower beds, bent to grab his chin with her index finger and thumb. Jason froze when her eyes landed on his, watching her inspect his face in total, scared stillness. After a second, she stood upright, turned and crossed the room to a skinny cabinet. More fae shuffled around the room, all of them ignoring us completely. When my gaze finally found Chloe and Mel, I let out a cry, raised my hand to get their attention. Chloe was being attended to by a creature that was maybe half her height and brimming with tentacles. Gray and vaguely person-shaped, it reminded me of a mass of octopuses having an orgy, but she wasn't bothered in the least by its appearance.

Two of the tentacles attached to its face wiggled curiously toward her as it leaned in to inspect her jaw. She was sitting, but she managed to wave her hand to let me know she knew I was there.

When I turned back to Jason, I let out a confused cry of shock. The redhead had returned and had bent him over the bed, her mouth on his, her hands tangled in his hair. Her dress had turned bright, eye-searingly red. Jason's hands lay on the bed next to him, but I could tell by the emotions pinging around his brain that he was into it.

After a minute, the redhead stood up, looked him over, considering her handiwork. Jason's face was back to normal: the swelling was gone, his nose unbroken. She'd even managed to clean all of the blood from his shirt. He blinked up at her, swallowed uncomfortably.

"Thanks?" he made it a question and she smiled. I felt a crackle of derision from her before she turned to me.

"You are injured?"

"No," I insisted, throwing my hands up. "I'm just—I'm not."

The redhead nodded once, twisted, and walked out of the room.

"Come on," I said, jerking my head toward Chloe.

Jason gave me a sheepish smile, embarrassed by the arousal throbbing through him. "I'll just hang here."

Chloe pushed to her feet as I approached and the octo-attendant stepped away from her. It turned and shuffled on multiple limbs toward the door we'd come through. Chloe started to follow it and I put a hand out to stop her.

"What are you doing?"

"You stay here. I'll be fine."

"Dammit, Chloe," I hissed again. She gave me a crooked, puffy smile, put her unbroken hand on mine. I felt her amusement and affection there, boiling under the bundle of nerves and anger her psyche had become.

"I'm going to be good as new, you'll see."

I watched her for a second, felt my bottom lip pull up in a quivering arch at the lie. We watched each other for a long moment before Chloe nodded once, a signal that I needed to let this all happen. I wasn't sure how to argue or how to stop her so I just shrugged. She smiled, sad and soft, and headed out of the room.

"Have you been here before?" I asked Mel. The three of us were sitting in the hallway in plastic waiting chairs that were weirdly normal for the myriad strange creatures milling about. Jason was surprisingly chill for someone suddenly confronted with the awful and strange truth about the world around him. I wasn't about to question it, if only because I didn't want to deal with having to calm him down again. Mel turned his head toward me, still leaning back against the wall.

"Not this one, but I've been to other fairy hospitals. They're all a little weird."

"Why do you even need them? I thought the scary ones were all immortal."

"Immortal, in many cases, though not all. And, sadly, immortal doesn't always mean untouchable. I'm quite touchable, in fact."

"Actually," I reconsidered, ignoring the slight slither of flirtation sliding out of Mel toward me. "I don't want to talk about all the things that live forever and want to eat my face."

"Like Dr. Howard?" Perplexed, stopped in my tracks, I stared blankly at Mel for long enough that he laughed. "You didn't know?"

"I know he's not human," I said, still thrown by Mel bringing up one of the other residents of our office building. "But … What is he?"

"Toothfairy."

"That's … a thing?"

"It's a thing. It's a disgusting but necessary and creepy thing."

"Do they really hoard kids' teeth?"

"They want all teeth, kids, adults, werewolf, human, it doesn't matter, they'll eat it."

"Oh god!" I yowled.

Mel laughed, so thoroughly amused at my disgust that his joy almost overtook me. I was grinning, even though inside I wanted to vomit at the idea of eating teeth.

"Let us never speak of this again!"

"Happy not to."

"You think Chloe's going to be okay?"

"I think she's convinced herself she'll be okay."

"I can't believe she's doing this," I said. Mel turned back to me, shock sparking through him.

"You can't? You're supposed to know her better than anyone. She nearly got you, me, and Jason killed. She's pissed and that's making her stupid."

"Nothing should make Chloe stupid. She's perfect. Perfect people don't get stupid."

"Then why are you always calling me an idiot?" Mel asked. I whacked him in the gut with the back of my hand. On a double-take, I looked him up and down real quick.

"They take care of you?"

"Nah. I didn't want to pay the fee and I refuse to let Chloe."

"Is it a lot?"

"It's … not money."

"What about Jason, what does he owe?"

Mel was quiet for a long time, eyes downcast, before he shook his head. "She said she came in owed a favor and she'll leave owing. I don't like the idea of the latter, but she can't be reasoned with right now. I'm … actually pretty worried about her."

"Me too," I said quietly.

Chloe strolled out then, whole and untouched, fired up with that acidic determination from earlier. She smiled at us, put her hands on her hips, and tilted her head once toward the exit.

"Come on, kids. Mama's gonna tell you a story."

Mel and I said nothing but we exchanged glances that spoke volumes.

We sat in Chloe's living room, Mel draped across the couch, Chloe and me in the two high-back chairs that flanked it. Poopy had not claimed either chair, and we'd dropped Jason off at his hotel on the way. Chloe had assured me, after he'd headed upstairs, that all of this would be a small, distant memory that his brain would probably never recall again. As far as he was concerned, we'd hung out, had a good time, and he'd gone home.

I didn't like the idea of Jason's brain being invaded, but hadn't I basically done that when I'd taken his panic and forced him to accompany me into the strange empty school? I didn't have a single stone to throw, so I gave up trying.

Chloe had made us all tea in silence once we'd gotten there. She still hadn't questioned the brick I'd been given, and I hadn't bothered to bring it up. It seemed a stranger diversion from the issues at hand, and knowing Izzy, it would come into play when we needed it. Mel had finished his tea, but Chloe and I still held ours, as if we needed the heat against some unfelt chill in the air. She didn't look terribly interested in the contents of her cup, though I couldn't blame her.

She hadn't put any sugar in at all.

Mel cleared his throat. Dropping his ankle from where it rested on his knee, he shifted, leaned over to touch her knee. "You fall asleep?"

"No," she said, looking up at him. Taking a deep breath, she straightened, set the cup of tea on the skinny table next to the chair. "I don't talk about this. It's difficult."

"We can find another way," I offered. Shaking her head, Chloe met my eyes.

"No. You both need to know what I'm about to say because … well, it might explain some things."

"Okay," I said. Swallowing my nerves, I put the teacup to my mouth, found it still too hot to drink. Chloe took another pause, breathed in deeply, stuttered twice, and then began.

"I used to have an older brother, Eli. He was eight years older than me and he—we looked alike." Chloe gave Mel a half-smile, though I could tell she wasn't really taking him in. "Same nose, same eyes. His mouth was bigger and he got our father's height, but you could tell we were related."

The fact that she was speaking in past tense made me want to jump to my feet and tell her to stop. I didn't want her to have to explain this to us. Whatever she was about to say, it was painful. She hadn't ever mentioned it before, so who was I to expect to hear it now? I could already feel my insides quivering in response to her emotions.

"Like I've said, I grew up in an area that had a lot of preternatural activity. Not everyone really noticed but my mother is a sensitive. She isn't on your level, Gwen, but she can see when something isn't quite as it seems." Chloe waved her hand, as if realizing she was saying something that wasn't relevant. "I don't know how Eli got into … the kind of trouble he got into, but it doesn't matter anyway. I was still young. He just wasn't around much and my parents were always worried, but they tried not to let me see it. I was twelve when he … died."

Chloe's jaw tensed, her expression closing down as she tried to hold in the tears. She could no longer look at us and it was making the guilt in my gut climb with clawed fingers into my throat. I wanted to help, even if it meant taking the despair into myself. I was clumsy as I set my teacup aside, sloshing some over the rim, but Chloe held up her hands, shook her head.

"Don't," she warned, sharp and quick, her expression threatening. I paused, halfway between her chair and mine. Mel flicked his gaze between us, finally landing it on Chloe as she spoke again, forcing herself to relax. "I don't want—I need to know I can still miss him. I don't want you taking this away from me, or making it any easier to talk about."

I felt my jaw work up and down as I tried to work out an excuse or an apology. When nothing came out, I felt Mel's hand on mine. He tugged me gently and I swallowed, took a breath as I tried to wall myself up so that, if I couldn't help her, I at least wasn't accidentally absorbing her sadness. I would be of no use huddled in the corner crying. I let Mel pull me onto the couch, rubbing my back as he gave her a nod to continue.

"I appreciate it, though," Chloe said, pulling her legs up to fold herself into a ball on the chair. "The desire to help."

I nodded and she continued.

"This spell that Kincade's done to steal Mel's soul, it's powerful. It makes you *feel* powerful, not just because you become more than human. When it runs through you, when it steals parts of another creature, you *know* it. You know inside that you are … incredible. It is a drug and it is dangerous. *It is addictive.* Eli … He couldn't stop himself. Once he started, I don't think it was his fault. He just kept taking, kept stealing. He went through creature after creature and it took him over. He nearly killed my father. They got into a fight and dad didn't know what was going on, only that Eli wasn't well. Dad tried to grab him, get him to stay and Eli just—" Chloe shook her head, eyes glassy. Mel must've felt me tense or prepare to jump up and go to her; he wrapped an arm over my body like a seatbelt, pressed me against the couch with the back of his forearm.

"Eli just tossed him across the yard. He hit a tree hard enough to break his back and Eli just left. Daddy was in the hospital and they never thought—" Tears spurted. "—but then there Eli was, two weeks later, with another set of stolen powers. He fixed it, he made it better, but he … couldn't come back after that."

Mel and I stayed still as a graveyard, watching Chloe relive something in her past that I was sure neither of us could ever understand. Even feeling the grief, the pain from my seat, I knew it wasn't comparable. Chloe blinked watery eyes, swallowed like she was trying to force a grapefruit down her throat and continued.

"The last time I saw him, I was twelve. He showed up at the house when he knew I'd be home alone, after school before mom and dad got home from work. I couldn't believe how he looked, how sick he was, even with the—with what he'd taken inside of him. But he promised he'd be okay. He promised he was going to get better, that he was done, that he wanted to come be part of the family again. He was … I mean, he … it was a few months later. When he … we got the call, when I realized he'd lied to me."

Chloe took her time, thinking, hurting, as I strained against Mel's arm without even trying.

"When Nysgrogh ..." Chloe began quietly, before shaking her head, not needing to explain. "I knew I had to get involved, that I had no choice but to stop her. Not just because she was a threat to you, but because of *how*. This is no different—no, that's not true. It's worse."

Chloe looked up at us again, her face wet, her jaw set. The despair was still there, swirling within her, the pain of loss a silver spear of electricity piercing my chest, but there was an anger brewing. She felt like a hurricane.

"Kincade is not better than my brother. He couldn't handle this and I know that means she can't either. We need to stop her. She's reckless, she's greedy, she's selfish and whatever she has planned, it won't stop with this. It won't stop with Mel; it won't stop with this plan." Chloe took a deep breath, let it out with a shakiness that I wasn't sure she'd noticed. "So, I need to do something ... dangerous."

"What?" I asked, feeling my world close in on me, blanket me in dark terror. Somehow, I knew what she was about to say before it came out.

Twenty-Two

"You don't have to do this," I begged as Chloe tucked her keys into her pocket. She'd barely slept in the hours after dropping her bombshell, and the only reason I'd known she'd gotten up at the crack of dawn and tried to leave was that I'd slept even less. She glanced over, her gaze flicking between Mel and me.

"Go see Lydia? I do if I want this to work."

"No," I insisted, grabbing her arm, frustrated and scared but not entirely sure why. "I mean the whole thing, taking someone else's soul to stop Kincade. There has to be another way."

"Does there?" she asked, shifting her footing, burrs of irritation pricking at my skin. "What else should we do?"

"I mean …" I trailed off, desperate for a moment, racking my brain for an idea. One skidded to a halt, making me jolt and grab her other arm, turning her to face me completely. "Nysgroph! The guy, the slick in the suit who came and dealt with her, let's call him! He knew soul stuff, right? He fixed me and the kids!"

The irritation in Chloe sharpened, twanging with frustration that rang in my ears like feedback from a microphone. "It's really not that simple. He had a stake in what was going on then. He needed to put a stop to what was happening for his own reasons. This has nothing to do with him."

"You can't even ask?"

"I don't know his number."

Her answer was flippant, her tone bitter, but something there wasn't right, wasn't entirely on the up and up. I frowned, letting go, not sure why Chloe was being so difficult about this. She gave me a moment, watching me intently before guilt swirled inside her, heady and thick. Closing in, she wrapped her arms around me, rubbing my back quickly and just holding on for a few moments.

"I can do this."

"You said it was dangerous," I countered. Chloe pulled away, meeting my eyes, petting my hair like a parent comforting a child. I jerked back.

"I can handle it," she tried to assure me, attempting a gentleness that I didn't trust and didn't appreciate.

"You said Kincade isn't better than your brother, that he got addicted, that he died because it's just that hard."

"He did and she's not."

"But you are?"

A slap of outrage whipped across my front, making me stumble back and cry out. Mel jerked forward to catch me, even though I was in no danger of losing my footing. I looked up at Chloe, hurt and shocked and watched as the shame and regret in her congealed into a sludge.

"I'm not doing this because I think I'm better than my dead brother, Gwen," Chloe said, her voice a quiet tremble. "I'm doing this because Kincade needs to be stopped."

She was correct, she meant everything she was saying but there was still something there I didn't like. She was determined, though, and I knew I wasn't going to be able to stop her, whatever happened. Lowering my gaze, I considered my options, realizing I really only had one.

"I'm coming with you."

"You shouldn't," Chloe started, anxiety creeping up to the edges of her psyche. "You're not even dressed. When was the last time you showered?"

"You can wait."

"Gwen—"

"*I'm* the reason you made it out of the club, remember? And besides, I can't stay in that windowless cave anymore. So, I'm coming with you."

"Me too," Mel said. "I'm not myself, but I'm sure you can find something to keep me busy."

"If nothing else, he looks good with his shirt off," I said, feeling Chloe settle, resigned that we weren't taking no for an answer.

"How does that help?"

"He can boost morale."

"What do you think Kincade is up to?" I asked as we drove north to Lydia's again.

"I haven't figured that out yet."

"Don't you think you should?" Mel asked. Chloe glanced at him in the rearview.

"I don't think I need to. I'll be stopping her soon enough."

"We didn't get the tracker on her, though," I pointed out. "And no one knows where she is. Even if you turn into the Hulk, how are you going to find her in order to smash her?"

Chloe was quiet for a long time and I got the feeling that this hadn't occurred to her. That couldn't be right, though. Chloe was organized to a fault, never missing a beat when it came to running my office and helping my clients. She thought of everything, especially if it was related to foiling my attempts to turn myself into a giant, bloated, blob filled with cake.

"I'll have to … grab something from Merrin."

"Something you could have grabbed without putting Jason in danger?" I challenged, feeling the fib in her words.

"Something that, at the time, seemed like it would cost me more than I was willing to pay."

"That's ominous," I groused, immediately wanting to forget the whole thing and make it someone else's problem.

"It's not what it seems," Chloe assured me. "I just need to owe a favor."

"What's *that* mean?"

"Whatever it ends up meaning, okay?" Chloe was getting annoyed at me again, but I didn't have the capacity to stop steering her in that direction. I needed answers.

"What if she wants you to throw yourself off a building?"

"She'd get nothing out of that. It'll be fine. I used to exchange favors all the time. This isn't my first foray into this sort of thing, you know."

"So you just promise to do … something nebulous in the future and she tells you where Kincade is?"

"At its very base, yes, that's right."

"And you weren't willing to do this before because it would cost too much but suddenly it's A-OK?"

"I didn't know the … lengths she'd go to before. And now she knows we're definitely going to hunt her down to stop her. Circumstances have changed."

"You should still figure out what she's planning to do with my wolf," Mel interjected, his tone calm, desperate to stop us fighting. "Or what she may have already done with it."

"For all we know she stole it just to be a bitch," Chloe spat, though she didn't really believe that. "Or because she wanted powers she didn't have. She's a greedy asshole, taking and keeping things whenever the opportunity presents itself. Maybe this is just something she wanted."

"This isn't like a teddy bear you see in the store, though," I pointed out. "This is a *soul*. This is … It can't be as simple as chanting a few magic words and tearing part of Mel's soul off like a banana off a bunch."

"It's not," Chloe agreed, some hesitation there.

"So she just … decided to do something tough just to have power?"

"You don't know Kincade like I do," Chloe argued. "You can't understand what type of person she is."

"I know what type of person she is. She's selfish, greedy, shitty, a liar, and would sell out her own mother for a candy bar. Am I about right?" I pressed on, not expecting Chloe to answer. "But she's also calculating and thinks about herself above everyone else, which means that, if this was dangerous and hard, she'd have to have a good reason to do it, right? She risked her life trying to kidnap a Lofriska but that's because she thought she'd get a shitload of money out it. So, we should ask ourselves what she's doing with Mel's wolf and, if it's too big a deal, you should sit back and let someone else deal with it."

"Like Owen?" Chloe asked, side-eying me with a smear of insult. I shrugged.

"Maybe. In any case, I don't want you putting yourself in danger for this if there are other options."

"Gwen—"

"Me neither," Mel asserted, leaning forward. "And since it's my wolf, shouldn't I get the final say?"

Chloe wanted to argue. She was combative, frustrated, annoyed, but nothing came out. After awhile, just as she'd done before, she relaxed, resigned. "Okay. Then we figure out what she's doing. But, in the meantime, I'm going to get the supplies I need just in case I'm still our only option."

I didn't like it, but at least she seemed to be stepping back from the edge of the cliff, if only a little bit.

This morning, Reginald had made the floor of the dining room his bed, the macaw was tucked away in the back room with the conures, and my little bird was warbling with joy over the risen sun. I felt a little stab of jealousy because I knew, just from the feel of him, that Sonny was much happier here than he'd been at my place. Before I had a chance to fall into a heap crying, Lydia gestured to the table looming over Reginald.

"Have a seat, I've made breakfast."

"You don't have to feed us," Chloe insisted.

"You're going to stay long enough for you and I to have a talk, so I figured it was only fair to feed you. Excuse me."

Lydia wasn't happy about us being there, though I had the feeling it had more to do with the reason why than anything else. I followed her direction and Mel followed me and next thing we knew, we were seated at the table next to the snoring dog, waiting for Chloe to join us.

She sighed, Reginald grunted and let out a rancid fart that pulled everyone's attention away from the situation at hand, and Mel winced.

"For perhaps the first time during this whole ordeal, I'm glad I don't have my wolf nose."

"He's usually restricted to his own food but I caved and gave him some lentils last night," Lydia said, carrying out a tray with waffles piled high with fruit. The fruit I could have done without, but, when she set my plate in front of me, I noted the sprinkle of sugar over the whole meal and it made me reconsider.

"Lydia, I know—"

"Not yet," Lydia chastised, shutting Chloe up as if she were her mother and not her peer. "First, let's have a nice breakfast together. Then Gwen and Mel can go visit the little ones. And we'll have a talk."

Mel and I glanced at each other, twinned in our nerves, but said nothing.

Despite Reginald's gas, breakfast was a lovely time, delicious and pleasant, filled with talk of Sonny's two visits to Lydia's home. I noted, after two of my own waffles, that Chloe hadn't asked to make sure there were no eggs in hers, so I could only assume Lydia was vegan too, or at least sympathetic to the cause. Chloe passed her third waffle to me without a word, and I wolfed it down in record time.

Once the plates were empty, Lydia leaned back in her seat, smiled at each of us, and then set her gaze on Chloe with a grim sort of determination. Excitement and nerves sparked in Chloe and she turned to us.

"You two wanna go see the birds, or take a walk?"

"You don't want us here for this?"

"I don't," Lydia said quietly. "If you please."

"Sure," I agreed, pushing to my feet. "Want me to clear anything?"

"No need," Lydia assured me. Mel and I locked eyes again, silence fell, and I led him back to the birds' room so the grown ups could talk.

"I think Sonny should live here," I said quietly, fifteen or twenty minutes later, seated on the floor across from Mel. He was holding Harold, petting him gently as if afraid to damage him. Sonny was nuzzled up under my hair, squawking occasionally, probably telling me about his adventures from the last twenty-four hours, or perhaps just asking for more snacks.

"Really?" Mel asked, surprise puffing out. "You love that bird."

"I do, but he's *really* happy here. He's happy at home because I spoil him, but I just … He's really happy here."

"When did you decide this?"

"Basically just now."

"You sure you're in the best headspace to make major life decisions?"

"No," I admitted, sighing. "But there's no rush. I can leave him here until this is all over and decide for sure about it after."

"Would you get another pet?"

"I don't think so," I said, watching Harold twist delicately on Mel's finger to make his way up Mel's arm. Mel tensed, not certain what was happening but nervous about interrupting it. I grinned, watching Harold settle in next to Mel's neck, likely enjoying the warmth. I felt Chloe and Lydia separate then, neither of them particularly thrilled, but during their whole intense conversation, no one had raised a voice or pricked an ego. Mel looked up, seeing Chloe as she stepped into the room.

"Are we ready?" he asked.

"Yep," she said, her voice a touch hollow. "Next step, Merrin's."

My heart sank into my stomach and started digesting the instant it hit. I swallowed thickly, wanting to tell her to go alone so I could stay in the nice, greenery-filled room with my pet bird and his new best friend. I couldn't do that, though, as much as I wanted to. Chloe needed me, if not to protect her from everything else in the world, then to at least keep her grounded in herself.

Once again, Evadne refused to let us see where they were living, so we were forced to meet in what Chloe called a "neutral place."

"This is a grocery store."

"It is indeed," Chloe agreed. "But we're not going shopping. Come on."

Mel and I followed her around the back, though he seemed completely unbothered by the odd turn of events. I reminded myself that, as an actual fae creature—or at least the descendant of one; I wasn't sure how that all worked—he had probably come across some pretty weird stuff like this before.

We passed one loading dock, heading toward a semi-truck backed up to the second one, and Chloe hefted herself up, grabbing the door to the cab, swinging it open as she leaned off the side like a pirate off the mast of a ship. Gesturing, as if we should be impressed by the condensation-drenched soda cup, ripped vinyl, and trash-covered passenger seat, Chloe invited, "Ladies first."

"What?" I asked, lost, sure I didn't want to sniff the inside of a cramped cab filled with sweat, body odor, and farts for eighteen hours a day.

Chloe rolled her eyes, climbed inside over the seat, and disappeared into the back. Mel followed suit, as if this wasn't all *very* weird, and I was left standing behind a grocery store at midday, wondering what the hell was going on. Figuring I might as well just get with the program, I grasped the door, hefted myself up, and swung into the cab, finding I was facing a curtain that I hadn't noticed from the ground. Swallowing hard, I pulled it aside and stepped instantly in a room that seemed the very definition of a Victorian parlor.

Stopping dead, my head on a swivel, I let out a long, impressed, wordless sound, admiring the vintage decor, low lights, billowing veils, high-backed chairs, and round, gleaming, dark wood table worthy of any seance. Chloe was leaning through a thin curtain at the back of the room, Mel was standing calmly off to the side, tense but not fearful. Chloe leaned back in, smiled at me, and then waved her hand at the table.

"Have a seat."

"Are we summoning the souls of my ancestors?"

"That could prove to be dangerous," Evadne said, striding on an icy breeze through the curtain, her hand behind her, fingers linked with Merrin's. "Considering your ancestors are most likely those who were banned many centuries ago by the queen herself."

"Peachy," I said, fighting the urge to turn around and run right back the way I'd come. Even if I fell face-first out of the cab and into the concrete, it had to be better than whatever was going to happen here.

Everyone took their seats, Chloe choosing to sit directly across from Merrin, who looked oddly lucid. She grinned at me, meeting my eyes directly, turned a similar, but much more pity-filled smile on Mel, and then took a deep breath.

"You're sure you want to do this?" she asked. Chloe glanced at Evadne, who was smirking in a way I *really* didn't like, then nodded once.

"I'm certain. It has to be done."

"Does it?" Merrin asked quietly enough that I think I only heard her because I was seated right next to her. Chloe didn't respond, didn't argue, just held her hands out palms down against the embroidered tablecloth. Merrin straightened, tilted her head back to look up at the ceiling, the bit of nervous hesitation in her disappearing in an instant. She lifted her hands, placed them in the same position as Chloe had hers, and began mumbling quietly. Evadne tucked her hand into her vest pocket, pulled out a vial of swirling, blue and purple liquid that reminded me a galaxy, and uncorked it, leaning in to press it to Chloe lips.

Without moving her hands, Chloe grabbed the vial with her lips, tipped her head back, and sucked it down. Continuing to pass easily, she slid into the seat across from mine.

Almost immediately she grunted, folding forward as if she'd been kicked in the stomach, and spat both the vial and a hefty amount of blood out of her mouth.

Olivia R. Burton

Twenty-Three

"Chloe!" I yelled, though Evadne fixed me with a frozen stare that rocked me back in my seat and kept me there. I groaned, pained by the icy grip of her disapproval, wondering how she could manage to strap me to my seat with a band of ice that I couldn't see and could only really feel within my ribs.

Chloe groaned, swore quietly, her eyes still shut, her body twitching, fury, excitement, and a bit of arousal whirling within her. None of it felt like her, every wisp and twist sharp or scalding. It was only after I took a deep breath and forced myself to read her over Evadne's frigid grip that I realized I wasn't reading her at all, but a werewolf.

"Kincade," I whispered, still confused, but starting to understand perhaps just a little bit of what was going on.

"Indeed," Evadne said, calling my gaze to her. She was watching Chloe with an eager fascination, a predatory, gleeful grin on her pale blue lips. "Pity we're missing the show. It looks to be a good one."

"What show?" I demanded, as Chloe grunted, slamming back in the chair. She growled, let out a loud battle cry and jerked forward in her chair. More injuries had sprouted across her body, her eye going purple and swollen with a bruise, her knuckles scraped and raw. I hard a snapping sound before she screamed and pain spiked out of her into me.

I wailed, wincing, feeling tears spurting to heat my cheeks against Evadne's glee.

"Stop!" Mel yowled, before he touched my shoulder. "Merrin, stop!"

"Pet," Evadne purred, disappointment chilling the room like a fog. "I believe she's seen enough."

Merrin stopped chanting, took a deep breath, and sighed out one last,

Olivia R. Burton

drawn out word that I couldn't understand. Chloe wailed in pain and when I could open my eyes against the assault of it all, she was hunched over, her good hand gripping the elbow of her other arm, which hung loose against her side.

"Stupid …" Chloe heaved, before groaning and forcing herself to sit up. Her mouth was bloody, her face purple, her throat bruised. She looked like she'd gone ten rounds with Ali in his heyday and all I wanted to do was grab her, comfort her, take her to a hospital, and have them drug her up and keep her down until I could find some other way of stopping Kincade.

"Are you okay?" Mel asked. Chloe mumbled something in what sounded like Russian and Evadne laughed. Instead of responding, though, she slid her hand over, slipped it into Merrin's, and pushed to her feet.

"Did you understand?" Merrin asked, not yet standing. Chloe rolled her one good eye up to Merrin, nodded shallowly, and then groaned again, coughing blood across the tablecloth.

"Chloe!" I cried, still recovering from just the echo of the pain she was going through. "What happened?"

"For a brief, unpleasant time, Nemain's Gavel got to sit in the body of the Battle Maiden. Mid-battle! Tell me, Gavel, ranked or pleasure?" Evadne asked. I frowned over at her, furious at her dismissive attitude toward Chloe's bloody, broken state, but before I could tell her off, Chloe whispered.

"Ranked. The selfish bitch has been using the wolf to cheat."

"It's hardly cheating if she declares it." Evadne's smile spread, revealing her snow white teeth as she tugged Merrin to her feet. "You should know that better than most, Gavel."

The look Chloe gave Evadne was harsh, even below the swollen, bruised skin, and I grunted at the insult and fury that tangled together, fighting like battling armies.

"Good luck. And please, send notice if you choose your final battle to be ranked as well. I'd bet a great many things to see what comes of it."

"Bitch," Chloe breathed as Evadne and Merrin disappeared back through the curtain.

Mel had to carry Chloe back out through the truck cab and, as we dropped to the ground, I realized that everything had changed. Night had started to fall and, yeah that happens pretty early in the winter, but it was much colder and quieter than when we'd slipped inside just minutes before.

"What the hell?"

"Fairy time," Mel sighed, careful not to jostle Chloe as he started heading back toward the car.

"What's *that* mean?"

"Pockets of Fairy move at different speeds than here on earth, which means you don't always … I mean, things … It's later out here than it would have been in there."

"*How?!*" I demanded, horrified by the idea of losing half a day to some otherworldly, Fairy bullshit. "Wait, we were in Fairy?"

"Yeah," Mel said calmly, his focus still on Chloe and her injuries.

"You drive," Chloe ordered. She was hard to understand, as if she'd stuffed her mouth with cotton. "I'll give directions."

"Drive where?" I demanded, hopping around to walk backwards in front of Mel, holding my arms out as if I could stop him. He stepped around me, but not before he gave me a look that told me to back off. He wasn't mad or angry, but he was worried and I knew it wasn't at all for me. "We'd better be heading back to that hospital."

"We're not, but I'll be fine just the same."

"Fine?" I demanded. "You look like you got thrown off a cliff!"

"It's fine."

"Chloe!" I shrieked, suddenly lost to my own anger and frustration at her stubbornness. "What the hell is going on?"

Chloe sighed, but it came out a pained groan instead of a dismissive huff. We hit the car and Mel balanced Chloe so he could open the back door and slip her in to lie on the back seat. Lacking any other options, I climbed in the front seat, turning to face her, kneeling like a kid about to get into a slap fight with siblings who hadn't been smart enough to call shotgun.

"You trust me, right?" Chloe asked, irritation singing. I nodded.

"Yes! Well, usually. Right now I'm not certain you're in your right mind."

"I'm fine."

"You're probably concussed with six different types of brain damage. What the hell hit you?"

"Technically nothing," Chloe said, making me want to hit her myself.

"Chloe!"

She moaned, shifting her position and draping her broken arm over her belly. Mel started the car, turned up the heater, and pulled away. Chloe doled out an initial, broad destination, and then rolled her unswollen eye to me.

"I had Merrin put me into Kincade's head so I could see what she was doing. It just so happened that she was in a fight with something … typically out of her weight class."

"What's that mean?"

"It means that when she got hit, I got hit. Only, I don't have Mel's wolf so what was, for her, a glancing blow, broke my arm, busted my eye."

"Oh my god!"

"I'll be fine," Chloe said for the billionth time, before wincing, grunting in pain as Mel hit a pothole.

"I'll slow down," he offered.

"No," Chloe said. "We need to get this over with as fast as possible. She

173

won't be in there for long."

"In where?" I asked. Instead of answering, Chloe just shut her eye, settling back as if enduring the pain she was in was suddenly taking all of her energy.

"Right here," Chloe said. She lifted her uninjured arm to point at an upcoming driveway, wincing immediately when her body punished her for the action.

"Don't move, goddammit," I snapped, my annoyance stemming from the worry I knew was sweating off of me in buckets.

"Pull up at the end of the driveway," she said, ignoring my protests.

The house we pulled up to was incredible. Sprawling and modern with high, glass, arched windows on either side of the front doors. It was lit elegantly with twinkling lights hidden well enough to give the illusion that the house itself radiated brightness. The lawn in front rivaled that of the White House in size and upkeep. Despite my entire attention being fixed on Chloe, I knew from the road up that it was on the edge of Mercer Island and I wouldn't have been surprised to see a yacht pulled right up to a dock in the backyard.

Chloe was already opening the door of the car before it'd completely stopped. I grabbed for her, but she was already too far away to catch. Mel exploded with exasperation as well, slamming the car into park as quickly as he could. He pushed out of the car, reaching for her. He couldn't quite manage to get his hands on her, either, before she collapsed against the driveway, but he helped her up immediately.

"Chloe!" I called when I saw her push against him, hating to be picked up. "What are we doing here?"

She ignored me, making her pained way up the three marble steps, between the Grecian columns to knock on the front door. Mel held most of her weight, but she moved her legs as if she was walking of her own, sluggish accord. I shook my head, intending to soundly kick her ass as soon as she was better and could take it.

The door opened, revealing a man who could not have screamed "butler" more clearly if he'd had it tattooed on his forehead. He was tall, skinny, big of nose, white of hair. His black jacket was waist-length in front with tails down the back, and he held one arm across his belly like he was holding in his own intestines. If someone had leaned in to whisper to me that Disney had drawn the man and then figured out the technology to bring him to life, I would have just nodded and believed it without question.

His eyes flicked to me, settled back on Chloe and, after a long silent inspection, he squinted, disapproval rolling out. Chloe swore quietly, leaning as far forward as she could without collapsing and growled, "Tell Badar I'm here, *servant*."

The man said nothing, though his emotions indicated he wanted to spout whatever the polite version of, "oh do fuck off," might have been. In fact, that might have been it.

Then, after a moment, he stepped back, gesturing for Chloe to hobble in. She did, still using Mel's strength to steady her, and I followed, not really sure what else to do. I didn't really want to wait in the car and, since I wasn't sure what Chloe was getting herself into, I felt like I should be present.

For whatever good it might do.

We moved through a long, marbled foyer, past art of all types, glittering chandeliers, closed, heavy mahogany doors, and finally into a large sitting room. Distantly, something sloshed against my empathy, so faint that I almost wasn't sure if it was real.

Then, startling the shit out of me, Chloe yelled, "Badar!"

The name echoed around the marble and I felt my brows jerk into my hair at the cavernous sound. For a few seconds, I heard and felt nothing except the disapproval of the unpleasant butler behind us. Then I felt someone else close in from our left.

My body felt warm, comforted. Suddenly, I wasn't standing in an expensive house worrying about my injured friend, I was lowering myself slowly and carefully into a hot tub on a tropical beach. The emotions flowed around me, soaked against my skin, filling up my every curve, licking along my flesh. I sighed out, turned to find a man of about my height step up to us. He was comfortable in jeans and a baggy t-shirt, his dark hair a bit mussed and wild. His nose was round, his eyes black. He looked Indian and he looked young, early twenties at most. His gaze ran over Chloe before taking me in.

When his eyes met my face, I let out a low giggle. He found it amusing, which only made the liquid of his emotions crawl like a lazy tide along my erogenous zones. My nipples went hard and I swallowed, took a step toward him before I realized what I was doing. He smiled and I caught sight of fangs.

"Badar," Chloe said, still sounding angry, which confused me, though not enough to pull my gaze away from him.

"Elise," he said, crossing to her. He wrapped an arm around her back, tugging her away from Mel, and led her toward a sumptuous living room. "You look unwell."

He had no accent, though he spoke delicately around his fangs. Chloe let him lead her to a couch, but brushed him off before she sat.

"I need your help," she demanded. He turned to look at us, gestured toward me vaguely with his hand. Before I knew was I was doing, I was closing in, reaching for his hand. He noticed my action and tipped his head to consider me.

"I was going to offer your friends refreshments, but this one seems eager for something else."

"Eager," I said with a giggle, as if it was the most delightful, sexiest word

I'd ever heard uttered. Chloe sighed and, even through the delightful sensations of just standing next to Badar I could feel her irritation.

"Gwen's an empath. Your emotions must be pretty amazing."

"Mmm. I have been told that they are pleasant." Badar gestured toward the couch. "Please, you must all take a seat. I'll have water, coffee, soda, whatever you'd like brought out."

"I don't have time for you to play host. I need your help," Chloe said. Badar let out a small sound, disappointed, appraised her for a long moment, and then nodded, taking the seat across from her. Mel hadn't sat yet, staring at Badar as if he wasn't sure what he was looking at but like he found his own ignorance was more annoying than scary.

Hell, I knew we were standing face to face with a vampire and I wasn't smart enough to be scared either. The last vampire I'd come across had injected me with his own paralytic venom and let a demon snack on my thoughts; I really should have known better than to be standing there, staring slack-jawed and practically drooling.

"Explain how I may help," Badar said when everyone but me was seated.

"I need your powers, just for a little while."

Badar lifted a brow, his face remaining pleasant. His emotions told a different story, suddenly coming to a boil around me. I twitched, rubbing at my skin as if I could knock away the liquid heat.

"My powers?" he asked. Chloe shifted like she would push to her feet, but froze with her butt barely off the cushion. Pain made her reconsider her bravado. Swallowing, she sat back down, shook her head.

"Not for free, not for keeps. I have plenty of items I know you'll appreciate. I just need you to let me borrow your powers."

"I'm sorry. I do not wish to spend even another minute sick or uncomfortable. I'm sorry you've traveled this far, but I really can't—"

"The Battle Maiden's running around with this one's wolf." Chloe jerked her good thumb at Mel and Badar's boiling emotions ticked up another few degrees. I whimpered, sure my skin was red and blistered at his displeasure.

"Is that so?" he asked, drumming his fingers on the edge of the chair.

"Unless I'm mistaken, you're not terribly pleased with her. She stole some things from you a few years ago."

Badar smiled and his amusement was thick, oozing along my skin like honey poured by a gentle lover. It cooled and soothed the heat, slinking between my legs to caress me again. I was three steps closer to him before he looked up to meet my eyes. I swallowed, feeling embarrassed that my body was being quite so forward, especially without my permission, and then looked around the room for a place to sit. I considered that maybe I should chain myself to the steering wheel outside.

Badar watched me take a seat in the chair nearest Mel and then rolled his gaze back to Chloe. He drummed his fingers once and then lifted a brow.

"What does she plan to do with the wolf?"

"She's already doing it. They don't call her Battle Maiden for nothing, and the wolf's giving her an edge she doesn't deserve."

"'Tis a pity for her opponents," Badar began, before glancing over as the butler approached, nose in the air. "Yes?"

"Your meal is ready."

"Thank you." Badar turned back to Chloe but when the butler shifted to go, Badar merely held up a hand, freezing him in his place. After a moment, Badar lifted a brow, addressed Chloe again. "What could possibly matter enough to entice me to lend you my health and strength to take her down?"

"There's a certain something tucked into Marv's inventory that could be very bad for you, should Kincade get hold of it."

"Is that so?" Badar asked. Chloe didn't elaborate, just held his eye, intense and commanding, despite her beaten, bloodied state. Badar watched her, something occurring to him that made his emotions boil again. His lips parted in a snarl and I felt myself go a little cold at the sight of his fangs. Despite his snarl, he leaned in, giving Chloe a compliment. "I've always liked your boldness, Gavel. Your mistress was mistaken to let you go."

"Will you help or not?"

"Very well," he said, pushing to his feet. "Have you the necessary components?"

"I've sent for them."

"We'll do it here, so that I may convalesce in the safety and comfort of my own home."

"Sure," Chloe agreed, her shoulders relating a bit. Until he spoke again.

"The matter of payment stands."

"I told you, I have—"

"A favor."

Chloe was quiet for a long time, staring at him as irritation burbled in her gut. She was listing to the side.

"I won't kill for you," she said after awhile. Badar laughed.

"I wouldn't need you to."

Olivia R. Burton

Twenty-Four

Chloe wouldn't let Mel and me into the room while things were happening and, in fact, banished us to a guest house at the far end of the giant property. I got the feeling she wanted to keep me out of it especially, which wasn't difficult with the distance she'd put between us. I couldn't feel any emotions around me except Mel's. Badar didn't even seem to have any garden rodents or birds on his property.

I wondered grimly if he'd sucked them all dry.

"I don't know what she's doing but I don't like it."

"I couldn't tell," Mel said, watching me pace feverishly. "I've never seen you move this much in my life."

"Shut up," I snapped, twisting to stalk back toward the far wall.

"Shutting up," Mel mumbled, settling back against the couch and looking around as if the art on the walls was suddenly much more interesting. I watched him as I paced, bothered by the fact that he seemed to care so little about Chloe. In fact, I realized, Mel as a human seemed to care about a lot of things a lot less. I stopped in front of him, glaring down at him until he looked up to meet my eyes, smiling, confused. "What?"

"What the hell's wrong with you lately?"

"You mean besides the fact that I'm so human I burned myself on coffee?"

"Yeah."

"I … don't know how to answer that."

"You don't even care that Chloe's in danger? You barely care that you're human, that half your soul is missing."

"I care," Mel protested. "Who showed up—who *woke you up* at an," he lifted his fingers in scare quotes, "*ungodly hour* to complain about said soul being missing? Me, that's who."

"I just mean you—I mean, you're just—Everything's different with you lately."

"Yeah. I'm human."

I rolled my eyes, realizing he wasn't going to understand. "Never mind."

Mel let me go back to pacing and I did, but kept my gaze on him where I could while avoiding running into anything. Mel as a human was a lot less intense than Mel as a werewolf and I wasn't entirely sure I liked it. Sure, it was nice not having my head explode when he walked into the room, but he also seemed much less passionate than I was used to. I wasn't sure why I enjoyed that side of him more, why I missed it now that it was gone, but I did. Something about Mel getting offended and picking a fight was sort of fun. I could only guess as to why—and what it said about me that I *like* getting into bickering, poking matches with him—but I was weirdly, sadly certain in that moment that I missed passionate, sleazy, slightly inappropriate Mel more than I ever thought I would.

My phone rang, making me yelp and jolt and swear and Mel laughed at my reaction, gesturing loosely toward me. "Phone's ringing."

I snarled at him, digging my phone out of my pocket and stomping to the opposite side of the room to answer it.

"Bad news," Owen said in lieu of hello. I interrupted him with a gasp before he could continue, remembering what Izzy had predicted.

"Oh god, you got shot!"

"How could you know that?"

"Izzy," I said with a sigh, swearing quietly under my breath. "I thought—he mentioned it and I should have called you to warn you."

"I don't know that it would have done any good. It's not a big deal, though."

"Getting shot isn't a big deal? You and I are two very different types of people."

"Thank god," Owen said, making me laugh. "It's just not the first time I've been shot and it won't be the last time."

"Don't say that," I complained, worrying about him more than I really needed to, considering the circumstance. "I already have a lot on my plate and trying to convince you to leave the mercenary business and live your life as my personal sex slave is just more than I can deal with right now."

"While I'm certain the benefits would outweigh the pitiful salary, that's just not an option for me. Not right now, anyway."

"Owen," I sighed.

"I'm fine. Or, I will be. I found a healer to fix me up good. Being shot isn't the bad news, actually. I have to cancel my visit. Or, at least put it off."

"For how long?"

"I can't say. The healer's willing to mend me, but I have to do a job in exchange. Then, right after that, I'm off on another. But, I'll do my best to keep in touch."

"At least text to let me know when you're whole. Send pictures if you're feeling saucy."

"Pictures of what?"

"Whatever. I'm like a Cherokee, I can use all parts of you."

Owen laughed and the sound warmed my insides through and through. I realized I really wanted a hug.

"How are things there? Is Kincade wrapped up tight yet?"

"Ugh. No. Chloe's plan went to hell so we're onto something else."

"What did she decide to try next?"

I went quiet, my insides going chilly again as I considered what should have come out of my mouth. I wasn't sure why I couldn't tell him the truth but I really didn't want to. Everything in my brain told me that Owen should not know what Chloe was attempting, though I wasn't sure why. They had a history, had worked together time and again when she'd worked in the Fairy world. I wasn't sure how much of her past he knew, though, because one thing I knew about their time as colleagues was that they were both extremely secretive about who they were and what sorts of things went on in their real lives. If Chloe didn't want Owen to know about her dead brother and the mistakes he'd made, or how that affected the choices she was making in dealing with Kincade, it wasn't my place to enlighten him.

"Izzy's around," I said, before sighing. "But of course he won't explain what exactly is supposed to happen next."

Owen was quiet and I got the feeling—maybe just because I was feeling guilty for lying—that he didn't believe me. "So Izzy's going to fix everything?"

"He got me a brick."

"A brick?"

"From Scotland. He took me to Scotland and now I have a brick. Of course he hasn't told me what I'm supposed to do about it, but some guy— well, some Fairy named Chiv is supposed to get it. I don't know when or how that's going to help, but I have a brick."

"You're not going to see him, right? Steer clear of Chiv. He's *very* dangerous."

"Oh, no, yeah, I know. I've met him. I almost peed myself."

"Give Chloe the brick. Keep me updated about Mel and Kincade. I have to go, I'm up."

"Let me know when you're whole again."

"You'll be the first."

We said our goodbyes and I stood facing the wall—eyes shut, body sore, emotions drained—for longer than I meant to. I heard Mel get up and approach and I turned to find him next to me, frowning down at me.

"Boyfriend got shot?"

"Owen got shot, yeah. He'll be fine, but … Everyone's hurt. I don't like it."

"Everyone will be fine," Mel assured me, lifting a hand to rub down my arm. I sighed, staring up into his face, considering that I wanted to lean in for a hug, to just fold myself into him and forget the world around us, but I wasn't sure that would work. The fact that I was willing to even consider such a thing without the magical necklace that dampened his emotions into oblivion was proof enough that everything was messed up and nothing was normal.

I felt a hot, simmering excitement off to the left, approaching from outside the guesthouse, back in the direction of the house. I turned, looking at the wall as if I could see Badar approach but, as the emotion closed in, as the heated, burbling glee reached the door to the guesthouse I realized it wasn't Badar at all.

Chloe stepped in, grinning at both of us. She had no fangs, but she was no less a vampire in that moment that Kincade had been a werewolf. My heart started pounding, my chest heaving as I realized my worst fears had come to pass. Chloe hadn't found another way to twin herself to Badar, to borrow his powers in some mild, temporary, safe, and smart way. She'd done what she herself had said no one should do. She'd done it without telling me she'd decided to do it, and now everything felt wrong and bad.

"You took his soul," I whispered. Chloe frowned, but her emotions didn't veer away from the glee she felt inside.

"I borrowed a piece of it. I'll be fine. I'll give it back."

She would, I knew, that wasn't a lie. Despite that, I didn't like the way she felt when she said it, the way she regretted it being the truth. The way she felt about having to go back to being just boring, human Chloe. If it was up to her, she'd have been lying. She would keep the vampire's soul, to keep his powers and his strength. Something inside Chloe, perhaps Badar's soul itself, I wasn't sure, didn't want to ever be human again.

"Come on. Let's go get Mel's wolf back."

"Where are we going," I asked, once my voice had come back to me. Chloe had ushered us into the car and we were speeding down I-90 toward Seattle.

"A party," Chloe said, smirking but refusing to elaborate. I frowned, fighting the urge to slap at her in frustration.

"A party?" Mel asked after a bit.

"Indeed. You know what today is?"

"Monday."

"It's the first day of Valentine's week."

"That's not a thing," I argued. Chloe grinned at me.

"Evidently it is. There are singles events happening all week and we're headed to one. Kincade, fresh from her victory, is celebrating by searching for some poor schmuck to satisfy her werewolf urges. We're going to make sure she fails. Well," Chloe purred, winking my way. "I am anyway. You two should probably wait in the car."

"I can't believe you did this," I said, watching her, frustrated with her casual attitude over something that had brought her to tears just hours before.

"I'll be fine, Gwen, don't worry. I can take her."

"I don't—this isn't about Kincade. This is—Wait. How do you even know where she *is*?"

"Don't worry about it."

"Chloe! I can't help but worry about it! How did you find out where she is?"

"I used my resources, okay?"

"What resources?"

"Myself. I found someone who could get the tracker on her without noticing."

My heart went to ice. "And … what did that cost you?"

"Just a favor is all. It'll be fine."

I sighed, realizing that she wasn't going to expand on that. She wasn't acting like Chloe and I wasn't sure if that was because she had the vampire in her or … if it was something worse.

"I thought taking souls was a bad idea," I said quietly.

"Borrowing them isn't as dire," Chloe said innocently, despite the fact that she was lying through her teeth. Stunned by her dishonesty, I felt my already frozen heart crack. This had to be the vampire in her, I reasoned. It was affecting her mind. I couldn't live with it being anything else. "It'll get back to him. As soon as I'm done with it, it'll go back. That's what they do."

"What about my soul?" Mel asked, when it was clear I had no response.

"That too," Chloe assured him, smiling at him in the rearview. "It'll take more time, just because it's been out there so long, but once we capture Kincade, we'll rip that sucker right out and it'll swim on home. In the meantime, I get to have some fun."

"Stealing souls is fun?" I asked, the ice in my heart spreading back to freeze my spine.

"Borrowing," Chloe corrected, sizzling with irritation at my judgment. I whimpered, tensing, leaning away from her despite the fact that the car was too small to actually get the distance between us that I would have needed to stop the burning pain. Noticing my reaction, she faltered, her irritation doused under gooey, chilly guilt. "I'm sorry. I should have left you at Badar's. I can take Kincade on without you two. I should have left you where you'd be safe."

"No," I said, shaking my head. I didn't want her alone, not in her state. Everything that had been happening since the beginning of this had affected her and I didn't like how. She needed me more than ever and, threat of injury or not, I wasn't going to leave her alone. "We should be there. For you, I mean."

The Graham Visitor's Center was jumping, despite the weather. The slatted patio roof had been covered to keep out the rain and heaters had been set out at intervals to make sure anyone who didn't want to sit inside could mingle in the open air. Tucked under cover was a coffee cart with a perky brunette whipping up hot beverages.

Lust, adoration, nervous giddiness, desperation, and discomfort jumped around between the groups and couples. I didn't see Kincade, but I knew she was here somewhere. I could feel the burning edge of the werewolf emotions through the couples, though it was joined by a familiar humming electricity, like standing too close to a live wire.

"So, what's going to happen here?" Mel asked. Despite the fact that he towered over Chloe, he still seemed small and insignificant next to her as she scanned the crowd. She took her time answering and, when she did, the smile she turned on him was withering.

"Do you think Kincade will be able to tell something's happened to me?" Chloe murmured as quietly as she could.

"What do you mean?"

"Smell. Do vampires smell different than humans?"

"I ..." Mel trailed off, shrugged. I felt Kincade move. I wasn't sure if she knew we were there or if she was just mingling. "Dirk didn't—well, he does usually but it was hard to get a read on him when he was with the demon. Mainly he smelled like blood."

"My blood," I commented with a sneer.

"Good," Chloe said, ignoring my commentary. "You two hang back. I'm going to get her, ask to take a walk. She's not an idiot; she'll know making a scene here, where no one's drunk and Vier isn't keeping anyone's mind muddled, is a bad idea."

Chloe slipped off into the crowd. Mel gave it a beat, let her get into the building before slipping his good hand into mine and tugging.

"Come on. I'm not just letting her run in there by herself."

"What the hell are we gonna do to help?" I asked. Mel didn't answer, just kept tugging me through the couples that had dispersed beyond the patio. I moaned quietly as we went, as the emotional buzzing continued to get stronger, making it hard to concentrate.

"Where are they?" Mel mumbled.

"I don't know, but—wait. I think I feel them—" We stopped dead at the edge of the patio as Kincade and Chloe came out of the building. Mel grabbed me, yanked me aside behind a pillar barely wide enough to hide one of us, let alone both. Chloe and Kincade curved around the side of the building toward the trees, calm in appearance, though both were crackling with anger. Chloe's rage was boiling beneath the surface, thickening like lava. Kincade's anger was razor sharp and shooting out of her like the needles of an exploding cactus.

"Maybe Chloe will convince her this doesn't have to end in bloodshed and we can just leave and no one will get hurt," I mumbled. Mel snorted, clearly taking my words as a joke. I sighed. I hadn't really believed it, either. Self-preservation lost to worry over Chloe, Mel tugged me back out the way we'd come. We followed the two of them up the walkway, into a small clearing barely lit by the moon and lights of the party.

The fight started in a blur. Chloe swung, Kincade dodged, both of them disappeared past a tree. I jolted toward them, caught up in their emotions, aiming to join them, but Mel grabbed for me. In the dark I couldn't follow their actions, but I heard the crack of the tree branch that someone tore loose. Before I knew it, I was right in the path of a bunch of pine needles nearly the size of my car.

"Oh—!" I managed, before I felt dewy needles crash against my face and Mel flush against my back as the force of the tree knocked us to the ground.

The world went black for a moment, though the stars so graciously came down from the sky to perform an interpretive dance right in front of my face. I felt Mel shift underneath me before his hand gripped my shoulder. Chloe and Kincade still grunted and swore, but there was no way to tell how things were going or who was winning. Even their emotions told me nothing, a mish-mash of glee, rage, frustration, and pain.

"Gwen?" Mel croaked. I couldn't answer. The stars had been joined by flashes of flying, skinny, toy-sized gargoyles with giant mouths and the teeth to match. Their ruddy skin looked reptilian and the beady eyes at the sides of their round skulls were solid black like coal.

Three of them were hovering over me, leathery wings flapping rapidly as they darted down close enough to be seen and then up and out of view. One opened its mouth to bear sharp fangs as it swooped toward me. I yelped and swatted, but the bastard just dashed out of the way, using its bony, tiny arms to mimic my action before looking to its friend and shrieking out a cry. I realized, as its stupid delight over teasing me clarified in my mind, that the electricity I'd felt through the crowd hadn't been the people at all. These things were everywhere and I had just not been able to see them until I'd been whacked in the noggin by a damn tree. I could feel blood oozing down my face.

"Gwen?" Mel asked again, groaning, shoving as much as he could manage at the tree branch pinning us to the ground. "Help. Help me push this off."

"No, no, no!" I yowled as another one of the creatures swept toward me.

185

I swatted, caught it in the side of the head. Shock exploded like needles and the feeling of its dry, scaly skin on the back of my knuckles made me wail. The two other creatures shrieked at me threateningly, before catching their buddy as it plummeted from my lucky hit.

As they hefted it up into the air, Mel asked, "What the hell are you doing?" and they screeched a battle cry into the night.

"Oh god, oh god," I moaned, realizing that Mel was right; we needed to get free before a hundred more of these ugly little shits showed up and ate our faces off. "Hurry, hurry!"

"I'm trying!" Mel insisted, shoving with the one arm that wasn't trapped between us. We got the branch to roll along my waist until it hit my thighs and Mel yanked his arm out from under me. We pushed up to sitting together, him warm at my back, nearly enveloping me completely as we both heaved at the branch. My panic gave me some sort of adrenaline-fueled super strength, dulling the pain of the tree rolling painfully down my shins.

"There," Mel sighed, relieved, as I pulled my legs out from under the weight and pushed to my feet. Then, as I took off like a lunatic, he yelled, "What the hell?!"

Mindless, I booked it, hoping I was aiming for the car, all other sense of reason gone. The cries of gleeful, terrifying, leathery, little bullies followed me.

Nearly lost in the darkness, I swatted at the creatures as they swooped me, grabbing at me with the curved, serrated claws, tearing at my clothes and hair. Abruptly, as I stumbled into a soft, wet hole and nearly snapped my ankle, they yowled in panic and flew off. I didn't get a chance to celebrate my victory, however, before I felt a slim, steel hand grasp my arm and yank me upward. Dizzy, burning with numbness, my stomach still tumbling, I groaned, trying to catch my bearings, relieved for the moment that the creatures had fled.

Then I realized that the pain and nausea that had overtaken me had nothing to do with running or being chased or being hit in the face by a tree. Kincade was pressed against me, her mouth against the back of my neck as she panted and laughed. I cried out, flailing as if I could claw at the air and pull myself out of her grip. She caught my arm, making me cry out at her touch. Her delighted, angry, bitter amusement scraped along my skin, making me cry out.

"Let her go," Chloe growled, appearing like magic in front of us. Her stance was defensive, her arms up and ready to attack or block, whichever would come in handy first.

"If I don't get her, they will," Kincade taunted, lifting a hand to circle her finger in the air. Confusion burbled briefly out of Chloe and, despite her expression remaining stony, Kincade laughed, sensing somehow what Chloe was feeling. "You can't see them? The cherubs? Entertaining, ugly little creatures. Surely you've seen them, even if you can't right now."

Abruptly, Kincade shifted her stance, grabbed my neck with steel fingers, squeezing and yanking me to the side so she could give one of the creatures a face full of rage. She bore her teeth and let out a low growl that didn't entirely match the intensity of a real werewolf, though it felt damn close. The creature shrieked, changing direction immediately, causing its pack to scatter. Kincade ducked back behind me, laughing uproariously at being able to intimidate the things. I felt myself pushing against her, choking myself impotently, mindless with the need to get away from her. She was going to scorch me alive, scrape my skin off, and leave me bloody and raw on the damp grass. Mel jogged over, limping slightly.

"Let her go," he pleaded, though we all knew it would do no good. Kincade only laughed, making me cry out.

One of the creatures swooped toward us again, snapping at Kincade like a nervous dog but she reached up in a flash, snatched it out of the air. It screamed and so did I, clamping my hands over my ears, tears streaming down my face at all the emotional input. I was going to die here, I realized, wishing I'd ignored Izzy's advice and just left Mel asleep in the hotel. I could have waited for Owen, had him fix things while I hid safely in my house with Sonny. Instead, I was here, hating life and wondering if death wouldn't be preferable to losing vision to the iron hands at my throat and the scalding emotions at my spine.

The cherub fought Kincade's grip, but she had it around its gaunt chest, her thumb tucked under its fat head. Chloe seemed to realize something that panicked her.

"Don't   " she tried to say, but Kincade was quicker.

"Little prick," she murmured into my ear before tugging the cherub in, shifting her thumb to press against it like a charmer about to milk a snake. Tiny fangs sank into the meat of my forearm before I'd realized what was happening and I shrieked. Struggling did me no good against her strength and, in fact, may have hurt me worse, but I couldn't help it. Then, the world was blurry, Kincade cupped my face in her hands, and I realized, staring at her in the romantic, moonlight, that she was hauntingly beautiful.

Olivia R. Burton

Twenty-Five

Chloe's anger was an erupting volcano but I didn't care. All I wanted to do was look at Kincade, to see her, to smell her, to be *with* her however she would let me. I wanted to share everything with her, starting with myself. Before I could stop myself, before I could contemplate the pain I knew I'd be in doing so, I yanked her into a hug.

Kincade laughed and I felt her arm slide around me. It was warm, comforting, despite the scraping pain of her joy. When she tugged me close, rubbing my back roughly, I twisted to rest my head on her shoulder, tuck my forehead against her neck. She smelled so good I barely cared that her skin was probably going to dry mine out and burn me like the sun.

"Someone's realized she wants to be with a winner," Kincade purred, stepping back, pulling me with her. "So, we'll just be on our way, what do you think?"

"Kincade," Chloe warned. Her anger was boiling, salty, drenching me in a way that reminded me I was definitely going to die here.

"Gwen, what are you doing?" Mel asked, circling around to Kincade's side. She let him, knowing he was no threat to her but when he reached gently toward me, I grunted out an unhappy sound, slapping him away. Frustrated, he stood there, holding my eye. "What did she do to you?"

"It's a love connection," Kincade purred, turning to face Mel. Her hands slid possessively up my body to tuck under my armpits and then, crushing my spirits and my ribs a little bit, she hefted me up and tossed me. "Well, she thinks so, anyway."

I barely had time to gasp before I felt Chloe's hands, and then wetness beneath my cheek as I hit the ground.

"No," I mumbled, trying to catch my breath in the damp grass. Kincade had attempted to flee but Chloe hadn't stopped to check on me, chasing her down and catching her. I could hear the sounds of flesh impacting flesh, but my eyes were not sharp enough to make out their actions. It didn't matter, I thought, getting to my feet, thinking of nothing but protecting Kincade. If I could just get close enough I could probably bash Chloe over the head with something and get this over with.

Then I could really get to know Kincade on a personal level. I'd realized she wasn't so bad, not like I'd thought before. She was beautiful, smart, resourceful, and she had to be into me. Why else would she have been stalking me, I thought, except to get close to me?

I was two steps toward the sounds of fighting before Mel's arm came around my waist from behind, his other a band over my shoulders. He lifted me into the air, not swayed by my yelling and kicking, my begging to be let down.

"No! I have to help her! She needs—" I yelped, cutting off when the cherubs turned to me as a group, their anger from earlier remembered in an instant. They swarmed, swooped in toward us and I swatted wildly, uselessly. I didn't have a plan, only the desire to get away from Mel and not get attacked, but I fought hard regardless of being aimless.

"What are you doing?"

"Let me go! She needs help—shit!" One of the creatures darted in and my swipe caught it. Working on instinct, I closed my fist around it, pulled my hand back to chuck it back toward its friends.

"Chloe can handle herself, we need to get—"

The sound of a body hitting the trunk of a very old tree startled us. It was too dark to see clearly, but Kincade was screaming like a mad woman. Mel stumbled, I jerked to see what had happened, and the cherub bit me. Teeth sank into the web of skin between my thumb and forefinger and I gasped.

"Gwen, are you okay?" Mel asked. The world shifted, my stomach heaved, and nausea took over. Mel, resourceful and competent even while human and trying to keep a dumbass empath from getting herself killed, noticed my body arching with a wave of sickness. Somehow, he managed to drop me, settle me onto my knees, and yank his arms out of the way as I vomited in the grass. I heaved until my eyes were crying and my throat was raw. My veins felt like they were on fire, my head was pounding, and before I knew it, I was empty.

I coughed, spitting into the grass, barely aware that Mel was crouched next to me, his arm across my back, his hands making sure my short hair stayed out of my face. I heaved once more, but nothing came up. Mel waited until a minute of stillness had passed before he leaned close.

"Are you okay?"

"I hope so," I mumbled, spitting again. Gently, Mel helped me, tugging me into his lap and cradling me. I groaned, closing my eyes against swirling colors and the urge to heave again.

Mel hefted me, holding me close, and walking us somewhere close by. When I managed to open my eyes enough to see without horking again, I found Chloe leaning over Kincade, who was face down in the grass silent and still. Chloe had wrapped a slim gold chain around Kincade's wrists and a silver one around Kincade's ankles. She was rifling through Kincade's pockets, tucking everything she found into her hip pack and into her jacket. When she stood tall, she watched Kincade for a moment before I felt a surge of anger that made me jolt, and sent a fresh round of nausea through me.

Shifting her footing, Chloe pulled back her leg, let free a kick that bent Kincade's body around her ankle and sent her across the grass far enough that Chloe stumbled and had to right herself. Kincade didn't flinch or react, her emotions an electric hum of unconsciousness. I could still feel the creatures hovering around, but they were intrigued, anxious, no longer interested in attacking but curious enough that they didn't want to leave and miss the show.

"We should go," Chloe ordered, hefting Kincade over her shoulder and stalking back toward the car. Mel shifted my weight, sighed and stood still for a moment, as if he didn't want to follow her. Chloe yelled back, "I'm your ride!"

Mel relented.

Kincade tucked into the trunk, we drove through the night. I felt drunk, but not a happy sort of pleasant, night out on the town drunk. Sick, nauseated, with the start of the bedspins drunk. Chloe was boiling with excitement and pride, Mel was sullen and nervous, and I just didn't have the energy to deal with any of it.

"Back to Badar's?" Mel asked. Chloe shook her head.

"First, we have to get Kincade handled."

"I thought that's what we were doing back at the mansion."

"Eventually. Don't worry, Ariel, we'll vanquish Ursula in good time. First, though, we have to hit Pioneer Square."

"Why in the world—"

"Chiv," I murmured, realizing that I'd left the brick Izzy had given me at Chloe's place.

"You're gonna shiv her?" Mel asked. my phone buzzed once, twice, three times in a row. I didn't want to get it, but the second I thought that, it buzzed again.

"No, Chiv," Chloe corrected. "Don't worry, you don't have to come down with me."

"Come down where?" Mel asked, glancing back to frown as I struggled to pull my phone out of my pocket.

"We need to make sure Kincade never does this again, don't we?" Chloe purred as squinted at my phone in the darkness. It had four messages from an unknown number but I knew once I read them that they were from Izzy.

Your brick
Is in
The console.
Don't you ignore me!

"The console," I said, struggling to sit up straight, before moaning and dropping back to my side.

"What?"

"The—in the middle there." I bonked the compartment with my knee. "Izzy got you a brick."

"A brick?" Mel and Chloe both said in unison, which delighted Chloe. She was already opening up the lid, reaching in, and pulling out the hunk of old rock Izzy had procured and somehow left in the car without us seeing him. I wondered why suddenly he was so against just appearing and, more importantly, why he hadn't come to canoodle with Chloe.

"It's from Scotland," I explained, taking a deep breath and pushing up into a sitting position again. I regretted it immediately.

"Izzy?" Chloe asked. Instead of answering, I fought off the urge to vomit, distracting Chloe. "What's wrong?"

"I feel really sick."

"You might have a concussion," Chloe said, worry burbling in her guts. I squeezed my eyes shut and shook my head. I'd never had one, that I knew of, but this didn't feel like it was centered in my head. Yeah, my tongue felt slightly swollen and my eyes were surely spinning in their sockets, but mostly it seemed centered in my guts. "As soon as I'm done with Chiv, I'll get you to a hospital."

"Will they be able to help?"

"A fae hospital will. Both of you."

"I'm not letting you—"

"Would you relax, Mel? It's all over. Everything's good now."

"I don't think it is, Chloe."

"Mel."

He was quiet for a long time, while I sat in the stew of sickness and misery, sinking back onto my side in the back seat. When I was down, groaning like a pregnant woman hauling her huge body out of a chair, Mel sighed.

"You can help Gwen, but not me."

"Your body, your choice," Chloe said, before giggling. She was the only one who found her joke funny.

"Just hang in there, Gwen," Mel murmured, reaching back to rub my hip comfortingly. I didn't want to hang in there. I wanted to hang my head out the parked car and vomit onto the sidewalk but I also didn't want to move. The door opened by my feet, someone grabbed my ankle and tugged, and Mel went, "Izzy?"

"I got her. She's got cherub poisoning," Izzy said, harried and worried. "I'll send you the address."

"The address for what?" Mel demanded as Izzy somehow managed to use his scrawny limbs to heft me out of the car. He slammed the back door shut as Mel opened his, possibly intending on chasing us down. "I got her, big guy! Make sure Chloe makes it back to Badar's!"

"How am I supposed to do that?" Mel called, but Izzy didn't answer. He was already folding me into another car, the same shitty Beetle as before, crouching in after me and slamming the door behind him. I groaned and dropped onto my side as he climbed from the back seat into the front and slid in, starting the car before he was entirely seated. Mel leaned in, knocking on the window and demanding Izzy answer him. Ignoring Mel, Izzy started the rumbling piece of junk and pulled away.

"Where are we go—Oh god." I groaned, ceasing all breathing lest it call bile from my guts up and out through my mouth.

"Gotta get you better. Shit's going down."

"What's—"

"Don't talk, you'll barf on my seats. You got cherub poisoning. Those little shits bite hard."

I groaned again, hoping he understood that I was asking a series of questions, even though I just sounded like a confused, zombie. He got it.

"You could sense them, right? The buzzing? They're always around in huge groups, biting, making people do dumb shit so they can feed on the energy. Like tiny succubi, but no upside. Once you got your noggin knocked you could see them, but don't do that again. You got Chloe to take care of and you can't do that if your brain is still sideways."

I moaned and Izzy sighed.

"Why you gotta ask the hard questions? Look, just don't do anything stupid for awhile and it'll work out, okay? Oh, I see how it is."

The nausea had spread, blacking out my eyes, tugging me down into a soft, thick, squeezing darkness.

I woke staring at the ceiling of a dark room. There was a jiggle of happiness to my left and sleepy discomfort to my right. I turned toward the happiness and found Izzy huddled next to my knees on top of the sheets of the hospital bed. Fists tucked under his chin, he grinned, reaching out lightly to poke my nose.

"Boop."

"Where am I?" I whispered, still scared to speak, even though I had no idea how much time had passed.

"Technically it's an office downtown. But for people like you, it's a hospital room. Friufert owed me one."

"What owed you one?"

"You're all better," Izzy said, ignoring my question. "But you needed a nap."

"Did I get better on my own or did someone help?"

"Friufert helped, but the nap was my idea. I'm eating your Jell-o."

"Hey!" I whined, despite the fact that I hadn't previously even known about the Jell-o and, for once, I had no interest in eating. I heaved myself into a sitting position as Izzy sat up straight, reaching over to a tray to grab a tiny snack cup of green gelatin. Before he cracked it open, he jerked his thumb to his left, my right. As he dumped the whole cup into his massive maw, I turned to look at Mel, draped uncomfortably over a plastic chair. His head had dropped back at such an angle that I was surprised it hadn't just snapped off. His ankles were crossed, propped up on the bed above heart level.

"Probably gonna be sore; he's still human," Izzy observed.

"For how long?"

"Can't say," Izzy said, and I got the feeling he literally couldn't tell me and not just that he wasn't sure. "Chloe didn't wanna get B involved and owe *that* favor. So at least she's not totally gone."

"Where is Chloe?" I asked, suddenly worried—suddenly *guilty* that I hadn't been worried until he'd mentioned her. Izzy's body language changed immediately. Shoulders slumped, he tossed the empty cup into a pile of plastic cups off to the side.

"She has to get better," he mumbled, settled into a hearty pout.

"What happened?"

"She took a vampire soul, that's what happened," Izzy spat, as if it was personally my fault. I tensed, feeling that, really, it probably was. I should have listened to him and to Owen and kept her out of it.

"Do souls ... Did it ... hurt her?"

"She needs time," Izzy said quietly. We stared at each other in silence while Mel snoozed heartily. I realized I wasn't sure how I'd gotten to where I was, what had happened with Kincade, or how Mel had gotten to me.

"How long have I been out? What happened?"

"Here, it's been awhile. Out in your time, only a few hours. And, well. Chloe got Kincade to Chiv, so she won't remember that any of this happened. He was pleased with the brick, really went to town with her brain meats so the rattle maiden's good and empty."

"Battle Maiden?" I asked, though I got the feeling he'd misspoken on purpose. Izzy waved his hand, snorting.

"Wrong series, sorry. Anyway, she won't even know that this nasty spell exists. Mel's soul is out in the ether, she's locked up until she recovers, and then she'll be set free."

"Then what?"

"Then what?" Izzy repeated, shrugging. "Then who cares? She'll go back to whatever she does best."

"That's it? What if she figures out that the spell exists, tries something nasty again?"

"Not how it works. Don't worry, cupcake. Chiv and Chloe took care of it. Speaking of cupcakes, I'm out. Tell Rupert I said hello."

"I hate that cat."

"That's okay," Izzy said as he dropped off the bed and got to his feet. He did a little stretch, like an old man preparing for his morning calisthenics, then took a deep, quick breath, and met my eye. "She's not bothered."

"So now what?"

"Mel's still human," Izzy said. I nodded.

"Yeah, which I'm sure he hates."

"But you don't hate it."

"I … think I actually prefer him as a werewolf."

"I knew you did!" Izzy lifted his hands, seal-clapping excitedly, before his attention swiveled abruptly toward the door.

"Oops. I have places to be."

"You're leaving?"

"Hopefully I don't see you for awhile."

"Thanks," I deadpanned, though I had a feeling I knew what he meant. He hadn't shown up in my life until shit started going wrong and, even though he was dating Chloe, I still seemed to spend the most time with him when there were problems that needed solving. With any luck, he'd skedaddle and we could spend some time apart, neither one of us solving hard problems.

Izzy saluted, turned on his heel, and darted toward the door. With barely a blip in his emotions and no comment or consideration, he shoved Mel's legs off the bed as he passed. Mel's entire body jolted, arms pinwheeling, head snapping up, eyes wide.

"What? Oh *fuck*," he groaned, tensing in place as if he'd just been hit with a paralyzing spell. "Shit, shit. Oh, that hurts."

"You okay?"

"I … Everything hurts. I don't know. What about you?"

"I'm okay. Izzy says so, anyway."

"He's here?"

"Just left."

Mel frowned, shifting to sit up. He cracked his neck, twisting and stretching, before getting to his feet and staring down at me. "How much did he tell you?"

"Broad strokes. He wouldn't say where Chloe is, just that she needs to get better."

"That's about all I know, too." Mel took a breath, setting his hands on his hips. "Izzy took you, speeding off before I could fight him on it, so I waited around for Chloe. She took awhile, but came back out pleased with herself, and told me to drive us all back to Badar's. I don't even think she noticed you were gone until I mentioned it, but she seemed fine with Izzy hauling you away. We headed back to the vampire's place, I got banished to the guest house again, but shortly after, Izzy texted me an address, said to come find you. I got here—to what looked like an office building, actually, punched in the code he gave me, and now here I am."

"Where's Chloe?"

"That I don't know."

"You just left her with the vampire?"

"Somehow I doubt it would have mattered if I stayed. She wouldn't have let me anywhere near what she was doing, and she wasn't acting very forthcoming about it all. And, honestly, I was more worried about you. What happened?"

"Apparently I got bitten by some cherubs."

"Oh, goddammit." Mel snarled, frustration rolling through him. "I didn't—couldn't even see them."

"Kincade could. She started it, snatched one out of the air and made it bite me."

"Sorry," Mel said, as if it was all his fault. "I can usually see them, but I guess I can't now. It didn't even occur to me to … I'm sorry."

"For what? You couldn't have stopped her. I don't think Chloe could see them either."

"Yeah, not all creatures can. We—werewolves can. I'm surprised you could."

"Only after I got hit in the head with the tree."

"Weird."

"Yeah."

We went quiet, staring at each other, contemplating the evening, for long enough that I got uncomfortable. Licking my lips, peaking under the hospital blankets to make sure I was fully dressed, I looked back up to Mel, locking eyes with him. "What d'ya say we get the hell outta here?"

"Please."

Twenty-Six

"Did they tell you how long you have until you're better?" I asked. Mel shook his head, taking the freeway onramp. Tuesday morning had dawned, Izzy was gone for good, and Chloe hadn't answered any of the texts I'd sent. We felt lost and ignorant, but at least we felt lost and ignorant together.

"No one can say."

"Will you survive?"

"I've done pretty well so far."

"Only because I've been around to save your stupid ass."

"Then you'll have to stay close, won't you?" Mel asked, catching my eye. I grinned, felt that swell of affection in him again. It didn't quite scare me off, but I did get a few butterflies in my stomach. Swallowing hard, hoping I could crush them, I took a deep breath, changing the subject.

"We should check on the cats."

"Pardon?" Mel asked, confused, worried for my state of mind. "You want to check on *cats*?"

"I'm not a monster," I argued, even as he laughed. "If Chloe's going to be gone, I need to make sure Poopy is fed and figure out how to get hold of the sitter she gets to check on Rupert when she's busy."

"Where to first?"

"Chloe's is closer and I don't think Poopy has an automatic feeder. I know Rupert does, at least."

"Got it."

We swung by Chloe's, I let myself in using the key she'd given me ages ago, and Poopy greeted us at the door. She was sitting just inside, staring up at us as if to say, "Finally." I cooed at her, promised her food, assured her that Chloe would be home safe soon, and got to dealing with making good

197

on my word.

Then, of course, I basked in her spectacular apathy as she perched on the edge of the counter watching me go about servicing her. Mel and I headed to the office next and he graciously went straight for Rupert so I wouldn't have to fear for my life. I double-checked my emails and voicemails to make sure that my clients were still aware I was out of the office until the next day. I felt infinitely lucky when I found that no one had called, disgruntled and angry at my absence. I thought about Sonny, still tucked safely at Lydia's and, as we shut and locked my office door, I sighed, making the decision once and for all.

"If you've got time, you wanna drive up to Stanwood with me?"

"To pick up Sonny?"

"Actually … I think I should say goodbye."

"Really?"

"I just think he'll be happier there. Something seems to come up to bite me in the ass a lot lately and apparently I'm not a fit bird mom anymore."

"You're fit enough," Mel said, a little lust puffing out. I rolled my eyes, whacking his arm with my hand gently, but not addressing the come-on.

"It just feels right, as sad as it makes me. But if you don't wanna go up with me, I can head up alone."

"I'll go, no big. I just wanna get home, shower, change, feel at least marginally like myself again."

"Same."

"We could save time and shower together."

I laughed, hitting him again, eyeballing him, curious if maybe his wolf was already making its return. I felt no buzz of werewolf emotions, but something was there that hadn't been since before Kincade had yanked out his soul.

"Just drop me by my place," I said as the elevator doors shut.

"You don't want me to *come* with you?"

We stared at each other, alone in the small box, lust filling the air around us but I kept my cool, swallowing and dropping my gaze. We still weren't out of the woods, I reminded myself. Chloe was as good as missing, Kincade was locked up, but would eventually be free to cause havoc again, and Mel was still human.

Mel was still a sexy, lusty human and I was alone with him in an elevator that could carry us right back upstairs to my office. I took a step back, which made him laugh, though he didn't mention why.

"I'll drop you off at your place," he agreed. "You can swing by and pick me up when you're ready."

"It's a plan."

The doors opened and we headed out to the car, our silence ringing in my ears.

Lydia and I spent an hour chatting easily about what had happened. She assured me that, from what she'd heard about the spell Chloe had used, it wouldn't have lasting effects itself. She was being honest, if leaving something out that I didn't have the heart to press.

She was more than thrilled to take Sonny off my hands and, when night had fallen and Mel had made noises about wanting to head home she flitted to the kitchen, coming back with a small vial of pink liquid in her hands.

"You should have this."

"What is it?" I asked, suspicious as I always am about anything magical.

"Just make a big plate of broccoli and pour it over."

"Excuse me?" She laughed, folding it into my hand.

"Just do it. I swear it won't turn your hair pink or turn you into a newt. It takes years to craft and mature but … something tells me you need it more than I do right now."

I said a long and drawn-out goodbye to Sonny, cried half the way home, and realized, as I pulled up to Mel's that I really didn't want to be alone. Sensing that, somehow, Mel spoke as the car slowed to a halt.

"You wanna come in for dinner?"

"As long as we don't walk about anything serious."

"No shop talk, only pizza."

"Sold."

Full on pizza and warm from the fire, I stood at the doorway to Mel's place, stalling my own departure, but not really sure why. Mel stood near, having walked me to the door, barefoot and stupidly sexy in his jeans and t-shirt. We stared at each other for a long moment, before I reached out not quite touching him.

"You'll be … good?"

"Eventually." Mel sighed dramatically, looking off into the middle distance. "Some day."

I laughed, glad to see that he was getting back to his old self, however slowly. We locked eyes again, and the air in the room seemed to thicken. Before my hormones could get the better of me, I took a step back, reaching back and grasping in the air a few times, missing the knob every time.

Mel leaned past me to open the door, but stayed near as the cold swirled in. We locked eyes and almost everything in me wanted to close the distance. We stood there letting the heat out for long enough that I felt Mel shift to shut the door, but I grabbed the door and stopped him.

Chloe's uncertain fate was still there at the back of my mind like a burr stuck in my shoe. As much as my hormones wanted to see how Mel the human stacked up against Mel the werewolf, I knew I wouldn't be able to really judge, to really concentrate, until I knew she was better. But, I thought, as I swallowed hard, ducking under his arm and stepping into the night, once she was, who knew where things would end up?

I was out to lunch with Rita when Chloe texted to let me know she was home. Being Rita, she was unbothered by my distraction, by my sudden need to excuse myself, and by my leaving her with the check. I kissed her cheek, promising her that we'd stay in touch, and she still practically kicked me in the butt when I didn't scram fast enough.

"Get outta here."

"I'm sorry."

"Don't worry, G-Spot. I'll give the band your regards. Settle whatever has your panties in a twist. We'll keep in text. Next time you can take me up on my offer and see us live."

I sped as fast as traffic would allow, tapping my foot impatiently as the elevator ascended, rushed straight to her door, and knocked with all my might. She answered within seconds and I flung myself into her arms the moment I cleared the door.

"Oh my god, you're okay."

"So're you," she said, squeezing me, kicking her door shut. I caught sight of Poopy perched on Chloe's desk watching. She didn't like what she saw, disapproval jabbing out of her like the elbows of an angry old woman, but I ignored her, squeezing my best friend until I worried she might burst. "How's Mel?"

"Fine." I pulled back inspecting her face, frowning when I saw that she looked tired and sick. "Probably. He hasn't let me know he's a wolf yet, and I haven't felt him around the office, but that could just mean he's back to himself and he took a week off to catch up on all the sex he wasn't having as a plain, boring dude."

"You haven't been checking on him?"

"He's a big boy," I lied, not wanting to admit that I had avoided him because of the temptation there. "I've been more worried about you. And I've been taking care of Poopy. And Rupert."

"Which I appreciate," Chloe said, guilt churned in her guts. She turned, leading me toward the couch, where we both sank down. Settling in, she took a deep breath, holding it for a moment. "I'm really sorry. About everything."

"I was very worried about you."

"I know," she whispered, shutting her eyes as sadness rolled through her. I felt my own breath hitch but, when I reached out to grab her hand, she tugged it out of my grasp, as if sensing without seeing what I was going to do. "Don't."

"I can help."

"You shouldn't. I was an idiot. I—No, that's all of it. I was an idiot."

"You were desperate."

"Which made me an idiot."

"But you're better now?"

"Better than an idiot?" Chloe opened her eyes, smiling at me, even as her voice broke. "I don't know yet. I feel like I'm still ... Um. I need some time. Is that okay?"

"Like, off work? Yes, yeah, of course. Whatever you need. Anything, just let me know."

"Even after I feel better, I may, um." Chloe licked her lips, nerves fraying, regret stabbing us both in the chest. "I will need to make good on the things I promised to stop Kincade."

"Okay," I whispered, realizing how hard that was for her to admit. She felt awful and, while part of me—a nasty, vengeful part of me that I wanted to shove down and ignore—felt like she deserved to feel bad, I still didn't want to make things worse for her. She'd done some dumb stuff to stop Kincade, but Chloe was a smart girl and I had to trust that she'd learn from her mistakes and things would be better from then on out. We were quiet for awhile before my curiosity got the better of me. "Kincade's really ... Everything's fine, right?"

"She won't be pulling that shit again, no."

"Did you run her out of Dodge?"

Chloe smiled but it was hollow. "The brick was good; Chiv was pleased. I was going to thank Izzy for it, but he hasn't been around."

"Not at all?"

"Nope. Last time I saw him was at Frigid."

"Can you call him?"

Chloe didn't answer, her gaze drifting to the far end of the room. I felt hurt swirl inside her, guilt, and shame and I tried to grab her again, aiming to suck it out. She surprised me, clasping my hand in hers and turning a big, fake smile on me.

"Everything's gonna be fine."

It wasn't a lie, not really. She meant each word as heartily as she could, but it still felt wrong and untrue, as if the universe was hiding behind the couch, planning to jump up and kick us both in the teeth. Wanting to join her in her optimism, I nodded, faking a smile just as intensely.

"Yes. It is."

"Good." Chloe said, squeezing my hand so hard it hurt. "Good."

Olivia R. Burton

Epilogue

I took a deep breath, tried to convince myself once more that knocking on this door wasn't stupid or unfounded. I was just coming to see a friend. Nothing had to happen with said friend except chatting, wine and, most likely, a lot of insult slinging.

I most definitely had not driven all the way out to this house in the woods just to have sex and maybe, if things went well, eat pizza.

"Well, now you're just lying to yourself," I muttered, before lifting my hand and knocking. The house stayed the same, the sounds of music wafting through the door. I waited a minute, before leaning over a crop of bushes to the left of the door and peering through a window.

Mel was stretched out on his back on the sofa, one hand tucked behind his head, the other holding up a book as he read. He looked good in a t-shirt and jeans, the blue in his shirt matching the blue in his eyes. His full lips were parted, his chiseled jaw tucked down against his chest.

Knocking again, keeping an eye on him, I grinned when he jolted at the sound, catching sight of me. Pleasure swirled through him as he smiled, getting to his feet, his book forgotten on the table. He opened the door, smiled at me, and we just stood there for a second, mutual enthusiasm pinging between us.

"This is a nice surprise," he said finally, stepping aside to let me in. I nodded.

"I'm glad you think so," I said, yanking off my scarf and unzipping my jacket. "I heard you were about to make dinner."

Mel laughed, shutting the door, watching me, unsure of my intentions as I stripped off my jacket and tossed it over one of the bar chairs.

"And what if I told you I already ate?"

"I would say you're lying," I said, pointing at him. "Don't forget, I can feel you, pal."

"Can you?"

Blushing, realizing my Freudian slip, I laughed, shaking my head. "You know what I mean."

"I'm sure you need to explain," Mel said, closing in. Darting away, squirrely and suddenly nervous about my own intentions, I circled the kitchen island, grabbing for the fridge, yanking it open and grabbing the first thing I saw inside.

"Chloe's fine," I said, changing the subject, hoping to ease the lust already throbbing through the room. Mel closed in, taking the glass container out of my hand and sticking it back in the fridge.

"I know," he said, tamping down his own eager lust at my presence. He swallowed, smiled down at me. "She called yesterday, said she wouldn't be back at at the office for awhile."

"Yeah, I'm praying no billing emergencies come up before she's back in fighting shape."

Mel laughed and we locked eyes again, but he cleared his throat, understanding that nothing was about to happen. Gently, deliberately, and with a delightful little squeeze that made me reconsider easing into what I had planned for later, Mel grabbed my shoulders. Pushing me back, he ordered, "I'll make food. You sit, don't help. But you're gonna owe me."

"I'll do the dishes."

"You'll do something," he said, catching my eye.

Mel and I sat diagonal from each other on his L-shaped couch, our plates abandoned on the coffee table next to Mel's almost-empty, third glass of wine. We'd hit a lull in conversation for the first time in a few hours and, even though I hadn't had as much wine as Mel, I was feeling a little tipsy. Looking him over, realizing I felt really, truly good for the first time in ages, I let my brain run away with my mouth.

"Can I ask you something?" I asked. Mel shrugged a shoulder. Taking that as a yes, I pressed on. "Do you ever chase your own tail?"

Mel laughed, amused rather than insulted as I thought he might be. "Sometimes, when I'm out visiting Julian and Sarah. You just get caught up with the pups and everyone does crazy things."

"That's cute," I said, chuckling at the mental image. Shaking his head, still grinning, Mel reached out and grabbed his wine to take the last gulp. When he set it down and leaned back against the couch, I jerked my chin at him.

"Can I ask you something else?"

"No, I don't lick my own balls."

I let out a loud shriek of a laugh before I realized what I was doing. Mel winced at the sound, amused but unpleasantly shocked at my volume.

"That's not—I wasn't gonna ask you …" Shaking my head, embarrassed at my own stupid behavior, at my tipsy brain steering me wrong, I shifted slightly on the couch, concentrating on what I'd really wanted to ask him and hoping I hadn't just scared him off with my dumb, buzzed brain.

"Say we've just met," I said after I'd calmed myself down. "You're human, I'm human, we're just two humans, being humans."

"Humans. Got it," Mel said with a nod.

Pressing on before I could lose my nerve, I asked, "How would you seduce me?"

Mel eyeballed me, delighted at my question, but took his time to answer. Warmth was spreading in him, a heady, lovely affection that I wanted to roll myself up in. Hoping I was headed right for such a delightful treat, I gestured. "Can't decide?"

"How drunk are you?" he asked after a bit, a nervous little note of panic singing deep inside him.

"I'm fine," I insisted, taking a deep breath. "You want me to say the alphabet backwards, or walk a straight line, officer?"

Mel was quiet for awhile, considering me, and I wondered if I was being too coy, if I should just throw myself at him, pin him to the couch, and have my way with him. After way too long, Mel took a breath, got to his feet, then paused, something occurring to him.

"What's the scenario?"

"I just told you. You're human, I'm human, we're just two attractive humans." I gestured vaguely into the air. He shook his head, worrycking into him again.

"No, no. Where—Are you sure you're not drunk?" I kicked out at him loosely and he laughed, giving in. "Fine. Where are we?"

"I'm sober! I know where we are!"

"In your little scenario," Mel said, laughing at my stupidity, pleased by it. "A man's got to work within his environment."

"Oh. Right. Uh …" I trailed off. "At a cafe. I'm reading, having coffee."

"I thought I was supposed to seduce *you*."

"Fine," I admitted, trying to frown, but laughing instead. "I'm playing games on my phone and eating copious amounts of chocolate."

"That's my girl."

Shifting, untucking my legs from under my butt, I sat straight, pretending to be sat in an uncomfortable café chair instead of on the squishy sofa. I mimed fingering a mobile phone enthusiastically, which made Mel chuckle at my terrible overacting.

He stood by the edge of the couch for a moment, considered me from his spot. He managed to make the inspection look curious and genuine, rather than creepy and possessive. It made me look up at him, meet his eyes. When

I did, he gave me a small smile, approached. I wasn't sure, for a moment, if he'd gotten distracted or if we were still playing.

"You wanna know something cool about this song?" he asked. I blinked at him, listened to the music for a second. He was back a step, respecting my personal space, just a nice guy who was interested in me. I shrugged.

"Sure," I said. He smiled, made it a little sheepish.

"Do you mind if I sit?"

I nodded, gestured to the couch. Mel dropped down next to me, held out his hand and introduced himself. His handshake was perfect, not greasy, not grabby. He didn't linger too long or squeeze too hard. He started speaking as our hands parted, making up some bullshit story about a band and their background, the song and its significance. I knew he was lying, but he was sincere about it, joking with me, engaging me without making me feel pressured.

I had to admit, it was impressive. With his werewolf emotions, I would have already been trying to smother myself with a pillow just trying to get away from him. As a human, though, I could see his appeal.

He wound the conversation down to the end before taking a pause as if trying to get the courage up to do what he was about to do. Smiling, he gestured to what I was assuming would have been my cell phone if it wasn't in my jacket across the room.

"Could I give you my number? I'd like to see you sometime, take you out to dinner."

"Your number?" I asked, a little confused. He nodded.

"We just met; I understand if you're not comfortable giving out your own."

"Wow," I said, staring at him, grinning. Other than the stuff he'd made up about the music, he was completely sincere. His body language was relaxed, comfortable, indicating a sweetness in him that I knew was there, deep down. He was confident but not overly so. "Not bad, Somerset."

"Thank you, Arthur."

"What would have happened if I'd told you I didn't want to hear about the music?" He shrugged, leaned back on the couch, unbothered by the idea of being rejected.

"I would have left you alone."

"And this works on all women?" I asked. Mel shook his head.

"You didn't ask me to seduce all women; you asked me to seduce you."

"Well. Mission accomplished."

"Yeah?"

"Yeah. I'd take your number and give you a call."

"Well, then now it's your turn."

"My turn?"

"Sure. I had to show off, it's only fair."

"You *like* showing off."

"Consider it payment for dinner."

"You're a cheap date," I said, making him laugh. Considering his suggestion, wondering how exactly the tables had turned and I was now expected to seduce *him*, I bit my lip. We watched each other for a long time before it hit me. Giggling to myself, still tipsy, I realized *exactly* how I would hit on Mel. Pushing to my feet, I locked my gaze to his, holding his eye for a few seconds. As the heat between us rose, I licked my lips, lifted a brow.

"You wanna go make out in the coat room?"

For a second, Mel was too stunned to react. His jaw worked fruitlessly before he shook his head, breaking out into a slightly embarrassed but giddy laugh.

"First," he said, before breaking out into another laugh. "I don't think a single building in the entire world has had a coat room in it since nineteen-sixty-six. Second, *that's* how you hit on men?"

"I'm not hitting on other men," I said, catching his eye again, letting the silence thicken around us. "I'm hitting on you."

"And you think I'm just that easy?" he asked, his voice quiet. I knocked my knee against his.

"Well, look at what you're wearing. You're asking for it."

"I've been asking for it for years," he observed. "You just won't give it." He was loose on the couch, arms still draped over the back cushions, legs spread. I'd noticed earlier than he was barefoot and that I found it strangely adorable, had since the first night I'd stayed over at his house.

Figuring that was as good an opening as ever, I leaned over him, reaching out to balance myself on the back of the couch. Eyes on mine, he watched me lean in, parted his lips. I felt a spike of excitement shoot out of him as I tipped my head and closed my eyes. Our lips met in a soft kiss that was betrayed by the emotions dancing through him. He was eager and relieved, thrilled and nervous.

He didn't made a move to touch me or pull me closer and I had a brief moment of worry that he was going to be just as timid this time around as he had been the first time we'd had sex. When I lowered my other arm to brace myself, though, I felt his hands gripped my shoulders, sliding down my back to my hips. He leaned up into me as the eagerness warped to arousal within him. I felt his hand slide down my body to grip the back of my thigh.

I followed the tug of his hand to lower myself into his lap, straddling his hips. As I moved my hands to rest along his shoulders, he moved his to cup my face. Abruptly, he bucked up against me, sliding himself forward on the couch so his groin was directly under mine. His lips were soft, his tongue gentle. I couldn't help but grind against him slightly, sucking in air somewhat desperately. I could smell him as I did and it made me press closer as hard as I could, suddenly frantic to breathe in all of him.

Some part of me realized that, not only did he smell like *Mel*—which was

not just the smell of soap and shampoo but also the heady smell of him—
but he also smelled like pizza, and I just wanted eat him up.

I couldn't quite fight off the smile at that thought and Mel noticed. Sliding
one hand to the back of my head and one down my shoulder, he pulled away
slightly.

"What?"

"Shh," I chastised, pushing forward again. He let me have one more kiss
before he leaned back, lifted a brow.

"Is something funny?"

"Just the fact that I'm once again trying to nail you and you're wasting
your breath asking stupid questions. Get with the program, Somerset."

To demonstrate, I dragged my hands down his front, grabbed his shirt
and slid it up, letting my fingers brush his skin as I did. He let me pull his
shirt off and then wrapped his arms around my back, yanking me close. The
kiss he gave me was aggressive, his grip tight enough that I could barely inhale
for a moment.

I felt his mouth leave mine as one of his hands curved up over my back.
He gripped the neckline of my shirt, his short nails scratching along my skin
as he did, and yanked it roughly to the side. I let out a small growl of
appreciation as his lips moved to my neck. He gave me a sucking, open-
mouthed kiss just under my ear before he moved to give my shoulder a soft
bite. I tipped my head back, scraped the nails of my right hand against his
shoulder as my left hand fisted in his hair.

I sighed and he let out a small sound, rolling it into a growl when I
squeezed his hips with my knees. I felt his arms unwrap from around my
body and the sudden coolness at my sides made me open my eyes. I found
him looking at my face and it was predatory, lustful. It matched the pure
desire pumping through him. When I lifted a brow in question, he smiled and
grabbed my shirt, tugged it upward. I didn't fight him as he yanked it over
my head and threw it to the side. Immediately, he jolted forward, gripping
the sides of my ribcage to hold me in place as he bit me hard at the curve of
my left breast.

My eyes rolled back as I ground my groin against his, my body moving
almost without my permission. My breathing was quick, my mind fuzzy. I felt
swollen and sensitive and needy. I wanted to run my mouth over him, to taste
his skin and commit the scent of him to memory. His hands slid upward,
thumb caressing the sides of my breasts through fabric as his mouth moved
along my chest, kissing my flesh through the rough lace of my bra.

When his mouth found my nipple, he let out a low moan, flattened his
tongue against it before he closed his lips around the tip. I arched against the
feeling, hissed in a breath when I felt his teeth close in a nip.

"God," I gasped, gripping his arms. I dug nails into his skin, scraped a
path to his elbow. Mel made a humming sound and it vibrated along my

nipple, made me buck against him. I was barely coherent enough to notice when his grip moved to unlatch my bra and I whimpered when he pulled his mouth away. He tried to slide my bra forward, attempted to pull it off, but I was overwhelmed. Moving my hands to his face, I cupped his jaw, tipped his head up and caught his mouth in a bruising kiss. The action seemed to distract him from getting me topless and I felt him grip my shoulders and pull me against him.

My heart was slamming against my ribs, fighting to match the pace I wanted to set. I was frantic to have him, to sate the growing need at the center of me.

Our tongues danced against each other, mine leading his through the music of my moans. I could barely control myself and the mewling growls I was pouring into his mouth were wild with excitement. Pulling away just enough to give his bottom lip a hard bite, I licked a line from his mouth to his neck, nipping his jaw along the way. I sank teeth into the skin there, gripped him like I could tear his pulse straight through his skin.

Mel let out a shocked sound and I felt pleasure spike briefly into pain.

I wasn't used to being gentle with Mel; I've known him for years and it's rarely occurred to me that he might be damaged, that I could injure him. Until the last week, it hadn't been an issue. Short of a chainsaw straight to his flesh, I wasn't sure I could've hurt him, no matter how I tried. His pain shocked me, jolted me back. Panting, I opened my eyes and looked down at him. I could see my teeth marks, hard, red welts on his throat. I blinked, felt my brows shoot into my hair.

"Sorry," I breathed.

Mel grinned, shook his head. "Now we're even."

Yanking my bra off, he wrapped his arm around my bare back, tossing the slip of fabric aside. I let out a surprised cry when I felt us lift, realized I was falling. I gripped his arms as he dumped me onto the couch, leaned over me. His mouth took mine, his hand caressing my side possessively. I closed my eyes, slid my hands into his hair and held on. His fingers tucked under the waistline of my jeans, slid along my belly, and then I felt the button give way. The zipper chirped and I felt him pull back.

I opened my eyes, met his as he gripped my pants and tugged them down my thighs. I lifted my hips, smiled up at him as he undressed me. He slid his palms up my legs before planting his hands against the couch on either side of my waist. As he leaned over me, I reached toward the button of his jeans, aiming to get him naked and finish this. Mel smiled against my mouth, reached a hand between us to catch my wrists.

"Excuse you," I murmured like an accusation. He only laughed, moving his mouth to my neck. Giving me a bite, he lowered his groin against mine. I wrapped my legs around his hips, slid my hands over his back, just enjoying the feel of his skin. He continued to nibble along my neck, licked a slow line along my collarbone, before laying a trail of kisses between my breasts.

I tried again to get at his pants and he stopped me. When I opened my mouth to protest, he darted over, sucked my nipple roughly. All that came through my lips was a moan. I arched against him, moved my hands back to grip his hair. His mouth was almost mean, his teeth tugging my nipple taut before he would let go and then lean in to kiss around my areola gently. I felt his fingertips dig into my hip, before his weight shifted.

I was still wrapped around him and I fought when he tried to pull away. As he moved back in to kiss my mouth, his hand left my hip, slid between us. His fingertips curved over me until he found my clitoris. I pulled away from the kiss, hissed in a breath, and squeezed my knees against him. Forcing myself to loosen my legs, dropping them away from his hips, I let him adjust his position. Catching my mouth again, he worked at the same spot until I was gasping, my fingers squeezed so tight in his hair that I could feel it hurting even me.

I let up the pressure and he moved his mouth to my collar, nibbled along the bone. Abruptly his fingers slid downward, two of them dipping inside to rub an even rhythm there. Bucking, I whimpered into the air, my hands moving to grip the backs of his shoulders. I scratched nails across his skin, groaned when I felt pain in him again.

"More, more, more," I demanded.

Close. I was getting so close to orgasm, my body was aching for it. Still working his fingers expertly, he leaned the heel of his hand forward, pressed it hard against the mound there. I pistoned my body against him, one hand dropping to grip the couch next to me, to vault me into the air as I arched my back. My other hand moved to his bicep and I dug my nails in.

I was whimpering, writhing, full, and overwhelmed. As I felt myself tighten around his fingers, cresting over that final, giddy roll toward climax, Mel leaned in, caught my lips in a kiss. I let out a high cry into his mouth, moved my hands to cup his jaw.

I came and he let me gasp, let me tear my mouth from his to tip my head back. He kissed along my jaw, licked my earlobe into his mouth and sucked back before leaning away. As my body tensed, squeezed his fingers, I shoved a hand down, grabbed his wrist.

"Too much," I moaned, tried to pull him away. I fluttered my eyes open, tried to glare but couldn't quite manage it. "Stop, too much."

Mel grinned at me, obeying my order. He moved, rested the heel of his hand on the couch as he leaned over to lay his body against mine. I bit his lip, ran my hands down his back lightly as I felt my body continue to spasm. I tucked a leg around the back of his thigh and then pulled him close into a full body hug. He let me, didn't try for more. He was aroused, excited, proud, but he let me kiss him, let me hold him. As I wandered through the satisfied fog in my brain, I wondered if I was really detecting something else from him, or if I was just too brainless to read my empathy correctly.

Deciding I didn't care, I enjoyed the closeness, relished the warmth of him for a while. As my body calmed, I cupped his face again, pushed him out of the kiss so I could look at him. He was smiling and I could feel affection, but it turned out there was something else there. I squinted at him, considered that he might be worried that was all I was willing to give.

"You're not getting off that easy," I said. He lifted a brow.

"Well, you did."

I snorted, shook my head through a sheepish laugh.

"That's not what I meant," I said, sliding my hands downward. He lifted himself off of me and let me reach his fly before he pressed forward enough to trap my hands. I sighed, exasperated. "What?"

"I just want to make sure—"

"I'm sure," I insisted, knowing what he was getting at.

"I—" I didn't give him a chance to argue anymore. Sliding my hands out from between us, I cupped his face, pulled him into a kiss. He let me, keeping it chaste at first. Wrapping my arms around his neck, I held on, decided to just enjoy the way it felt to kiss him. I wanted more and I wasn't going to let his insecurity ruin things again.

"Unless you don't think you can perform." Mel narrowed his eyes at my challenge, thrusting his hips against mine, making me squeal in delight.

"Oh, it's on," he growled, wrapping his arms around my back, he pulled me against his body, braced himself on the couch. "Hang on."

I let out another squeak as he pushed up, holding me easily against him as he twisted and walked toward the bedroom. Grinning, he leaned in, gave me a quick kiss on the mouth.

"Do you need props?" I teased as we entered the bedroom. "Instructions tacked to the headboard?"

"Shh."

The lights were off and he didn't bother to turn them on. He just crossed the expanse between the door and the bed, held me against him as he lowered us both onto the high mattress. Pressing his lips to my chin, he kissed gently downward, his mouth open over my skin, sucking slightly as he moved. Leaving a trail of cooling, wet flesh, he made his way down my body, gentle as he went.

Abruptly, his hands gripped my hips, fingertips digging in, before his tongue followed the path his fingers had taken earlier. I was still sensitive from the first orgasm and the curling smoothness of his tongue was almost immediately too much. Crying out, I reached down, tangled fingers into his hair, arched my breasts into the cool air.

"No, no—okay! Yes," I cried, squeezing my thighs around his head. My breathing was ragged, my voice high. When I concluded that I couldn't take anymore, that I was about to fly apart or implode, I yanked on his hair, unconcerned with being gentle. Sighing out a laugh against my skin, he attempted to kiss his way back up my body. I growled, impatient.

"No. My way."

Grabbing at his shoulders, I tried to haul him up, reaching between us when he was high enough. I grabbed at his pants, undid the button with what I considered Olympic level speed, and pushed at the zipper. Heart pounding, I shoved at the hem of his pants, caught his mouth in a kiss. He held himself above me with one hand, his other moving to help me in my task. Desperate, I shifted my legs, used my toes to shove at the denim until I could bend forward even more and get a grip on his dick with my hand.

He shuddered, breathed out an uneven sound, and I felt the smug amusement he'd been running with dip toward worry. As far I was concerned he had nothing to be worried about.

"Now," I ordered, giving him one rough stroke before I shifted my legs to help me angle my hips upward.

"Indulge me a moment," he purred, reaching between us to grab my wrist. I opened my eyes to glare at him in the dark, but I couldn't see his face. Sighing, I opened my fingers, let him free. He pulled back, stood up.

"Dammit, Mel."

I heard him fussing with his pants, taking them completely off before I felt his grip on my upper arm. Roughly, he tugged me over onto my stomach, ran his hands possessively down my body to grip my hips. His fingers were pressed hard enough that I could feel it in my hipbones and he took his time standing behind me, the desire in him turning selfish.

As I swallowed, still shocked at the sudden change in him, he yanked me downward, pulling my legs completely off the bed. I realized, quite happily, in that moment why his bed is so high up off the ground.

One hand still dug into my hip, his other slid, curved over my ass and between my legs to tease me again. He waited until I let out a whimper before he moved to clear the way for his cock. I gripped the bed as he slid inside, as he pressed his hips against me. He was slow when he pulled back, hard and fast when he thrust in. I moaned into the bed, shoved myself against him. His rhythm remained consistent at first, his hands sliding up my body to grab hold of my waist.

Squeezing my thighs together, I arched against the bed, reached a hand to grip his fingers as he fucked me. Every time he slid out, slow as a glacier, I let out a whimper. When his hips hit mine, I sighed out.

"Faster, faster," I demanded. I felt Mel's amusement, but it was falling fast behind the arousal building within him. He was playing it cool, doing what he could to prove himself, to prove *to* himself that he could satisfy me. Instead of giving in to my demand, Mel slid in just as slow as he'd pulled out. Pressing our bodies together, he slipped a hand under my pelvis, down past my belly. When he tucked his hand between my legs, I moaned into the bed.

I felt him bend close to me, mold himself against my back. He kissed my shoulder and I turned my head, giving him the side-eye.

"You're just pissing me off, now," I said, voice breathless and hitched as he continued to move his fingers against me. I felt his teeth as he smiled into my shoulder, hissed in a breath as he moved to scrape a wet line along my spine.

It was another torturous eternity before he slid his skilled hand out from between my legs and moved to once again grip my hips. Shoving against the bed, I arched my back, pressed back into him as hard as I could. He started slow again and I moaned into the blanket, frustrated. His pace quickened, though, and I could feel another orgasm winding up at my core. It twisted, tightened, tensed my lower half. With every thrust into me, I could feel it building in him, too. His emotions merged, tunneling down a bottleneck from amusement, desire, glee, and affection to end firmly at the crackling heat of arousal.

I could feel the moment he was about to go over and it made me gasp, made me shove at the bed and squeeze my thighs. Mel slammed against me, his hands tightening against my skin so hard I knew I'd have bruises. We stayed frozen for a second, both of us concentrating too hard on the shared feeling of orgasm to even breathe.

When I gasped, I felt Mel stumble slightly behind me, leaning his weight against me for a moment. He swallowed, letting out a ragged breath before he yanked his hands away from my hips. His sudden worry was distant, drowned out by the feeling of my own pleasure.

"Did I hurt you?" he asked, collapsing against me.

"Ohh yeah," I moaned. I was limp on the bed, arms stretched boneless out to the sides, cheek pressed against the soft blanket. A drip of confusion rippled the pool of satisfied happiness in his mind and he brushed the hair off my cheek, kissed the back of my shoulder.

"That's okay?"

"Oh yeah," I repeated. Mel chuckled against my back, kissed me again.

"I'll … keep that in mind."

"For next time," I purred. Eager pleasure and glee rippled through Mel, tickling my spine and making me realize what I'd just promised. Yeah, I thought, lounging in content satisfaction.

For next time.

Olivia R. Burton

About the Author

Olivia is a vegan thirty-something living in New Mexico with a clowder of cats and a stink of litter boxes. She enjoys vexing her kitties, cooking, watching action movies, and making up collective nouns for things that don't already have them (like a "stink of litter boxes"). You can find her and all information about her different series at OliviaRBurton.com.

Gwen Arthur Novels

Visit OliviaRBurton.com for more information

www.ingramcontent.com/pod-product-compliance
Lightning Source LLC
Chambersburg PA
CBHW072050170626

46813CB00004B/1286